Top 10 Romance of 2012, 2015, and 2016.

— BOOKLIST: THE NIGHT IS MINE, HOT
POINT, HEART STRIKE

One of our favorite authors.

— RT BOOK REVIEWS

Buchman has catapulted his way to the top tier of my favorite authors.

— FRESH FICTION

A favorite author of mine. I'll read anything that carries his name, no questions asked. Meet your new favorite author!

— THE SASSY BOOKSTER, FLASH OF FIRE

M.L. Buchman is guaranteed to get me lost in a good story.

— THE READING CAFE, WAY OF THE
WARRIOR: NSDQ

I love Buchman's writing. His vivid descriptions bring everything to life in an unforgettable way.

TARGET OF ONE'S OWN

NIGHT STALKERS 5E ROMANCE #4

M. L. BUCHMAN

Buchman Bookworks

Receive a free book and discover more by this author at:
www.mlbuchman.com

Cover images:

Stylish blonde girl © Y-Boychenko | DepositPhotos

Racing square background © vska | DepositPhotos

Black Hawk Night Vision © New Jersey National Guard

SIGN UP FOR M. L. BUCHMAN'S NEWSLETTER TODAY

and receive:
Release News
Free Short Stories
a Free book

Do it today. Do it now.
http://free-book.mlbuchman.com

Other works by M. L. Buchman:

1

The view was awesome from up here. To the far north, the mountains of the Hindu Kush were jagged ice points etched across the limits of the horizon. To the south, the arid wastelands of Pakistan.

At the New Year, all of the peaks were sheathed in layers of snow; only the valleys were barren. Scattered villages, even nomadic groups, showed up as bright spots in her infrared vision, but with little of note in between. It looked like a half-finished artist's painting—ever evolving, never complete. Midnight silence reigned, so near perfect that it echoed. She could almost smell the dry desert air—so clean and clear that it was like cool water on a hot day.

For now, she floated above it all like some disembodied alien: seeing but unseen. Her favorite state. As if she was finally forever disconnected from—

"Zoe?"

Lieutenant Sofia Gracie's voice slammed Zoe back into her chair. One moment she'd been soaring through the night at sixty-thousand feet, so completely in tune with her twenty-million-dollar Avenger stealth drone that she might as well have been up there. The next, she was back in the "coffin"—as drone control stations were called—staring at the command console for her bird. The air so sterile that it had no scent at all. The vast silence replace by the soft whir of ventilation fans.

Her soul had been in the sky over southwest Asia, but her butt was undeniably planted in Fort Rucker, Alabama.

Some remote pilots got all wound up, "It's not a drone. It's a remotely piloted aircraft—an RPA." Whatever. As long as they let her fly, she was cool with anything folks wanted to call it. She didn't even mind when they said she wasn't really a pilot. All they were doing was proving that they were ignorant dweebs—stroking their massive egos to compensate for tiny, Air Force pricks—and were so not worth speaking to ever again.

She'd left the Air Force behind and good riddance. Zoe had answered the call to become an RPA pilot for the US Army's 160th Special Operations Aviation Regiment and not regretted it even once. She flew with the Night Stalkers, the very best helicopter pilots anywhere. No one could debate that. Not even the Air Force jocks with their big jets…and tiny pricks.

And while she didn't fly rotorcraft, there was no question that she flew with them, over them. She was their all-seeing eye. Her view was a multi-screen array that had once made her head hurt, but now felt second nature. LIDAR (high-resolution 3D laser-scanning radar) on one monitor with image resolution down below a meter even from this altitude, infrared night vision on another, visible light on a third (which wasn't much on this moonless night deep in Pakistan), and finally the RPA's operations and weapons status. Each screen itself multi-tasking with superimposed readouts of relevant data: terrain, targeting, friendly assets, and the like. Keyboard and a pair of joysticks—flight (not the running-away kind) and fight—completed her world.

Zoe glanced over at Sofia, sitting in an identical seat beside hers.

Just once she'd like to look at her commander and not feel inadequate.

Sofia was a tall, voluptuous beauty that her Army coveralls did nothing to hide. Her smooth Brazilian accent made her sound even more beautiful than she was—which was saying something.

Zoe stood five-four on a good day and had all the curves of a computer screen. Of course, they were making curved ones now, which... She sighed and reported. Sofia had been busy on a command frequency while Zoe was doing the flying.

"Air space is clear," Zoe told her. "I'm seeing no ground forces on the move. Couldn't even see our people if they weren't linked up." The Night Stalkers 5th Battalion E Company was on the prowl tonight and really didn't want to be seen as they were deep inside a "friendly" country without permission. Of course, being invisible was their specialty. The only completely stealth helicopter company in the US military, they truly ruled the night.

It felt odd to be flying here. The fact that she was sitting in Fort Rucker, Alabama, half a world away from her team, was nothing new. But she hadn't flown over Pakistan since joining the elite Night Stalkers.

Back when she'd been flying Predators for the US Air Force's 27th Special Operations Group—out of a coffin at Cannon Air Force Base near Clovis, New Mexico—she'd flown over Pakistan and Afghanistan all the time. The hours had been brutally long and the missions emotionally gutting. Authorization to fire in the face of collateral damage—dead civilians—permitted in order to take out a Tier One target. Women and children traveling with the target were deemed by command to be guilty by association and therefore expendable.

"Keep it smooth." Sofia's reminder to stay focused. Maybe she'd learned that from when she walked fashion runways in exotic climes. If she had. Sofia never talked about her past, but it was easy to picture her there.

Zoe didn't talk about her own past either, but that was because she couldn't imagine anything more boring—other than the one part she refused to remember.

Her mother was a stereotypical legal secretary and her father a Pismo Beach, California, car mechanic—a business he'd started with his high school best friend and next-door neighbor. It was a family she'd *never* belonged to. Their conversations weren't exactly what Zoe would call intellectually stimulating. Thankfully, they also hadn't been strife-laden, just…dull. Which so wasn't right for descendants of the great filmmaker Cecil B. DeMille—not even if they were distant ones. As their only child, it had been up to Zoe to amuse herself. For the last nine years it had amused her to fly drones for the US military.

"Two minutes to perimeter."

This was a smaller mission than normal. The 5E only had four birds aside from her Avenger: a massive twin-rotor Chinook helicopter (the cargo van of Special Operations Forces), a heavily-modified DAP Black Hawk (the most lethal rotorcraft weapons platforms anywhere), and a pair of Little Birds. The last two didn't have the range to strike this far from any support so were parked in the hangar alongside her coffin in Alabama.

In the heart of Balochistan Province in "friendly" Pakistan, a ground team had identified a major arms dealer —perhaps *the* major arms dealer. Not only was Hathyaron ("Weapons" in Urdu) supplying the Taliban in Afghanistan, but he'd been doing it since the Americans had first arrived. Hundreds of millions of dollars for weapons and ammunition had flowed through his hands every year.

The bastard had slipped the net more times than bin Laden. He'd left behind booby traps that had decimated teams. He'd mailed informants' heads to the US embassy in Islamabad—with the tongues cut out before they'd had their limbs removed at the neck. This just had to be the night they took him down.

Zoe scanned again.

Still a whole lot of nothing.

More nothing than there should be. No shepherd boy. No traders camped with their mules by scattered campfires. It was as if the land had been undressed.

"It's quiet." Now that she thought about it, almost nothing had happened at the target compound in the four hours she'd been in position.

"One minute to deployment," Sofia announced as she scanned her screens carefully, then they shared a look.

Zoe keyed her mic. She could broadcast without pinpointing the 5E's aircraft for any enemy. They could hear her transmission, which would cover a wide area—encrypted burst signal, of course—but the mission team wouldn't respond, to avoid their response giving away their position.

"*Carrie-Anne*, this is *Raven*."

The big Chinook helicopter of the Night Stalkers 5E was

named for Carrie-Anne Moss, who had played Trinity in *The Matrix*. Their own RPA, *Raven*, had been named for Marion Ravenwood in *Raiders of the Lost Ark*. Their whole company was named for dangerous women—just one more reason to love flying with the 5E.

"It's *too* quiet."

LIEUTENANT COMMANDER LUKE ALTMAN echoed the call to the rest of his team.

The two leads on his team, Nikita and Drake, grunted out acknowledgements and shouted the message down the line. Six DEVGRU SEALs—SEAL Team 6's actual name, the Development Group—and six SilentHawk prototype hybrid-electric motorcycles in the cargo bay of a pounding Chinook helicopter. Just because it was stealth on the outside didn't mean that it was quiet on the inside. The US military wasn't big on wasting weight on sound insulation that could be better spent on ammunition or fuel.

The bay was eight feet wide, thirty long, and red as the devil's armpit with the night operations lighting. The helo flew fast and furious, mere meters above the Pakistan countryside to avoid detection, slewing them side to side with every tree or tall boulder.

Not his issue.

His issue was the takedown mission.

He considered dismissing the warning. What did coffin-heads really know, locked safely in their stateside boxes?

But he'd recognized Chief Warrant Zoe DeMille's voice. Not hard to do, since the only other person who could be on the circuit was Sofia Gracie, with her lush Latinate tones that so evoked her tall, lush body. That was his type of woman: long, leggy, and built. She wasn't big on talk and that was fine with him. But they'd tried it once. Not even enough spark to get them past drinks. Strange. In the past he'd always been able to ignore such shortcomings, but that had shifted recently. He'd be damned if he knew why, but for some idiot reason an awesome body wasn't enough anymore.

Zoe DeMille was the polar opposite of her commander: five-four, flat, and sassy, with hair somewhere between yellow, gold, and white except for black roots down the center. Kind of cute, in a punch-you-in-the-face style.

She'd even gone into the field with them once when an undercover mission called for it. Without her instincts, that mission might have gone down hard. She was no fighter, definitely not built for it (he could bench press her one-handed if she was a free weight), but just maybe she was a warrior despite that.

If only she didn't make it so damn hard to take her seriously. He was always having to discount her flighty civilian lifestyle for which he had no respect at all.

However, her job *was* to be their eye in the sky—especially as the helos were racing along, nap-of-the-earth at better than a hundred and fifty knots—in territory they were *not* supposed to be in. From their low flight altitude, they couldn't see anything past a few hundred meters—a view only two seconds into the future. And to fly even a drone with the 5E meant she was one of the best in the military at what she did, no matter what the woman herself was like.

"Thirty seconds," Nikita pointed out. It was the way his Number Two asked questions, by not wasting time actually asking them. Thirty seconds to their planned insertion point five miles from the target. He'd studied the files and was only too aware of what might lay in wait for them at Hathyaron's compound.

Thirty seconds meant a mile and a half out from that; they'd be audible any second if someone was waiting for them at the outer perimeter.

"Too quiet" because the information was bad and the target would be a dry hole? Happened often enough. Some leak could have spooked the target and they'd be gone. But the intel had come from The Activity—the Special Operations Command's own intelligence service—and those guys just didn't miss.

The other answer was that Hathyaron's instincts—which had kept him alive for so long—had him either bugging out or digging in a ground team so deep that they were invisible.

Which meant they were flying into a trap.

He flashed a signal to Nikita and Drake to prep the team for landing as he turned and called up to the pilot, "On the ground, now!"

"Wel-l," the Chinook's pilot, Major Pete Napier, drawled out laconically like only a true Coloradan ranch boy could, completely belying his radical actions to slow down and land. "Don't that beat all. You SEAL boys never do know what you're wanting, do ya?"

"Just don't put your wheels down, Napier. Might suck if Hathyaron put landmines out this far."

"Might at that," Napier agreed pleasantly as he hovered a hundred feet of helicopter to a stop less than a meter over the dirt. Danielle had sure mellowed his ass by marrying him. Pete "The Rapier" Napier was a changed man since he'd hooked his copilot—no less skilled, just less of a pain in the ass.

The rear gunner lowered the big rear ramp to reveal the night.

Napier had found what looked like a goat trail to hover over.

Luke gave no outward sign. He stood at the edge of the lowered ramp and tried to read the night. He flipped down his night-vision goggles. The NVGs revealed low brush and scrub, nothing of interest—probably not even a goat.

The night was cool—just below freezing. His breathe was as cloudy as a cold winter's day in Maine. Aside from all of the dust being churned by the rotors, it smelled clean. He liked the crispness on the air; it wouldn't be hiding anything. In Beijing or New Delhi the air hurt to breathe no matter what temperature it was, and it had a stench all its own that masked all other scents. He'd have to get well clear of the helo to listen to the night, but he could get to like this place if it wasn't filled with assholes who wanted him and his country dead. Even from here he should be able to see the heat signature if a man had walked through here in the last twenty-four hours. Or if some asshole had come out to bury IEDs along the path.

Nothing.

There was a dead feeling to the air despite the rotor's downwash; a feeling he knew.

"Dry hole," he bet himself, but he didn't tell his team because he wanted the vigilance to be at full-mission high.

"Saddle up," he called aloud, wondering if Napier's Coloradan was rubbing off on him. Better not be—Maine lobsterman and Colorado rancher just didn't mix. Same as Maine farmer and Texas rancher.

Old Maine joke.

A Texas rancher is surveying a Maine farm and says, "Well, shoot, son. I got a ranch so big takes me all day to drive 'round it in my car."

Mainer looks at him for a long moment before replying.

"Had a car like that once." Knocks his pipe out against his fencepost and refills it. "Got rid of her."

Saddle up? *Yeesh!*

2

*I*n fifteen seconds, six members of DEVGRU had slipped down the ramp on their silent hybrid-electric all-wheel-drive motorcycles, jumped down the meter of distance aloft that Napier was holding twenty tons of helo, and sped into the night. The big rotors' downwash drove at their backs as they accelerated down the trail, leaning hard into the throttles.

The helo would pull back to some safe location and was no longer his concern. They were Night Stalkers, so he knew they'd be there when it was time for their extraction. "Anytime, anywhere." It wasn't just a motto for them—it was a permanent mission plan.

Luke punched down the trail. He particularly enjoyed missions where he could integrate a motorcycle into the scenario, and these were particularly sweet machines. It took him back to his days racing dirt bikes along the Maine logging roads during long summers. Even though his team was all SEAL trained, no one could keep up with him as he jumped gullies and goosed it hard to climb narrow upward twists. Having all-wheel-drive made the SilentHawk bike exceptionally tenacious. The infrared headlamp lit the terrain brilliantly in his NVGs.

And still the ground remained evenly cold—no stray heat signatures bigger than a rabbit.

The SilentHawk could run over level ground at eighty with no noise except the tires in the dirt, and the chain. You could converse at normal volume while running at full tilt, except for the wind noise. On the goat trail, he rarely dropped below forty until he reached the edge of the original landing zone.

He grinned to himself at beating the others by a full thirty seconds. Not something he'd ever show, but it felt good. Long way from aging out.

Weird to think of that. He remembered older SEALs talking about it, but had never thought about it himself before. He had a decade in. By the end of the second decade, most SEALs' bodies had been so hammered to shit by constant training and hard missions that they just couldn't sustain it anymore. The thought marked some halfway point that he sure wouldn't care crap about for long while.

Parking his bike, he moved fifty meters down the trail and surveyed the night. He knew these smells. Less iron in the dusty soil and a little more moisture than Afghanistan—which meant it didn't catch in the back of his throat or hurt his nose as much. Growing up in the Maine woods, almost everywhere else he'd ever fought was drier—except for his time in Central America with Zoe DeMille. But the bit of moisture in the Pakistani air meant that it carried scents farther than a truly arid desert. No mules. No spent cordite. No hidden enforcer drinking too little water meaning that his piss would be sharper on the air.

The night animals were behaving normally. The heavy wingbeat of a lone owl passed by to the south and a mouse or gerbil skittered along twenty meters off to the northwest.

Nobody had disturbed them and few but a SEAL team operator could be here without doing so.

No lurking guards.

Dry hole.

The others were waiting back by where he'd parked his bike.

"Moving?" Nikita asked about what he'd found. It had always been Drake who had been the talker of the couple, but their year together since he'd made the jump from flying with the Night Stalkers to fighting with the SEALs had made him quieter rather than drawing her out.

"Ahead slow. On our toes." *Ain't gonna find shit, but no dying in case we do.*

He pointed at Nikita and Drake and waved them down the trail.

Nikita had been the first woman to make it into ST6 through the front door because she was just that goddamn tough. And Drake had proven himself in Honduras, getting Nikita to fall in love with him while he was at it. How did that shit happen?

He'd been there and seen it go down.

He'd given away the bride, for crying out loud, since her dad had gone down ugly years before.

Luke still had no idea how that kind of shit happened.

And their skills? They'd become his absolute go-to pair in the entire squad because they coordinated like no one else. It had taken going through hell and high water—and a fair amount of very fine Scotch one night—to convince his commander to sign off on them both remaining on his team. The results had spoken for themselves.

Signaling "No Relation" Coogan to follow him left, he knew the last two would ride to the right as they came in on the target. Coogan had protested one too many times that he was no relation to somebody and the tag had stuck. Not to the actor who'd played Uncle Fester in *The Addams Family.* Not to Coogan's Irish pub in New York or Coogan's tavern in Boston. "No Relation" was also the newest member of the team and Altman liked keeping him close for that reason. Better trained than dead, though he'd transferred over from another ST6 team so he was no slouch.

Nikita and Drake would know to move slower up the middle to give the two pincers time to sweep wide. That would also allow them more time to check out what was happening ahead.

Apparently the answer was nothing.

No landmines, no tripwires, no claymores, bazookas, machine guns…not even a damned potato gun. They rolled into Hathyaron's compound, scaring up a grand total of squat. Only a caretaker they startled awake…who insisted he was alone. Carrying no weapon except for a Makarov handgun so old Luke wouldn't dare fire it for fear it would shatter in his hand. And no radio. Guy was too frightened to be faking it, swearing up, down, and sideways that he knew nothing. He'd just been told to come watch the place starting this evening.

Fuck all! That's what was here. Luke knew it happened, but it didn't make it suck any less.

No need to tell his team to check it out, they were already on it. And he'd bet good money that they weren't going to find a single personal item: no clothing, photos, none of that. He knew that because they wouldn't if it were him.

He climbed off his bike in the center of the main courtyard and studied the soil. This had never been an arms depot—Hathyaron didn't work like that. He was a broker, never actually touching the goods himself. You needed a hundred thousand rounds for an AK-47 or a dozen Strela-2 man-portable missiles? Maybe a Russian Tupolev Tu-22M jet-bomber? He quoted a price and had someone else get his hands dirty with the delivery. It was part of what had made him so hard to find.

Luke studied the heat signatures while the rest of his team moved in. Footprints, some six hours old that must belong to the caretaker, and a few real faders were probably closer to eighteen—about dawn on New Year's Eve. No obvious booby traps. Meant Hathyaron hadn't been spooked; he'd planned to leave. The question now was for where, because the place felt as if he wasn't planning to come back.

The soil hadn't been stirred up by helos. Rather, a lot of tire tracks. Mostly size 245 tires with all-terrain tread appropriate for a Toyota Hilux or a Range Rover. Some narrow P205s for the ubiquitous Toyota Corollas that seemed to be taking over the world. Crap! That's what his dad had always driven. Gutless little rattletraps that just wouldn't die no matter what you did to them. At least not until Luke had pulled the plugs and dumped iron filings into the cylinders, which had destroyed the rings on the day he left for good. Did the same to the bastard's lobster boat on his way out of town.

But there was one heavier pair of tracks.

It wasn't like Hathyaron to have a truck big enough to run 275 duallies with similar tires on the trailer it towed. By the depth of the impression in the loose soil, he'd estimate that whatever he was towing was below the maximum gross weight, but it wasn't exactly light either—there was only a slight bulge of side tread from the flexed tires imprinted on the soil.

The tracks led out the compound's front gate and turned toward Peshawar. He followed them to their source around the back of the main building and up to a massive workshop building.

Everything about the compound was traditional Pakistani —wealthy but traditional. It wasn't some heartless concrete fort like bin Laden's place. The man had lived here. But he'd hear, if he didn't already know, that this place had been found and raided. No way was he coming back here any more than Luke was ever going back to Maine.

He peeked through the workshop's window with his NVGs, but what he saw made absolutely no sense.

Zoe had slid the *Raven* down to thirty thousand feet for better resolution. At six miles up, she could read the tags on a car's license plate. If there'd been a postcard in decent light, she could have read the address. She set one of her cameras to a wide area view so that there'd be no surprises if someone else approached. She set another to auto-track the first bike off the helo *Carrie-Anne*. That would be six-four of Lieutenant Commander Luke Altman, a full foot taller than she was. He *always* led from the front—except for the one time she'd forced him to follow in Drake Roman's wake.

She'd done it half because the mission called for it, but half to see if she could convince the bull-alpha SEAL to take a secondary role. She still wished she'd had some way to make a photographic series of Luke's various frustrated expressions on that mission—*The Many Grimaces of Lieutenant Commander Luke Altman.* A bestseller for sure—or at least some great fodder for her social media channel.

Her vlog had begun as a way to show her parents that there was more to life than an under-stimulated, *so-boring* existence. Of course, her actual career was almost entirely classified as top secret, so she couldn't use that at all. She'd started developing her feeds on herself—creating a persona that had been comfortably distant from herself—long before she joined the military. She'd spent a year trying different hair colors and cuts—frequently surveying the results with her various followers. Eyeglasses (all decorative, of course), clothes, shoes…she'd done the research and created an entire flighty persona that had nothing to do with her real personality. Yet it had taken off in a *huge* way. Her loyal following of budget-conscious hopefuls were near fanatic.

Over time, she'd become more comfortable in the role than in the person. Did that mean that's who she was becoming? That…persona on the screen? That didn't sit very comfortably in her, but she didn't know what else to do with it.

The Cutey-Edge had changed its name when she'd joined the military.

The Soldier of Style: Living in the Cutey-Edgy Budget Battlespace.

She never mentioned joining, it was simply a better name. Fan numbers had skyrocketed. Her fan group, *The Soldier of Style Brigade,* was far larger than a mere brigade. It wasn't the 1.3 million of the US military, but it was fast approaching the half million active personnel in the US Army.

Outside the military, she doubted if one in a thousand

believed she actually was a soldier. On the inside, she'd sometimes run into someone in the PX or a chow hall who would startle to find her actually on a military base. Rather than telling them she was a Chief Warrant Two with a top secret unit, she always told them she was just a clerk in Army intel—they'd know not to question her about anything. Or they should. Those who did were quietly reported, even if it cost her a fan every now and then.

Her online reputation had garnered her more than a few dates, and a serious pile of inappropriate propositions from: married men (some of them officers—whose wives she tipped off), overeager teenage boys (especially during her "experiments with leather" series), and the like. *Nothing* interesting, never mind long term.

She wanted a man...*not* boring. At least she knew that much. A writer, maybe an artist. Someone she could understand and who understood her. Someone so not like *The Many Grimaces of Lieutenant Commander Luke Altman.*

Altman had never mentioned her alternate, social self— he barely appeared to recognize her soldier-self from one mission to the next. At first it was understandable, the 5th Battalion E Company was new and the Team 6 SEALs only occasionally flew with them. But over time, the bonds had tightened and it was rare for the 5E to fly for anyone other than ST6. Still, Luke remained a puzzle; no tease elicited more than an infinitesimal frown. Definitely not an artistic, self-aware sort of person. Too bad for Altman that she couldn't stop herself from needling him because he was her polar opposite.

Way back on his first mission with the 5E he'd said he was married. To her mind, that also made him a safe target to tease. Actually, it had almost become mandatory. She'd imagined his home life.

"Welcome back from your latest life-threatening mission, dear."

Manly grunt.

"Did you have a good time?"

Another grunt. Then a beer and ball game before hitting the weight set. Better yet, a man cave with the weight set, the big screen TV, *and* the beer fridge. There he'd gather with his SEAL buddies and be…guys.

Such a charming image Zoe wanted to barf.

Yet hadn't he gone on a date with Sofia once? What kind of married asshole did that? He didn't wear a ring, but that didn't mean anything in Special Operations. Spec Ops guys didn't like things that could catch or conduct an electrical charge to an explosive trigger…or reveal the least thing about having evolved to Cro-Magnon rather than Neanderthal— never mind modern humans.

But there was no questioning that Luke Altman was one of the best warriors in the military and it would pay to keep an eye on him. Not hard at all. He might not be the artistic type, but he definitely wasn't a burden to watch.

So, while ninety-five percent of her did her job, looking for some clue as to where Hathyaron had gone, the other five percent followed Luke's progress. Racing ahead of the others to the outer perimeter, then walking away from the heat signature of his parked bike.

Again with the other five SEALs, entering the compound.

His unmoving stance in the center of the deserted site as the rest of his team moved ahead with rapid precision. His very stillness an anomaly that echoed along her camera feeds.

She and Sofia had had the *Raven* RPA circling high overhead since late afternoon and there'd been no movement. The Activity had reported Hathyaron's position two nights ago. Thirty-six hours, and they'd lost the biggest arms dealer in Pakistan somewhere in that window. Satellite overpasses were less consistent than drone coverage, and he must have left during one of the gaps in coverage—he'd know when those were, of course. He'd survived far too long not to. The Activity's call had sent them rushing from Italy where they'd been running missions into Libya, taking out ISIL infections one at a time.

Luke's heat signature was on the move again. Afoot by his speed. Yes, the tiny radar image of his stealth bike remained in place. She followed him around the main house —a two-story structure of typically four-square stucco design. He continued to an outbuilding almost as big as the house.

"*Raven?*" It was the first transmission of the night from the mission team.

"Yes?" Zoe answered, knowing full well what he was asking. Making the man actually speak was half the fun—he was pure gruff-warrior-hero to the core. He'd always looked it too. Clean-shaven with dark hair just long enough to look charmingly scruffy, fitting his roles when he had to go undercover, but not so long that he'd feel non-military. He wasn't like some Delta soldiers who took hairy and bearded permission to untidy limits and beyond. Never attractive to her. She liked Luke's neatness. No wasted actions. No wasted words. And certainly no wasted looks at her—even if she hadn't been watching for them.

"*Raven.*" He said it like *Du-uh!*

"Yes?"

"Zoe! Are there any damn stray heat signatures you can

see on this building before I walk into it?" He snapped it out like a single-word curse.

"Nope!" Could she sound anymore facile and airheaded? Probably not. Her normal games never worked with Luke. Maybe it was because he had the sense of humor of a rock.

His helmet's camera feed came online and she split-screened his feed with her drone's eye view of his position. Sofia took over the piloting and flight status consoles. It was fun how seamlessly two women could fly together.

She kept wanting to ask men if they ever did that, but the pilots who had sufficient security clearance that she could actually discuss her job with, counted very close to zero. She should ask Danielle or Pete Napier next time they were back in Alabama—except the Captain and Major were a little daunting in their perfect synchronization. Besides, maybe it was because they were married. Rafe and Julian in the lead DAP Hawk would just assume she was flirting. So not with those two self-proclaimed comedians!

For now, she was the eye in the sky protecting Luke's back.

The insides of the outbuilding were so bizarre that she had to blink as if that would clear the monitor's view. It was an auto shop. No, it was far more than. It was one that would put *any* American service garage to shame. The equipment was all top-of-the-line gear and it gleamed. In a land where dust penetrated everything everywhere, this shop looked surgically sterile.

She recognized the gear from her father's shop catalogs— he'd certainly never been able to afford even half of this. It was as if someone had driven up a big, red, Snap-on tools van and stocked one of absolutely everything. Rachet sets, welding gear, computerized emission testers, wheel alignment lasers…everything—right down to the girly calendar, even though Snap-on had stopped those when Zoe was a little girl (Hathyaron had the *Sports Illustrated* swimsuit one instead). She could practically smell the fine sheen of oil wiped over the sparkling tools to protect them, the latent hint of heavy weight motor oils, and the sharp tang of lubes and greases.

"Wow! Stop moving so fast." Luke was just scanning the room, turning his camera as fast as he was shifting his gaze. She couldn't see all the cool toys when he didn't focus on them for long enough.

"It's car shit, DeMille. What do you care?"

I had such a boring childhood that I used to read Dad's catalogs for fun. Nope! Not going to find her saying a word about thinking this was cool.

Luke turned to leave.

"Wait. Go back!" She'd seen something. But what?

Luke turned back more slowly.

"Stop there!"

"Didn't know you were into cars, DeMille." She wasn't looking at the tools anymore, though she could tell by the angle of view that he was.

"This place isn't mere cars, you goof. Look at the poster."

"So?" The view shifted and centered on it. The poster hung in the place of pride, centered above the workbench. It was black, with a few silver lines that suggested an Arab wrap around a man's head and shoulders. Below it simply said, "Dakar" and the date.

"It's the Dakar Rally, the toughest car race in the world. The Tour de France-scale ultimate endurance race of motor sports."

Luke took a step closer to it. She could feel him squinting at it in confusion from ten thousand miles away.

It was the announcement poster for the most amazing race ever. And the next run started in just a week.

"Well?" Luke was back to his one-word sentences again.

"Wait a sec," Zoe did a quick search of her social media fan base to confirm something, then looked back at the image of the poster Luke faced.

"DeMille." *Wasting my time here, DeMille.*

She composed a quick message to Christian Vehrs. He was one of her superfans—and a racer in The Dakar Rally.

"It means…" Zoe dragged it out to buy herself a moment.

Christian pinged back immediately, announcing that he was always at her service.

"…that we're going to Dakar."

"Fine print says the race starts in Argentina."

"Uh-huh. Which is why you and I are meeting in Dakar, Senegal, in twenty hours. If you want Hathyaron, get your cute ass moving."

Luke just offered one of his questioning grunts.

Sofia looked at her in some surprise.

Zoe offered her a conspiratorial grin—woman to woman, even if she wasn't half the woman her commander was. "Gotta keep him on his toes," she whispered even though she hadn't keyed the microphone.

Sofia's smile didn't quite buy it.

Zoe wasn't sure why she'd thrown in that last bit. She wasn't a woman who watched men's asses—that was more of a cliché from *Sleepless in Seattle* than reality as far as she was concerned. Though, being a SEAL, his *would* be exceptional. Didn't mean she was actually interested.

Also, drone pilots simply didn't go into the field. But she'd done it once for the Honduras mission and was suddenly itching for an excuse to do it again.

"Really?" Sofia's arched eyebrow—lovely, of course, and only one raised, something that Zoe couldn't do no matter how much she'd practiced in the mirror as a kid—looked very skeptical of her motives.

Zoe nodded, *Yes, it is necessary.* She long ago learned not to look at her motives too closely because she never liked the answers. Not since she was eleven and—

So not going there!

Sofia shrugged her acceptance—she'd make sure it was square with the company commander.

Zoe keyed the mic to Luke. "It's on the westernmost tip of the African bulge. The farthest point into the Atlantic, if you're wondering."

"Know my countries."

"Learned them in fifth grade like a good little boy?"

"Learned them by reading the models' profiles in *Playboy.*"

Zoe couldn't help glancing down at her own chest, well hidden by the pilot's uniform she always wore when she was flying. Well, if that didn't just put her in her place. Not a photographer anywhere would waste a single shot on her. Not even for an issue on the hot women of the most secret helicopter regiment anywhere.

Poop!

3

"*W*hat the hell?" Luke flapped his carboard sign at DeMille as she breezed off the plane in the Blaise Diagne International Airport in Dakar, Senegal. No mistaking her, there couldn't be two people like her on the plane—or anywhere, for that matter. Petite, blonde, outrageously flamboyant in bright yellow clothes, and a smile bigger than should be physically possible.

"It means precisely what it says. And hello to you too, Luke."

He flipped the sign to look at it again, as if it would make more sense this time. It didn't. It had been included along with his plane ticket and false ID that had already been waiting at Bagram Airfield by the time he got out of Pakistan and back into Afghanistan.

Zoe DeMille, Personal Assistant. In large black letters.

"Not your goddamn ass—"

"Keep your voice down, Luke."

"It is down," he struggled to rein it in. "I'm not your goddamn assistant, personal or otherwise."

"We *are* low profile here," she ignored his protest.

DeMille was anything but low profile. She wore oversized sunglasses—despite it being past midnight—with thick, plastic, yellow rims and pale yellow lenses. Her sundress— again past midnight, but he was pretty sure that's what women called them—was sunrise yellow with blue butterflies sewn on to flutter about the skirt's hem. The combination made her blue eyes stand out, despite the ridiculous tinted glasses. The dress stopped just above her knees, revealing surprising legs. He'd remembered being surprised the first time he'd seen those legs too. DeMille wasn't the size of woman that a man expected to have good legs, but she did.

He very slowly crumpled the sign in one fist, then folded his arms over his chest.

"Oh, you're so cute when you get like this that you just slay me. I swear on my favorite cat's grave."

"Isn't that supposed to be your mother's grave?"

"Not dead yet. Duh."

Teach him to open his damned mouth. Figured she was a cat person. As if there was something wrong with a decent dog. Day he retired from the military he was going to the pound and getting himself a prime, Grade A mutt. Nothing wrong with a dog.

Though there was definitely something wrong with this airport. The country had a perfectly serviceable airport right in the heart of the city, a city that now accounted for over twenty percent of the country's population and more every day. So what did they do? They built a brand new airport sixty kilometers into the desert that was close to absolutely nothing. Open more than a year and the nearest hotel was still over thirty kilometers away—all one of them.

The airport terminal was a shining multi-story edifice

with four jetways, three of which stood empty. His plane had parked far out on the tarmac, then everyone had been crowded into buses for the drive to a small door at the bottom of the steel-and-glass terminal.

He'd watched three planes debark over the last six hours as late morning became late afternoon, which accounted for all four flights that were scheduled for today. Not one had used the jetways, except DeMille's of course. She'd strolled off the plane at the head of the line—which meant her pint-sized frame had traveled first class while he'd been crunched in coach.

"You rich or something?"

Behind her came a line of majestically dressed men and women in what he assumed was traditional attire. It was clearly one of those countries where people still thought plane travel was special and dressed up for the occasion. A heavy matron, in full head-wrap matching a floor-length dress of strongly patterned gold on red, stepped from the plane slowly but with immense dignity. A pair of tall, very handsome daughters tended her either side as soon as they were clear of the jetway.

He'd been watching people unload all evening, for lack of anything better to do. The Senegalese weren't as generally dark as the Nigerians, but they were close. They were a damned handsome race. Tall, shining white teeth, clear skin. And the Senegalese definitely knew how to build curves on their women. He wondered what the cultural rules were like about picking women up in bars here.

"Not rich," DeMille dragged his attention back down to her level. "The girl at the ticket counter is a fan and gave me a free upgrade to First Class."

"A fan." He used a tone that had quashed the hopes of new recruits for the rest of their useless little lives.

She just offered him a cheery, "Uh-huh."

Keep that up and he was going to start calling her Tweety Bird: small, yellow, terminally cheery, and far too cute for her own good.

Well, he knew a fan of what, but he sure as hell didn't get it. He didn't work with anyone without investigating their background. Her service record was so stellar that it was hard to believe it wasn't faked—except she was one of only two RPA pilots selected to fly for the Night Stalkers 5E, which said she'd earned every bit of it. But it was Nikita who had shown him Zoe's social media profile.

The Soldier of Style: Living in the Cutey-Edgy Budget Battlespace.

It was catchy. Funny even. Didn't mean he understood any of it though.

When he asked if her number of followers was considered a lot of fans, Nikita had taken him to the US Army site. Okay, so the Army was still outpacing Zoe DeMille, *The Soldier of Style,* in popularity. But not by as much as he'd expected—or liked. He'd investigated the site, but couldn't make any sense of it. Too foreign to his way of thinking. He'd finally asked Nikita to break it down for him.

"She plays it clean. Not a single word about her day job. It's as if she's two people, one RPA pilot and one constantly reinventing herself. This site and her fans are all about the latter." He'd tried to watch one of the videos, but gave up halfway through because he didn't recognize the woman at all or understand what the hell she was talking about. The only thing she had in common with Chief Warrant Zoe DeMille was blonde hair and a thoroughly cheerful attitude. But the overexcited-by-fashion bit he didn't get at all.

Old Maine joke.
Three blondes out walking in the Maine woods.
First blonde, "Oh look, deer tracks."
Second blonde, "Those aren't deer tracks, they're moose tracks."
Third blonde is still looking down, puzzled by the tracks, when the train hits them.

Zoe DeMille's online persona in the "Fashion Battlespace" was absolutely the third blonde. Why would he want ditzy?

Not that she made a whole lot more sense in real-space either. She was one of those women who looked permanently twenty, except for her service record and those eyes—when they weren't behind yellow-colored lenses.

He remembered those eyes from Honduras. They'd seen things so clearly, and in ways that they never taught in SEAL training. He'd been trained in threat assessment, but DeMille had been deeply attuned to emotional nuance so subtle that even after she pointed it out he often couldn't see it—yet she'd been proven right every time. But this wasn't some phony battlespace. Nor was it a real one. Senegal was one of the very few peaceful countries on the entire continent—not a single war since it gained independence from France in 1960.

"Why the hell are we—"

"Zoe!" The loud cry had Luke slapping for a weapon that he wasn't wearing.

"Christian!" Zoe cried back, pronouncing it to rhyme with Shawn, before tossing her massive electric-blue purse—it matched her dress' butterflies for crying out loud—to Luke and letting herself be enveloped in a big hug by the interloper. He was mid-height, slender, elegant in Armani or some such shit—you could smell the money on him from his leather loafers to his professionally trimmed beard—*coming in with a little gray there, dude.*

"To meet you in person! It is such an honor." Well, at least the suave bastard wasn't sleeping with her. Not that he cared. Or had any reason to. *Le Dude* was so French that he should be in a Parisian café…in a movie…anywhere far away from here. Right. Senegal was a former French colony. The French colonialists had differed from the British: the Brits ruled, the French married in. An attitude that still hadn't changed even in the post-colonial era.

"What are you doing on this side of security?" Zoe was standing so close that they looked to be the oldest of friends on the verge of *becoming* lovers. Had they had online sex or whatever that was called?

"Oh, I couldn't wait. So I buy a ticket, *oui?*" He was one of those Frenchmen who was too handsome and knew it. They always made Luke want to squish them like a bug.

Zoe acted like such things happened to her all the time. She looped an arm through this *Christawn's* and walked off chatting away happily.

Squashing him like a bug could be a kindness.

———

ZOE COULD BARELY UNDERSTAND a word Christian was saying. It wasn't his accent; her high school French had left her ear well enough adapted to easily understand his heavily-accented English.

It was that watching Lieutenant Commander Luke Altman of SEAL Team 6, without watching him, was *so* distracting. A reflection in the darkened glass of the broken water-bottle vending machine. Another against a window facing the night.

She ached to pull out her phone and snap a picture, even just for herself.

Tall, rugged, pissed as hell about being in Senegal without her telling him why—there just hadn't been time to tell him about Christian's connection to The Dakar Rally where Hathyaron must have gone—and toting along a foul attitude and a bluebird Michael Kors purse. It was actually a knockoff, all her budget could afford, but she'd always liked it. Watching Luke carry it through the Dakar airport now made it her absolute favorite. Maybe that would be her next hair color, though she'd become attached to the daffodil-blonde—which her fans still favored too. It was time to stir them up, but not blue. Maybe she'd go to a true white next.

Focus, Zoe! Never something she did well when she wasn't flying.

At the baggage claim, she handed Luke her ticket. "You know which one, Luke," as if he was indeed her personal assistant.

He offered her a narrow-eyed glare. She barely managed not to giggle as Christian led her aside. It would be obvious once Luke saw it on the baggage carousel, but he wouldn't know that.

"So, who is this Luke?" Christian asked in a barely lowered voice as he led her away. "Should I be terribly jealous?"

"He *works* for me, Christian. He doesn't sleep with me." Despite her teases on just that point during their last mission together, he hadn't done a *single* inappropriate thing. Ever. Of course not, why would he? Why would a man like him, who could choose any woman he wanted, be at all interested in someone like her? Even if he wasn't married.

He'd said he was, but she'd seen him head off on a date with Sofia. Her commander hadn't said a word afterward and they'd given no other signs of being together. Just a *Wham! Bam! Thank you, Ma'am?* That didn't sound like Sofia. That totally sounded like a SEAL and she wanted none of it.

"Ah. That is good. Your fans would be very disappointed if the lovely Zoe settled for such an angry man. You need a French lover."

"Like you?" Would she be interested? He was far closer to what she was looking for than the SEAL commander. His charm was as thick as his accent, both undeniably inviting.

"Ah, my wife Leola is Senegalese. She does not have the French view of such things. You will meet her. Meek like a lamb in public. But her name, it means lioness. Curiously, her name is Italian even though she is a pureblood native." He shrugged it off. "She is fierce in the home."

"And in the bed?" She felt decidedly voyeuristic for asking, but as he was French, he took it in stride.

"One look at her and you will know how she is in my bed." His tone spoke volumes.

Zoe only had to look around to know that the Senegalese women were all shaped far more like Sofia than like her. Would Luke treat her differently if she had a real figure?

Now there was an odd question because she couldn't think of why she'd possibly care.

She glanced back to see him carrying her massive zebra-striped suitcase. He ignored the wheels and simply carried it as if it weighed less than her handbag. She'd been unsure of what the future held, so she'd packed her civilian clothes—

with enough changes to satisfy her fans for at least a week—and a full military kit except no weapons.

Luke didn't notice her glance. He wasn't looking at her or Christian. His anger apparently forgotten, Luke Altman appeared to be ever-so-casually looking at nothing—which Zoe knew was when he was looking at absolutely everything. A man strolled by him—*close* by him. Moving well into his personal space, which was almost shocking. No one got close to Lieutenant Commander Altman unless he was playing a role. She'd certainly been deep inside his personal space for much of the Honduras mission—atypically so, even for her. It had felt natural at the time…still did in memory and—

If she hadn't been watching, she'd have missed the handoff.

Luke had been wearing a small, efficient backpack before she'd burdened him with her handbag and suitcase. Now, after the man had brushed by him, Luke also carried a small satchel—the handoff so smooth that it had nearly been invisible. They were outside airport security, so she'd wager there was at least a handgun and a good knife in the newly-acquired satchel.

A warm shiver slid over her skin. Knowing that an armed Team 6 SEAL was watching her back felt surprisingly good. Whoever said that having a highly-protective male in your life was going out of style needed to have their head fixed—if she'd had one in her past, her present might have been so very different.

Zoe filed the idea away for her next media post.

4

"*W*hat the hell have you got in here, DeMille? You know this country never gets below 70, right?" Luke heaved the suitcase, as heavy as a field pack, into the back of the Frenchman's waiting car.

"A Vega II?" DeMille sounded passionately breathless, and was utterly ignoring him. No, purposely ignoring him. It wasn't an accident that she hadn't told him why the hell they were in Senegal, Africa, together. He hadn't missed how often he was a target of her quick tongue.

Altman looked around—Vega was a star in Lyra he'd used to navigate a few times on hikes—but it wasn't even sunset. DeMille was staring at the bright red car.

"Oh, Christian," she whispered, like saying thank you after amazing sex.

What the hell?

"I bring it out special for you, dearest Zoe. I knew you would appreciate her."

"The 1962 Facel Vega II. Oh, with the manual four-speed," still in that tone that was supposed to be reserved for the bedroom.

It was a long car that might have been sleek half a century ago—so retro it was almost modern. Two doors meant that emergency egress from the back seat was poor. It looked like some primitive had been trying to design the future but reality had passed him by.

DeMille was busy emoting over original leather. She rapped her knuckles on the wooden panel, which sounded metallic—which she apparently knew beforehand.

When Christian opened the hood, she scurried to look. "The Chrysler 383 cubic inch Typhoon V8." She held both hands to her heart.

"She will go *very* fast," Christian might be talking about the car or about DeMille.

It didn't sound as if she was faking it for the Frenchman's benefit. It sounded as if she actually knew something besides blue handbags and zebra suitcases filled with ten tons of girl-shit.

Why was it so hard to remember that she was an Avenger RPA pilot? She had skills, even if he only understood the one of them.

Not that he understood a thing about piloting either— except for the data feed it provided. *That* he understood perfectly because it was a new key to survival and victory in modern warfare. And no one provided it like the 5E's RPA team. The fliers of the 5E were amazing and he loved what their stealth-equipped aircraft could deliver, but at least half the reason he'd shifted most of his mission load to them was because of their RPA team.

Sofia and DeMille. Two seriously skilled women, who were so different that it was hard to believe they were the same species, never mind the same gender. Sofia was everything a woman should be and DeMille was…

She was talking gear ratios. The damned Frenchman was practically drooling. Well, whatever turned your crank. Christian's hand rested casually at the small of her back as if she was the pinnacle of desirability and not…

Shit!

DeMille was like a woman designed just to confuse the crap out of men. Thankfully, she wasn't his problem. Except she was. She'd dragged him to bloody Senegal. While he didn't know what was going on, he'd bet she was way out of her depth.

One of the airport "freelancers" came over with some hustle in mind. He knew the type. Hanging about and always vying to make an extra buck wherever they could. Rather than pull a gun on the guy, he gave him a friendly-seeming grab on his forearm. Pinching the ulnar nerve point, he turned him about and sent him on his way, letting him wonder how long it would be until his arm started functioning again. Take about thirty seconds, but Luke saw no reason to tell him that as long as he didn't come back.

The late-afternoon light blazed down out of the dusty blue sky. The parking lot could hold only a few hundred cars —smaller than the average American grocery store—but it was mostly empty. No sign of long-term parking lots, apparently not needed. Palm trees and irrigated grass made it appear First Worldly.

Turning away from the airport toward the near horizon dispelled that impression completely. Palm trees gave way to twisted scrub and cactus growing from the achingly dry red-brown sand. He twisted a foot and felt the slickness of blown sand over the tarred pavement. Just enough to make him compensate if he was turning a corner at a dead sprint or on a speeding motorcycle. He filed that away against future need.

Done showing off his car, Christian waved Luke toward the back seat. It wasn't small-car cramped, but neither was it the back of his Silverado pickup's Crew Cab. DeMille was half the size, but he was the one crawling into the back— stupid two-doors. How did she keep making him do shit like this?

She settled in the front passenger seat and at least had the decency to slide it forward…then she tipped the seat well back. He reached out to grab the lever and pop her upright, but the back of the seat hit the center of his chest before he could reach the control.

Which left him staring at the top of her dark part and the cascade of blonde hair falling to either side. It looked thick and soft, perfect for a man to run his hands through and—

He was *not* thinking such shit about Chief Warrant Zoe DeMille. Just plain and simple wasn't happening.

She tipped her head back to smile up at him upside down as if she could read his thoughts. Worse, he wouldn't put it past her. It would explain some of why he always felt off balance around her.

Her position also provided a very pleasant view down the front of her sundress that revealed enough to show that, while she didn't wear a bra, she was very definitely female.

Whatever.

Shit! Now he was sounding like her. Given the choice, he'd rather sound like Napier, despite his new-found Colorado-pilot-Joe Friendly mannerisms while flying his Chinook.

DeMille had placed him here. In Senegal. No idea why.

And no way to ask without revealing DeMille's game. Or maybe she and Christian were in on it together.

If she was wasting his time, he'd see that she was busted but good and—

Except that wasn't like her.

So, she did have some clear purpose but enjoyed trying to get a rise out of him by not giving him even a clue. *Fine.* Let her try. He pulled on his shades against the lowering sun and stared out the window to watch the desert give way to concrete buildings. Lots of them. Most of 'em empty.

Damned weird country.

ZOE STARED OUT THE WINDOW. She'd fallen into a strange science fiction novel. *The Half-built Apocalypse* or something like that. Her first ever trip to Africa, first out of the US other than some training trips to Canada and Ramstein in Germany. And that lone mission to Honduras. She'd flown all over the world from the safety and comfort of her coffin— most of the time ten miles up, but to see Africa in person from ground-level was overwhelming. She'd thought it would be so easy, like slipping down to Honduras on a luxury cruise boat had been.

Not so much.

At the airport, she'd focused on Christian's Vega II partly because it was amazing, but partly because everything else was wholly disconcerting.

She wasn't so parochial that being one of the only three white people in the entire airport was affecting her, but *everything* was different.

The clothing styles had started it. Men wore button-down white shirts, dark trousers, and leather shoes. That was fine.

The women were swathed from neck to ankle in form-fitting dresses that came in a wild array of colors and patterns. It had taken her a long time to notice among the wild oranges, reds, purples, golds, and every other color both in and out of nature that no two were alike. The colored patterns of the material—which would appear wild in the extreme elsewhere—somehow belonged in Dakar. They were remarkably modest in that they covered the women from throat to ankle, but they also displayed them elegantly.

During the flight she'd been particularly captivated by a teen across the aisle who would be wearing jeans, a slogan t-shirt, and Converse in any Western culture. Instead, she wore leather sandals and a stop-sign-red dress with a massive bloom of multicolor painted flowers flowing upward from her hip to curl around her breast and also spilling down over the skirt. It made Zoe's own efforts to push "The Cutey-Edgy" appear timid and reserved. And it made the girl breathtakingly beautiful.

Once away from the airport, the women's lush fabrics were the only color to be seen.

She'd never seen anything like what was passing outside the window, not even the desert towns near Clovis AFB.

Christian was racing the big car along the road like a cross between a luxury liner and a cigarette racing boat. The divided highway—three lanes to either side—boasted perfect pavement, concrete dividers, Western-style exit ramps, and clusters of little orange and yellow taxis that were mere flashes in Christian's wake.

To either side of the pristine highway was an entire city under construction. Mile after mile of three-story apartment blocks, malls, a massive sports arena, and more. And no sign of a single person or car on the side roads except for construction vehicles. Only the highway had traffic and no one using the big, sign-posted exits and on-ramps. This couldn't be normal, could it? She had no way to judge.

Anything.

It had seemed like such a good idea at the time. Hathyaron goes to race The Dakar. Superfan Christian Vehrs lets Zoe and Luke go undercover at The Dakar Rally as his "assistants." They find and take out Hathyaron. Done. Simple.

Except Christian was still in Dakar, Senegal, rather than preparing for the start of The Dakar Rally in Argentina. And now it was all going to hell and Luke was going to just flat out kill her for screwing it all up so badly.

How much of her "instant plan" had been an ego trip of "Zoe knows best" and how much had been real? Was it too late to declare a mission abort? Could she ask Luke? What would he think of her if she did? This empty city was scaring her like an echo of a bitter emptiness that had devastated her so long ago. A city with no life. No purpose. No—

"Yes, dearest Zoe," Christian must have noticed her distraction. "It surprises all people the first time. The president, he decides that the city must grow, so he is building the city before the people come. A vast city far from any services."

At least he didn't appear to have noticed her rising terror before she could throttle it back down—something she had too much practice doing.

"Scam?" Luke asked from the back seat. He'd made no response to her laying the seat back to tease him and now it seemed even more foolish to return it to upright, which left her craning her neck to see over the dashboard. Which felt even sillier.

Christian shrugged. "It is Africa. There is always someone else's hand—how do you say—on the pot? It is so normal, we don't even bother to look anymore."

Luke offered one of his grunts, apparently exhausting his verbal capacity by unearthing an actual word.

She tipped her seat upright and continued watching ahead. Still no detectable reaction from Luke Altman and there was no passenger side mirror on the old car so that she might catch a glimpse of him without turning. The man was a brick—almost literally. Solid, dependable, and just as exciting. No tease penetrated his formidable facade. Had she ever seen him smile?

So the question was, why did she keep trying? He wasn't like her father, content with his small garage and his quiet life. Her father was an open book, a gentle man with gentle thoughts who loved his family and his cars. Yet she couldn't leave the inscrutable SEAL alone. Maybe because she needed a distraction.

Luke thumped the back of her seat, as if he was punching her shoulder. Not about raising her seat, she'd already done that. So why? To remind her of something? Nothing that she could think of.

After the team had cleared out of Hathyaron's compound, there hadn't been time for any planning. There'd barely been time to shower and pack—there was always a sense of flying in a coffin that she had to wash off immediately after any shift. Cold, chill efficiency. As if she had indeed flown the *Raven* directly rather than remotely. She could feel the kerosene of the jet fuel drying and tightening her skin even if she couldn't actually smell it.

It wouldn't bode well if Luke knew that her plan had just imploded.

They finally moved out of the Half-built Apocalypse area and rolled into outer Dakar, the scenery changed only a little. One-story buildings of gray concrete topped with tin roofs were scattered among baobab trees—the fat gray tree trunks sported thin branches with few leaves, looking like forlorn rocket stages dropped end-on into the sand. She only recognized them from having read *The Little Prince* in high school French class.

In the city itself, there were few cars, almost all old, and not all that many scooters. Sheets up on roofs drying in the hot wind indicated that there were finally a few inhabitants. The flat terrain revealed a city with a few taller buildings yet they never seemed to come closer despite their considerable speed.

Focus. There *was* a reason she was here and, short of bailing out of a car going over ninety, she was stuck in a bucket seat of her own making. She didn't want Luke giving her some other unsubtle reminder.

"Christian. You have raced The Dakar seven times, right?" Maybe he knew Hathyaron personally.

"Nine," Christian suddenly lit up, as if he hadn't already been glowing before. Some part of her had been keeping up with his inane chatter about how Zoe was his wife's style guru and how her energy and vitality had captured his imagination as well.

"Ever won?" The conversation killer asked from the back seat with two whole words.

"One does not win The Dakar so easily," Christian replied in a huff. "One survives it. The big sponsors, they command resources that we amateurs can never bring. There are over three hundred entries, and four winners each year. This is not some simple party; it is the Dakar Rally."

"Which isn't in Dakar?" Luke had all the tact of a turnip.

"Alas, no." And Christian looked so sad that Zoe reached out to pat his arm.

AND NOW DEMILLE was getting all cozy with the guy? Holding onto his arm while he was driving at twice the speed of any other traffic?

Hadn't Mr. Suave said it was such a pleasure to meet her in person?

Luke sent a secure text to Nikita: *Investigate relations: Zoe DeMille, Christian Vehrs, Dakar, Senegal. Check whatever that site was you showed me.*

They waded into Dakar—the city, not the race. The capital of Senegal, it might seem a Third World city, but only on the surface. Buildings weren't falling apart, they were being built and painted. It was being worked on in a thousand different ways.

After a while, he managed to sort out the new construction from the old. Only after a building was finished did it get a coat of paint. He'd been in enough concrete block towns to appreciate how rare such attention was. They were done up in pastels, mostly pale yellows and equally dull blues, but they were painted. No wild Indian paint jobs here.

The city proper had crazed traffic. The rotaries— probably used instead of traffic lights because the electricity was too unreliable—were so narrow and tight that it was hard to see how a truck or bus negotiated them even without the clutter of bicycles, scooters, and taxis ignoring any rational sense of navigation. All of the vehicles came in the same color—dust-coated red—no matter what their actual paint job might be, but they were there. It meant that they had moved beyond strictly foot-and-moped culture that so much of the Third World never made it past.

However, they still changed lanes as if they were fresh out of the moped era—with psychotic abruptness most SEALs wouldn't attempt. Any opening over half a car-length long was an excuse for hard acceleration, even if a pothole the size of Kansas awaited them.

In his experience, few cities anywhere had pedestrian dress codes. Paris required a certain amount of chic—most of it black. Seattle had a dress code of never looking dressed up. Dakar did as well. Men all wore the ubiquitous slacks and button-down shirt. Some women were in the evocative dresses and others dressed similarly to the men, but all decently attired. There might not be much money here, but there was a pride in who they were. In how they carried themselves.

He also didn't see any beggars on the street. Little kids selling neatly folded packets of peanuts they'd toasted on a small propane burner using a steel wok, but not begging. Fruit stands could be merely a single pile of bananas. One woman sold mangoes into which she'd jabbed a wooden stick and was peeling with a small machete. He'd make a point of keeping an eye out for where these vendors were, in case he needed to grab a machete on short notice.

The stark poverty was missing. Which was interesting. As if that low, painful layer had been scrubbed clean from the city—or perhaps never been there.

They plunged into the city. Suddenly the massive length of Christian's car commanded attention. But it didn't do him any good as the congestion pressed them down to a slow jog. It let Christian babble even more in his tour-guide role.

No obvious connections outside social media, Nikita pinged back. *He responds to almost every post by Zoe, but so do hundreds of others. He's one of the most consistent, though always in his wife's name as he claims she is the true fan.*

He started to type back: *Is hundreds good?* But figured Nikita wouldn't have mentioned it if it wasn't. Zoe. First name basis. Of course Zoe had been Nikita's maid-of-honor, so it made a certain sense.

Luke stared at his phone, waiting for further information, but there wasn't any coming in. He could feel Nikita doing that almost-smile of hers that she'd picked up since marrying Drake. Just daring Luke to ask the next question.

To hell with that. He stuffed the phone back in his pocket.

"The *Deux Mamelles,* the Two Breasts," Christian suddenly had Luke's complete attention. He slipped his hand onto the hilt of his hidden knife—five inches of hardened steel. While not quite his Winkler blade, if that man tried to grab DeMille's breast, he'd find that hand pinned to his own thigh—hard.

Christian instead waved his hand to take in the surroundings rather than making a pass at DeMille, which drastically increased his projected lifespan. But he wasn't indicating some well-endowed woman on the street either— and there were a lot of those to see now that they were barely crawling.

"They stand above Dakar like guardian angels."

Luke decided he had to be talking about the two hills. They weren't much to look at, maybe a hundred meters tall. However, with the severe flatness of Dakar and the flatter Atlantic Ocean beyond to compare them to, they were indeed prominent—and kind of breast-shaped. The far one sported a tall lighthouse in traditional white like an oversized nipple. The near one had some crazy monument that was half as tall again as the hill it stood on. A powerful man, holding aloft a child pointing out to sea, and forty meters of bronze babe on his arm with her hair and skirt billowing out from high on her long thigh.

But what Luke really noticed was that DeMille's hand still rested on Christian's arm. He remembered the feel of that from the Honduras mission where they had posed as a couple. She'd often kept her hand in the crook of his elbow when they were in public, as if it was the most natural thing in the world to her. Natural to *her* maybe. So foreign to him, even undercover, that he could almost feel her fingers there even now. The only people who ever touched him were the occasional bar babe, for the brief encounters that entailed, and soldiers who needed a few lessons in hand-to-hand combat.

Except it was this Christian guy she was touching.

Fine. Not as if he had any claim on her himself. Or interest in her.

The Frenchman just damn well better not touch her in return.

*Z*oe struggled to make some sense of her surroundings. Everything had gotten so disorienting that even that slightest contact with Christian was the only thing that kept her from flying apart. She'd stopped as soon as she caught herself, but she missed that tiny bit of human contact badly.

They were seated on the verandah of what she supposed was an upscale Italian restaurant. The food was good—though not up to Pismo Beach standards, or even Fort Rucker DFAC standards—but the Fort Rucker Dining Facility had some seriously good cooks working the line so maybe the comparison wasn't fair. Ahead of her lay the Atlantic: nothing but the Cape Verde Islands five hundred kilometers over the horizon until the ocean slammed up against The Bahamas. The sun was easing down toward that watery line in a sky that should be painfully blue but was tinted gold with a hazy red dust.

The ocean didn't smell of ocean. Nothing here smelled right. There was the faintest hint of sea salt, but none of the rich sea-ness of Pismo or the murky thickness of the Florida panhandle just south of Fort Rucker. Instead of the smell of garbage, which she'd expected, there was the smell of livestock.

"But we're in the heart of the city," she'd protested when they'd been stopped along a major road while five cows had moseyed through the intersection.

"That is Farouk's herd," Christian had shrugged negligently. "They make most of their living in this area. Everyone knows them. Phillipe's goats wander less, but you can sometimes see them down that street."

As if on cue, she'd looked and there they were, sorting through the garbage to see what was edible. Apparently almost everything was, as every member of the small herd was chewing away happily except for a pair of baby goats chasing each other in circles.

When they'd arrived at the restaurant, it was almost as disorienting. It was thoroughly Western in design, furnishing, and menu. The verandah perched over a craggy beach with the Atlantic rolling away from them forever.

Between their table and the ocean were tiny patches of sand that had been leveled within rock-walled terraces and were graced with picnic-table sized, open-side thatch roof. There was nothing inside them except more sand, but it might get them clear of the sun during the daytime.

Laughter floated up from a group on the second one past the end of the verandah. Most were astonishingly tall and handsome black men. A group of four white women sat close together—chatting happily away like close friends. She could hear snatches of English and French and some language she'd never heard before, but couldn't make out any of their words from this distance. Their easy way with each other calmed her nerves better than a good belt of scotch—which truthfully just tended to make her sleepy.

Zoe wondered what it would be like to just stand up, descend the stairs, and join them. They were her age, dressed in jeans, flip-flops, and long-sleeved shirts open over t-shirts. They had no particular style, no overt fashion among them. They were…so much themselves.

She would be embarrassed to wear her clothes among them, though they didn't look like the sort to care. She didn't like the feeling but couldn't seem to look away. She made sense in her own world. But her "sense" seemed uncomfortably senseless in theirs.

As she, Christian, and Luke were served with their main courses—hers was seafood carbonara—the group below was also served by someone who had been cooking out of sight under the thatched roof. Great round platters like giant pizza tins were set out. Rice, dark brown with sauce, had been spread in an even layer with a small fish and some vegetables in the center. Everyone gathered around the platters with a spoon and set in to eating, some kneeling on the sand, others sitting cross-legged.

"Watch them," Christian said softly—the first time he'd spoken in less than a merry bellow all afternoon. "They will only eat what of the *ceebu jen*—it means fish and rice and is the national dish—is in the triangular area in front of them, like a slice of pizza."

"But the fish lies in the exact middle." Even as she spoke, someone dug into the fish with his spoon and pried loose some meat. He nudged some into the triangles adjoining his before pulling some in front of himself.

"Everything in this culture is shared. It is called *teranga*. A rough translation is: 'the more you share, the more plentiful your bowl will be'."

Zoe looked back at their own table. They each had their own section of table, their own napkin, silverware, glass of wine, and white plate of food.

The silent meal continued below them. "They don't have much to say to each other."

"The Senegalese believe that you should do one thing at a time to improve your enjoyment of it. Eat, talk, play music, make love. These are all separate."

Rather than looking at Christian, she caught herself watching Luke, who was already well started on his spaghetti and meatballs.

"Your assistant never talks, so for him it is not a problem," Christian announced smugly before cutting into his eggplant parmigiana.

A wave of sadness washed over her. An old familiar cloak that she had spent a lifetime fighting against with bright colors and outrageous looks.

Why was that simple action of the group below affecting her so?

She had friends. No, *they* had friends. She had…fans.

Zoe had Sofia—who was her commander.

Nikita was a friend. As much as the lone female SEAL had female friends. She spoke almost as rarely as Luke, which probably explained part of why she fit into the team so well. Though they rarely saw each other outside the start or end of a mission, she supposed that Nikita was her best friend. She'd certainly told Nikita things she'd never told anyone else and knew that Nikita had done the same. But perhaps Nikita was also her *only* friend, and that was a very sad thought.

There were the other women of the 5E—who Zoe liked

and respected—but she was "other." Peggy, her best friend in high school, had explained "otherness" to Zoe. She had a nurse mom and a cop dad. Zoe's own parents, with their "normal" occupations of secretary and car mechanic, didn't stand out. But Peggy talked about how people always treated her parents as if they never belonged. People lowered their beers at a party when her dad showed up—as if drinking was bad even with friends when you weren't driving. Others set down their greasy burgers and over-dressed potato salad when her mom sat with them, even if her plate held the same.

Zoe was "other." She flew with the 5E, except they flew helicopters into foreign countries and she flew an RPA jet sixty thousand feet above them from a box in Alabama. They constantly risked their lives beyond the front lines and she risked getting a sore butt from too many hours in the coffin's command chair. They didn't treat her differently, but she was and knew it. They told tales of wild countries and wilder missions. She watched them from her eye in the sky.

Or maybe Zoe had no one she could just let her hair down with because she was broken inside. She knew that, but it was completely out her control to fix. That internal breakage they each possessed had created the bond between her and Nikita.

She was so sick of being "other." Of being broken. Of being…

So sick of herself.

Teranga? She'd show them goddamn *teranga*.

She jabbed her fork into one of Luke's meatballs and hacked off a whole chunk.

He stopped his own fork with a large twirl of spaghetti halfway to his mouth and watched her, hawk-eyed.

She made a deliberate show of stuffing the whole piece into her mouth and chewing.

Luke made no other action except to watch her as his spaghetti slowly unraveled back into his bowl—his expression as unreadable as the moment she'd thrown him her purse and he'd caught it.

Fine! Whatev! She sipped some wine to clear her mouth and spun some of her own pasta onto her fork.

Still Luke didn't move or look away. What did those trained eyes see? What thoughts did that bland expression mask? Not even the hints that most men gave as they told her all about themselves. Luke revealed nothing. He was seriously smart—they didn't forge Team 6 SEALs from dumb jocks— but there was no way to read what was going on in that head of his. Not that she wanted to know.

Zoe sighed and turned her focus back to Christian, pasting on her best smile.

6

*L*uke decided to grind out another five klicks. The sun was just cracking over the sprawling city and the dawn temperatures were running about seventy Fahrenheit—fifty above the chilly midnight mission in Hathyaron's Pakistani compound. A welcome respite. It wouldn't become too hot and humid for running here until May or June.

But it felt like he was part of some damned cross country team. Nothing organized, but there were a lot of guys and a few women out for a run in twos and threes. He'd never been in a country so filled with runners—no one jogged here, they ran.

Then between one heartbeat and the next he was running alone.

The muezzins' call echoing from the minarets of the mosques cleared the streets. On the next arm swing, he tapped his fingertips against his SIG Sauer P239 compact 9mm handgun just to make sure it was still in his waistband.

It was hard to believe the low religious violence stats for

Dakar. Ninety-five percent Muslim, but if they decided to marry a Christian, it wasn't much of an issue. Highly tolerant. At least some damn place on this planet was—he'd fought in enough of the others. He'd grown up in a deeply bigoted household, which was crazy in Maine because the state was far more Christian white than Dakar was Muslim black. So who had Dad and his buddies been fighting against?

People from away?

Maine was so insular that someone was called a Person From Away if they'd been born "over the line" in a New Hampshire hospital, even if they'd lived the next ninety years without ever leaving Penobscot Bay.

His old man was cracked in the head. Too bad he'd survived whatever it was that had done that to him.

Luke kept pounding along the road, which was giving it the benefit of the name. There were only four or five paved roads in the Ouakam neighborhood where Christian Vehrs lived. Christian was really starting to piss him off, even more than DeMille—which was saying something.

He sure couldn't wipe out the memory of that brilliant laugh in her blue eyes as she'd stabbed up a piece of his meatball. She'd done it as if challenging him. The last fool to challenge him had been a recruit six years ago and Luke'd made the guy eat dirt for being an asshole.

DeMille had taken some of his food without his permission and he hadn't known how to respond. Still didn't. Take some of hers? Stab her hand with his fork? What?

And the smile on that woman. Half the time it made her look like a sixteen-year-old imp up to no good. The other half it made him want to do things so that he'd see it again, because when the cute rubbed off, there was a woman in there somewhere. A woman that a part of him recognized, and he wasn't thinking about his dick. Okay, he wasn't only thinking about that.

She did something to him. He could pal around with his team just fine. Knew how to flirt with women. Except DeMille.

Shit! He was starting to babble like an ensign after his first actual combat mission, which was beyond sad. Like DeMille had planted a hex on him.

Focus on the run.

There were a few sidewalks, but it was safer to run on the verge of the road. The sand was often several inches deep with low drifts of plastic garbage and concrete rubble at the crossroads, but the sidewalks were inconsistent with gaps and shifting surfaces. As the morning traffic built, his route was more and more pushed onto the backroads. They were all deep, gritty sand and tougher running. He didn't mind the sand—just made for a better workout—but the twists and turns, with streets ending abruptly or running into a blank wall without warning, made it harder to sustain momentum.

Everywhere there was evidence of the good and bad. New building projects marked every street, backed by another road-ending open sewage ditch or a load of deep red sand someone had dumped in the middle of the road by a construction site. It was so fine that it left a taste of iron rust thick on the air for a dozen meters around. The bootstraps that the city was hauling itself up by were plain to see.

Most of the residences were walled, making it hard to tell what was really going on inside—but there was definitely more than met the eye.

Christian Vehrs' place last night had been a shocker. He lived behind a random steel door in a white concrete block wall that looked no different from any other on the quiet back one-lane. The door had required a sharp kick to open after it had been unlocked, the hinges squealing with grinding sand.

Despite the low theft statistics, a second house door with another lock stood just inside. It opened onto a large room with cool marble floors and Western furnishings. A sectional couch wrapped around a monster big-screen TV that was set to a moderate blare of a soccer game. An inner courtyard thick with trees and bushes was open to the sky. Between a banana and several mango trees, a twenty-foot swimming pool had been sunk into the ground. On three sides, Christian's two-story home wrapped around the courtyard.

Were their private oases and family areas hidden away behind all of Dakar's sterile concrete walls?

The fourth side of Christian's home was a large blank wall with no windows and only a small door.

"Ah," Christian had said. "That is for tomorrow. Tonight is for relaxing and drinking."

Nothing he or DeMille had said swayed that determination. And Zoe still hadn't offered a single clue as to why they were here. No, she had. She'd gotten Christian talking about the Dakar Rally...briefly. But he'd ever-so-smoothly changed the subject before it went far. She'd said they had to come here after she saw the poster for The Dakar. And Christian had raced The Dakar—nine times.

And Zoe had put that together how fast? Under twenty seconds. Perhaps under ten.

Did he trust her? As much as any woman. Which wasn't saying much except for Nikita. And yet Nikita trusted her. Friend of a friend was one thing. Trust? That belonged only to his own action team. He didn't even like integrating with other ST6 squads on a mission and he understood them a whole hell of a lot better than he understood Zoe DeMille.

Luke turned the corner at a European-style bakery that offered a glass display case filled with French pastries and a sign offering pizzas that he'd have to remember how to find later. A cinnamon roll sounded good, but he opted for another lap up and over the Two Breasts.

Christian's wife, Leola, definitely had a pair of those— custom-designed to satisfy a T&A man. Pretty and half her husband's age. Her frank looks had made it clear that he was welcome to come find her if Christian was out.

He didn't know if it was for his own protection or DeMille's that he chose to stretch out on the cool marble outside Zoe's door last night. He'd slept in far less comfortable places, so that was fine.

In the middle of the night, he'd heard the soft pad of feet slapping on the cool marble. He prepared to roll away from the door so that DeMille didn't trip over him. But the footsteps weren't coming from the crack under DeMille's door, rather from the direction of Christian Vehrs' room.

Luke had pretended he was still asleep.

Christian had almost stepped on him before stumbling to a halt. His curse in French didn't sound polite, even if Luke didn't understand it. He'd stood over Luke for long enough that he was mere seconds from earning a hard upward fist in the nuts before he finally turned around and returned to his wife.

How naive and trusting was DeMille that she'd landed them here? Luke was far bigger than Christian, but the man could overwhelm a woman of DeMille's size easily.

Luke was again blocked off the sidewalk and onto the street by a roadside nursery of hundreds, maybe thousands of small tropical plants and a few man-tall trees. It was just a fifty-meter stretch along the road and a few meters wide, but the pots were all touching so there were a huge number of plants. No gardens on the outside of homes, so his guess must be right about there being a lot more courtyards like Christian's inside the city's unrevealing white walls.

A taxi carwash was a hose at the side of the road. For a brief instant, each small Toyota or Ford was its proper color again—two men with whisk brooms cleaned sand out of the inside. By the time one rolled past him a hundred meters later, its color was already hazing with the sticky dust.

He entered the roadway up to the Mamelles lighthouse. It wound a full time around the hill in a steady climb, just like tracing a finger so slowly around a woman's breast, starting at the ribs and spiraling up to…

Too long in the field. Way too long in the field when he realized he was picturing that glimpse of DeMille's breast. First, they were kinda minimal issue. Second, she was… something. Irritating? Yeah, that was it. Just like watching too many Tweety and Sylvester cartoons in a row.

His Maine sense of humor kicked in and made him feel better. .

A tourist asks: How can you tell if a boy moose is attracted to a girl moose?

Cain't say, but wouldn't want to be gettin' in his way.

Imagining tiny Zoe DeMille with a massive rack of horns at full charge could almost make him laugh. Thinking about being the man doing the charging at DeMille…

He kicked harder on the climb. The circle of the two-lane paved road was just tight enough that he could actually lean into the curve. At the top of the hill, he slapped a hand on the old lighthouse that towered a half dozen stories above him. On his way back down, he forgot to account for the thin coating of sand over pavement and almost flew off the trail into a nasty looking tangle of thorny acacia bushes all snarled with wind-blown plastic.

That would teach him to think about DeMille's breasts. Or DeMille.

Twelve hours in Dakar and he'd had enough of this shit. It was time to get something moving if he had to pin Christian to a wall and beat on him to get it. He blew off the end of his run and turned to cross straight over the second breast beneath the African Renaissance Monument to return to Christian's home.

Time to make sure DeMille hadn't gotten herself into trouble in the hour he'd been gone. If she was even awake yet.

Then to find out what trouble she'd gotten him into.

⸻

IF one more Dakari man tried to stop her and convince her that she should marry him, Zoe was going to murder him. It was as if they couldn't help themselves.

Oh look. Pretty white girl. She must be rich. I must flirt.

At least she hoped it was just flirting, but she'd grown sick of it in the first hundred meters of her run and that had been five kilometers ago.

She'd pulled on a wedding ring for her morning run… which seemed to make no difference at all. At least they weren't aggressive—confrontational but not threatening. But they kept getting in her way.

Asking Leola if there was a gym nearby had earned her a disinterested, "Not at this hour." Zoe wondered if Leola's expression was unreadable because of cultural differences or if Leola just didn't care. It didn't seem like anger. Or curiosity. It certainly wasn't the fandom that Christian had claimed on her behalf.

Zoe needed Christian, but she wasn't dumb enough to trust him. He could just be a superfan who didn't want to admit it. Or was he something worse—something she'd had far too much experience with? It was the first time her professional career had needed her public image and she didn't like the feeling in the least. Lines that should never have been blurred were actively converging—the story of her life.

Last night she'd slipped the carbon fiber knife out of her suitcase and kept it beneath her pillow—it wouldn't pass an x-ray machine, but metal detectors didn't see it. Self-defense rule: don't brandish it unless you're going to use it. Twice pulled, twice bloodied. Not wanting a third episode, she'd also rigged a primitive alarm system using two chairs on either side of her bedroom door. She'd linked them together with three of her belts so anyone opening the inward-swinging door would snag the belts and drag the chairs noisily across the marble floor.

The only sound had been someone moving very close by her door just at dawn. She didn't hear the person arrive, but she heard them depart without knocking or trying the door. By the time she'd ventured from her room, she could feel the absolute stillness of the house. Which had sent her back for a quick change and a run.

She'd have invited Luke along, but she didn't know which room was his. There was an idea in the back of her mind but she couldn't seem to tease it out. If *felt* as if there was some way to recover the situation, but she couldn't make it conscious. Maybe with Luke's help... Except he was still asleep.

Usually a good workout helped her think, but her run had instead earned her nothing except jillions of marriage proposals.

Now she was trying to pump up the energy to do some serious stairs work. Trotting around Dakar, and dodging tall handsome natives with hopes of a rich foreign wife, hadn't really lent itself to the kind of workout her elliptical delivered.

But then she'd spotted the stairs up the front of the African Renaissance Monument. One quick trot up and down had revealed two hundred and four steps, level and in good repair. Eleven flights unevenly broken up between landings, mostly in groups of seventeen or eighteen. Good. More of a challenge.

Back at the bottom, she closed her eyes for a moment and breathed deeply to make sure she was as well oxygenated as possible.

Then she spun for the stairs and slammed into someone.

"I'm. Not. *Interested.*" It took all her control to not shout it in the man's face. "I don't want to marry..." The "you" dribbled off as she looked up into Luke Altman's face. He hadn't even had the decency to waver when she'd slammed into him. He was just that substantial.

He crossed his arms and looked down at her, then raised his eyebrows at her in a question.

"I don't want to marry you either," she snarled at him.

"Good to know." They were so close she could feel the soft morning breeze speeding up slightly to slip between them. Two bodies creating a Venturi Effect just like an RPA wing's flat and curved surfaces creating lift. And with Luke's impressive biceps and chest, it was sadly apparent which one of them was the flat one.

"Go away. I'm working out here."

He waved a hand for her to proceed.

Screw him. She breathed deeply once more, then turned and began double-timing it up the stairs. Her legs were long enough—barely—that she could have done them two-by-two but that wasn't the point of the workout. Hitting every step clean, she was soon racing upward.

Only when she turned at the top did she realize that Altman was right there with her.

"Enjoying watching my butt?"

"Did enough of that last night."

At the airport was the only time he'd been behind her—for about twenty meters. Great. Like one look at her was all a man needed before he got bored.

She turned and ran back down.

"Go away," she said at the bottom turn before heading back up the stairs to start her third lap.

Luke came up beside her and matched her step for step. He didn't run up the stairs or climb them. He flowed. He had built-in laminar flow as if he was only touching the steps for guidance to steer his flight up the steps. He did the same on the descent. Ten stories twice, she was definitely beginning to feel the burn, but she wasn't going to give in yet. Definitely not with SEAL Commander Altman beside her.

At least he kept away the *Marry me* jokers. They were there, also working the steps hard with their long legs and lean muscles. But now she was "with a man" so they treated her differently. She didn't *need* a man's protection. She didn't *want* a man's protection. They'd certainly done crap at protecting her when she could have really used it.

She turned to face him on the red-brick plaza at the base of the stairs.

"Okay. How do you do that?" She asked partly because she wanted to know, but also to buy a moment to catch her breath without letting Altman see how badly she needed to.

"Do what?" But his smile said he totally knew.

"Asshole." She started up a fourth time.

As she hit the second landing and started on the next flight of twenty steps, she almost fell and ate the brick. Luke had placed a large hand at the small of her back.

"Try not to shift against my hand. Keep your body stable and let your legs do the work."

She'd have asked why, but she was running way short on breath—far more than the climb should account for. Maybe the interval timing of landings and descents was chewing her up a lot faster than the predictable continuity of an elliptical exercise machine.

At first it felt as if he was rubbing his hand up and down her back. Not an unpleasurable sensation—even if he was married. Even if he'd grown bored of looking at her ass in the first thirty seconds. Her efforts to stop the motion only made it worse.

"Stay on your toes."

"This isn't. Ballet. Class," she managed to huff out.

"Not ballet. A stable core from which to shoot accurately."

And she watched Luke sideways as they hit the next flight. His motion was so smooth, even with her jostling against his hand, that he would indeed have a very stable motion from which to shoot accurately while on the run.

With the gentle pressure of his big hand, she had a reference of what her upper body was doing. It was going up with each step, but it was doing it in noncontinuous, bumpy fashion, shoving upward as she reached for the next stair, then easing down as her foot settled firmly on the step. It made her feel like she was a bobble-head doll version of herself.

By the sixth flight, she was getting a feel for it and by the top one, she felt a little as if she was floating upward on a strong thermal rather than driving upward under full thrust. Her legs burned even more, but the feeling of smooth flight was more than energizing enough to compensate for it.

Another lap down and back without a word.

Halfway up, he slid his hand away. And again she almost went down, losing every bit of the smooth rhythm she'd found. She held it together until the top step, then more collapsed than sat.

Her lungs were heaving. Five laps? Six? Ten stories each. After a 5K run. That definitely counted.

"You'll get it." Luke looked as if he was barely breathing.

If she had a cooler of ice water, she'd dump it over his head right about now. Or bury her face in it.

"You work out. It shows." *Wow!* He was using whole sentences. Only two or three words, but grammatically intact.

"Hullo. In the Army."

He shrugged. Because of course a Team 6 SEAL had no need to respect anything in the Army. Especially not an RPA pilot.

"I repeat: asshole. Bet you've been called that a few times."

Again the maddening shrug as if to say, "Maybe." Or perhaps as if he didn't care.

"Bet your wife calls you that." Except it didn't come out funny the way she'd meant it.

Luke's fulminating look might be the first true emotion she'd ever seen on his face.

"Sorry. That was—" unforgivable. "Sorry."

But she was talking to herself. He was already halfway down the steps in that floating motion of his—at triple the speed she'd been moving. So smooth that he disappeared from view long before he was out of sight. He just blended in and she could no longer find him in the gathering crowd below.

"Smooth, Zoe. Real effing smooth."

She stared out at the Mamelles Lighthouse and the broad sweep of the Atlantic. Beneath the morning sun, it was a dark blue with a hint of green. So different from the dark Pacific and the turquoise waters off the Florida beaches she went to on leave—because she sure as hell didn't go home.

No question she was out of her depth here.

A tall Senegalese man, in green tennies and gym shorts that left little to the imagination, reached the top of the steps and sat down beside her. His smile revealed brilliant white teeth.

"You look so very sad," he said in a deep, pleasantly French tone. "Maybe you should leave him and marry me. I make you very happy."

It wouldn't be the dumbest thing she'd done in the last thirty-six hours.

Or even the last thirty-six seconds.

Crap!

THERE WERE some things Luke didn't need to explain to anyone—least of all to someone like Zoe DeMille.

67

He stood in the cool shower and tried to soak the heat out of his body.

It wasn't working.

Marva Hernandez had been everything he wanted. Exotically dark, fantastically built, and hungry for a SEAL. They'd met at McP's Irish Pub and Grill in Coronado. They'd started at one of the outside tables, a cluster of tall tables under the cool trees perched on Orange Avenue. Their group had been thick with SEALs and bar babes.

Even in that crowd Marva had stood out. Maybe that's why Sofia, DeMille's commander, had been no turn on—too much like Marva. He hadn't thought of that but it made sense. Except he hadn't gone after many others lately either. The game had gotten old and maybe even gone stale.

But Marva had everything a twenty-eight-year-old, newly tagged SEAL lieutenant commander deserved: sun-kissed Central American skin, topped with just a hint of her country's lush accent. Marva had done her best to make her speech pure Californian after coming to the US as a teen.

Long dark hair had rippled down to the middle of her back. Her short shorts and that clinging tube top had promised so much—and they'd delivered in McP's bathroom stall when he took her up against the wall later that first night.

Luke turned the shower water colder, but it was already as low as it could go.

The heat wasn't in his groin. He could feel it steaming off his head.

Two years married, his first mission with the Night Stalkers 5E had finished fast and efficiently—something he'd since learned wasn't chance but rather a trademark of the 5E.

He'd meant to surprise Marva by coming home early.

He had.

The first thing he'd seen when he walked into their home was her magnificent breasts, clutched in another man's hands as she rode him hard. A damned petty officer second class from Blue Squadron.

The petty officer went wide-eyed with shock. Screwing an officer's wife wasn't a court-martial offense, but it could easily be a death sentence.

If Marva noticed Luke's arrival, she ignored it and finished what she was doing—crying out in that near-panicked release that she'd said only he could give her because he was just that big and good.

When she came down, that lovely toss of hair and arch of back so burned into his memory that he could still see it now, she'd finally turned to him and waited for his response.

"Back early," were the only words he could think to say.

She'd rolled her eyes at him. "Asshole." Moments later she'd tried to cover it with the typical, oh-honey-this-was-just-a-mistake bullshit, but he wasn't buying it for a second. That one word had burned between them and he could still feel the searing brand of it.

SEAL officers didn't beat the shit out of enlisted men— not if they wanted to stay in the military. No one would say shit if he flattened Marva, but Luke had seen too many beatings of women in his youth to ever do it himself.

Instead, he'd tossed them both out the door without clothes or car keys and called for the MPs to come haul their asses away when they made a fuss—it was base housing after all. Three hours later, he'd dumped every single thing that was hers or the asshole's into his pickup, including their wallets. He'd towed her car—that he'd paid for—to the nearest used lot that offered him cash on the spot, transferred all except one dollar out of their joint account, and swung through the dump on his way out of town to empty the bed of his pickup.

Luke had wanted a photo of Marva's glittering smile each time she greeted him home. It would keep him company on missions and he'd had his phone out. Instead, he'd instinctively snapped a photo that went in with the divorce papers that left her nothing. He'd forwarded a copy to the asshole's wife, which had cost him everything too. And the asshole's commander, which had made no difference at all. There were *many* reasons Luke only trusted his own team.

He lay his head on the ornate brown-and-gold tile wall of Christian's shower. It still hadn't chilled him down.

Asshole. Bet your wife calls you that.

"Go to hell, DeMille." She couldn't do it soon enough for him.

7

*Z*oe stood in Christian's garage and tried not to keep checking every dark corner. Her nerves were only slightly mollified when Christian rolled up the big outside door to let in the morning sun. There were still too many dark corners. Too many places where she could be dragged out of sight and—

Gathering every fiber of strength she possessed barely overpowered that horror of memories. She had made a whole woman out of that broken girl. It was so unfair that she wouldn't stay lost in the past where she belonged. Everything about this mission was unearthing that young, naive, trusting version of herself from her restless grave and Zoe hated it. No shower, no amount of scrubbing, no amount of wishing to make that girl go away had sufficed.

Garage! She shouted it to herself in panic the moment Christian led her and Luke in here.

Don't focus on the garage! There'd been a time she'd loved her father's garage. As a little girl, she had known what tool her father wanted before he did. Could do the fussy work of rebuilding a carburetor by the age of ten better than Dad could.

Focus on that!

This wasn't the garage where Dad's best friend from childhood, "Uncle Bob," was co-owner. Where—

She was half a world away from Pismo Beach.

Senegal. They were in Senegal.

Surely she was safe here.

In Christian's garage the dark corners weren't dangerous shadows, but rather pools of cool concrete-enclosed space inviolate to the soaring temperatures outside. The structure was as big as a whole wing of his house—which made sense as it was the fourth wall of his courtyard.

She also took comfort in Luke standing close beside her, even if he was still not saying a word. Her attempt to apologize once more didn't even earn her the narrow-eyed inspection of when she'd hijacked a piece of his meatball last night. Someday he'd learn to use his words. And someday frogs could be princes. SEALs? Not so much. That thought almost made her smile.

The garage wasn't quite the fantastic setup that Hathyaron had hidden away in Pakistan, but it was pretty amazing anyway. Over a dozen cars were parked here, and the Facel Vega II was not the only rare prize. A Plymouth Hemi Superbird and an even rarer 1981 Talbot Sunbeam rally racer also graced his collection. She wanted to go visit each one, but the vehicles in the service bay were why they were here, so she forced herself to focus on those. Which wasn't hard; they looked amazing.

The working part of the garage had room for three cars, a lift, and an impressive array of tools. The parts rack alone was a thing of beauty—ultra heavy-duty shocks and other suspension parts, spare body panels, an extra engine... It screamed off-road rally racing even without the cars.

She wrapped her arms more tightly around herself, still feeling chilled by the space. But the cars helped pull her out of the darkness. All three in this area were Dakar Rally racers.

"They're awfully pretty."

One car was in pieces. A somber black man who was introduced as Ahmed the best mechanic in Dakar was rebuilding it.

But the Renault and Citroën looked ready to roll. They were only recognizable as such because of the prominent logos on their hoods. These bore no other relation to the manufacturers' production cars—custom-built for world rally championship races. Like most WRC vehicles, they were designed to tackle cross-country racing where roads were just a distant memory.

There was a certain romance to them. Wide tires with deep tread to run on sand or rock. High body metal for ground clearance revealed massively oversized suspensions. The roll cage was clearly visible inside the body to protect the driver and navigator in the event of a roll or flip.

"You've upgraded them both to Brenthel Baja kit suspensions." Even without the factory stickers, she'd have recognized the configurations from the dune buggies her father had built for racing the Pismo Beach dunes.

Most of what raced there were just ATVs or the hopped-up buggies that were little more than an engine and a roll cage. But every now and then a serious racer would come into the shop and want their car or truck jacked especially for the sand. If they had the cash, they went for the Brenthel kit.

Independent front suspension, solid axle rear—both rugged enough to take the pounding.

"Oh, Zoe. You make my heart go wild. That is how I first find you, is that picture of you at Huckfest."

Huckfest was the annual truck-jumping competition that had run for years on the Pismo Beach dunes. Huckfesters had showed up by the hundreds, with fans in the thousands, to win bragging rights for the longest and highest jumps. The five years it had run had overlapped with her wild teenage years. She'd taken her revenge—mostly on herself, she'd finally understood—by sleeping her way through the camps.

She already knew the gear from her dad's shop, so she could speak the lingo. The men had found the combination of that and the string bikini on her sylph-like body irresistible. She'd flown with more than a few of them. The summer after her senior year she'd gone for a record of her own—"I'll sleep with you if I can jump with you." She shuddered to remember how many jumps she'd made during the two-day event.

A few of the photos, thankfully not any of the bad ones— at least not the *really* bad ones, had been unearthed by her fans and posted to her feeds. There were some skills she wished she'd never learned.

Christian waved a hand at the Huckfest photo's place of honor just above his own swimsuit girl calendar. It was her, the only woman and dressed in that trademark lemon-yellow bikini, at the center of a long line of male Huckfesters with their arms around each other's shoulders, grinning like idiots for the camera. At least she'd finally developed some breasts by then.

She was a head shorter than any of the guys. Well, she wouldn't be revealing the truth behind that photo, she'd screwed every one of them—some before the photo and some after. As if filling in the gaps had made that part of her more rather than less complete. Even did the twin brothers together to squeeze everyone in.

Definitely time for a change of subject.

"Why are your cars here, Christian, and not on a ship bound for South America?" She knew The Dakar started in less than a week and they should already be underway.

Luke twisted to look at her. She could see the light bulb flash on over his head. Hathyaron. The Dakar. Undercover. Each piece fitting except for Christian being in Dakar, Senegal, rather Mar del Plata, Argentina.

Christian sighed dramatically as he ran a loving hand over the smooth hood of the dark red Renault. The Citroën was appropriately lemon—*citron* in French—yellow.

"My doctor, he says my spine will not survive The Dakar so soon after last year's crash." He blushed as if he was less of a man for having impacted his disks. No, it wasn't a blush, it was anger. "I tell the doctor he is a criminal, but he insists that he will report me to the race association if I try to drive. They would take away my FIA license. So here my beautiful cars sit when they should be racing. It would have been my tenth Dakar, I would become Legend."

Legend was the label—and fee discount—that they gave to drivers who had started ten or more races. It was obvious that Christian didn't need to worry about the ten percent discount off the thirty-thousand-euro entry fee. Not when the shock absorbers on each car cost over ten thousand apiece. It was his ego that radiated fury.

Zoe had researched both the Dakar Rally and Christian on the flight over—the free First Class upgrade had thankfully included free Internet.

75

She'd already known about the former being the most demanding car race in the world. Five thousands kilometers —in vehicles that made Huckfest jumpers look like kids driving Tonka trucks—over terrain that made the Pismo dunes seem little more than sand ripples on the beach.

She'd also found a video of Christian utterly destroying what now must be the pile of parts that Ahmed was working on. Christian had jumped a dune, catching serious air—too much air. He'd flown off the top of the steep-backed dune with his nose almost straight up toward the sky. What had appeared to be a smallish dune from the front had turned out to be a catastrophically far fall on the back.

The car had landed tail first, shattering the rear end. Then the front end had slammed down so brutally that it had folded everything except the driver's roll cage in half. The car had tumbled down the dune like a shattered donut—spewing parts in every direction.

His navigator had only broken his ankle, but Christian had to be airlifted out.

"Maybe you should listen to the doctor." ·

His fury glared from his eyes for a moment, then she could see him visibly struggle for a long moment before he smiled and looked at her.

"If that is what my Zoe thinks, then I will accept it."

But she'd seen the look in his eyes as his rage had turned briefly on her. It was a look that said he was capable of anything. She casually laid her hand against the handle of her knife where it lay flat against her opposite forearm under her blouse.

While he struggled to regain control of himself—soothing his male ego by showing Luke all of the features of his cars— Zoe was left with a problem of her own.

Two cars in Dakar instead of at The Dakar.

An injured driver.

Her entire plan for hunting Hathyaron the arms dealer while embedded undercover in Christian's support team had just gone up in smoke. What had seemed like such a brilliant idea when she'd thought it up had turned into a boondoggle —something she'd wager Luke Altman wasn't a fan of. And something that even if he didn't report to her commanders, she'd have to.

She didn't have a Plan B. Needing one fast wasn't helping her think clearly.

Luke Altman was tolerating Christian's ego, but that wasn't going to last much longer.

Unable to remain in place among all the shadows, she stepped out the garage door and onto the street. Christian's garage door opened onto a typical Dakar street. It was reddish sand and under twenty feet wide. Two cars could pass, if one edged onto someone's front stoop—narrow mosaics of colored stone swept clean several times a day. Occasional trees dotted the roadside, but the only one she recognized was a bougainvillea vine because of its lovely dark purple blossoms showering the street with its only color.

The sand itself was gritty with bits of broken-off concrete from construction work. A small group of men were working a few buildings down. One was mixing concrete in a plastic bucket. He dumped it into a battered steel mold. Another man thumped it a few times with a board to settle the slurry, then flipped it upside down in the sand. When he lifted it clear, a concrete block, complete with its two large central holes, joined the rows of the ones they'd already made.

That explained the grit already wheedling its way into her

sandals. And the grit she felt inside seemed to make her blood flow sluggish and painful as well.

Across the street, two men sat with ropes in their hands. The ropes led up to pulleys attached to the building's third story, then back down to street level. Finished—and she hoped dried—concrete blocks were loaded into slings, then tugged up to the roof by the men with the ropes. Occasionally a fresh bucket of mortar was sent aloft to the men laboring on the third story. A half dozen others were sitting around, appearing to have no purpose other than visiting with the workers—perhaps their friends lucky enough to actually have a job. In a country where a living wage was $150US a month and unemployment hovered around twenty percent, there were plenty of friends to hang out.

The work slowed at the site as more and more of them began watching her. She wore long pants and a knee-length caftan of spangled sunrise colors that Emilio Sosa had made for her when she'd interviewed him for a post after he placed second in *Project Runway*. She was decently covered—far more than usual—but she'd felt the need for it after this morning. Even that didn't hide her from their attention. The question was obvious on their faces, *Is she single? Would she marry me?*

She wanted to smack the lot of them. And smack herself for believing this was all going to be so easy.

In the other direction, the back lane led toward the main road, a street busy with buses, taxis, and the constant interweave of pedestrians. Across the street she could see a lone tree. Its bole was painted red and blue. Beneath the overarching branches a group of people sat. Friends. Laughter. One making tea with long dramatic pours from one cup to the other. And musicians. Even from here she could hear the music: a guitar player hunched over his six-string as if he was nurturing it, a drummer with his instrument clamped between his knees, and a flute player who swayed with the music.

In moments she forgot about the construction workers and let herself get lost in the music. The flute arced above the noise and hurry of the street; it seemed to float, echo, and beckon. Her heart leaned toward it until she almost stumbled forward.

"He's a *griot,*" Christian said softly, coming up beside her, wiping his hands with an oily rag. "Music is very important in Senegalese culture, and some are born to the music as their destiny. The skill is inherited. His father was a *griot* and his father before him."

"He had no choice?"

"Music is not to be denied. Like a bard of Druid Europe, he holds great power. Traditionally, when he died he would not be buried, but rather placed inside the hollow center of a baobab tree that his music may live on. Though I don't think they do that anymore."

A breeze stirred up the cloying scent of oil and grease from Christian's hands. Splotches of oil darkened his knuckles. They reminded her of a past so dark that—

If only she could just answer the flutist's call. She would run down the street and never stop. She could taste the bitter adrenaline in the back of her throat, so sharp she wanted to cough it out, but feared she'd vomit out her breakfast of over-strong coffee, omelet, and Nutella on baguette instead.

The shadows of the garage behind her and the promise of sunlight ahead of her. She'd race away until—

Zoe turned and looked back into the garage. She could see, by how studiously Luke wasn't looking her way, that he was intently keeping track of exactly where she was. If she tried to run, he'd be on her in a flash.

Did that make her feel better or worse?

Trapped?

Protected?

Borderline hysterical?

But it wasn't him or his fine backside that was attracting her attention. Not even the impression of his palm on the small of her back that she could still feel resting there.

It was the cars.

The cars. The empty street. And her desperate need to escape.

8

"*C*hristian?"

    Luke could feel Zoe's voice through the street noise as much as he heard it. It resonated in some way that confirmed her identity through instinct long before he could have actually recognized it. It was down at the level of a SEAL training gestalt—simply known. When had that happened?

Maybe because, while putting up with Christian's ego, he'd pieced together DeMille's plan...and how it had just broken. The key had been the change in her when she'd entered the garage.

Tweety Bird DeMille—again dressed in yellow—had flown away and suddenly a very serious woman stood in her place despite the flowing clothes that made her look almost ethereally pretty. When she'd asked why the cars were still here in Dakar, he could hear the deep importance of the question. Then her vast disappointment at hearing of Christian's injury was far more than mere sympathy warranted.

And that had been the key to her plan. She'd intended to use her crazy fandom thing to get inside the Dakar Rally undercover to chase Hathyaron.

Chief Warrant Zoe DeMille had never been stupid. He didn't understand her most of the time, but she was as sharp as any Spec Ops soldier. He remembered how fast she'd put it all together while he'd been standing in Hathyaron's compound in Pakistan. No more than a long pause over the radio and she'd thought up and implemented the whole plan.

She wasn't being some gushing fan of Christian Vehrs; she was trying to use the fact that *he* was a fan of *hers.* A plan that had been shot to hell because the guy had busted up his back.

Yet she did her best to appear like a flighty airhead, running on no more than two moosepower. Moose were one of the dumbest animals on the planet—two moosepower was still dumber than a turnip green.

He remembered a young bull that had walked into town and accidentally stepped on a low sports car—except it was an old ragtop. Its massive hoof had punched through the cloth roof and the flooring on the driver's side. Each time it tried to lift its leg, the tendon at the back of its knee caught on the inside of the roof, making it impossible for him to withdraw his leg. So, he had stood there, looking perplexed, while Officer James had tried to figure out how to help half a ton of stupid wild animal that slashed his massive rack of horns at anyone who got close.

He already knew DeMille was smart enough to be flying for the 5E, damn it.

From now on, he was going to proceed on the assumption that she did nothing by accident.

Had she leaned her car seat back into his chest to heat

him up by looking down the front of her dress? No. That didn't fit. But she certainly enjoyed teasing him. Though he still wasn't sure why, she must have some reason. Didn't she?

"Christian?" DeMille's voice was sweeter than fresh-boiled maple syrup. Okay, here came Plan B. *Go for it, DeMille.*

"Yes? What can I do for you, my Zoe?" That possessive was going to get Christian in trouble yet. Luke just might leave him with far more than his back screwed up.

"I've never driven a WRC car. Is there somewhere I can try? I'd love to video that for my fans."

And Christian lit up like he was Sylvester who had finally caught his Tweety Bird.

What the hell? What kind of a Plan B was that?

Luke glanced at the cars. Two seats: driver and navigator. No rear seat, not in a race car.

Whatever naive ideas DeMille might have about being in control of Christian Vehrs, she was dead wrong. The man was dangerous. Luke hoped that she didn't end up wishing she was dead because of—

"Maybe we could drive somewhere together," she made it a statement, not a question.

Hadn't he just seconds ago thought she was smart. She was being an idio—

"No, wait, your back. How about if Luke and I each drive one. You could ride with Luke and film me for the post."

Okay, not as stupid as he thought…maybe. He still didn't see where she was going with this.

"What do you think?" And suddenly she was up close to Christian with a hand placed on the bemused man's chest, pleading upward into his face as he was most of a foot taller.

It should be ridiculous, but somehow DeMille made it coy and cute.

Yes, cute as hell in the yellow drape thingy over loose slacks and blouse. She was also more concerned about clothes than common sense. These were high-performance race cars —what the hell would she know about those?

"Oh, it would be so fun to drive even a little way." "Oh, it's such a beautiful car that you've built." "Would you really let me drive one even though I've never done a rally drive?" "I have to go change! I can't drive in these clothes." And she was gone, running back into the house.

Christian never got in a word edgewise. She'd accepted his agreement without him ever agreeing. She'd simply kept hammering on every one of Christian's weak spots to keep his head spinning.

DeMille better not try that shit on him, but it sure worked on Christian. The man was in a daze as he prepared the cars. Luke settled in to wait for Zoe, but didn't have to wait long.

He'd leaned back against the hood of the Renault, partly because it was comfortable, but mostly because it pissed off Christian.

But he jolted to his feet when DeMille reappeared in three minutes flat.

She now wore a form-hugging zip-front sleeveless shirt sealed up to her neck—with such a big-toothed zipper that it was easy to imagine pulling it down. The material—like her running shirt this morning—revealed there wasn't a single thing wrong with her figure despite her slenderness. Her chest matched her, complementing her slim waist and good shoulders. Black jeans hugged her hips down to sensible shoes. A yellow leather jacket was slung over one shoulder with a casualness that said she absolutely knew she was on display. Not just on display, but loving it.

She posed by the cars and did one of those coy smile things as Christian snapped pictures of her. They conferred quickly over the display on his camera and Christian plugged it into his phone to post two of the photos immediately.

DeMille had leaned her shoulder against his as she dictated the captions for him to type in.

For all that he'd known Zoe for three years' worth of missions, he'd never really seen her as a woman until she was lying back on the Renault's red hood, perfectly outlining her bright yellow clothes. Did she also have a red outfit in case she'd wanted to pose on the Citroën? What if his car had been blue or green? At least that would explain why her suitcase had been so damn heavy.

Five-four of pipsqueak shouldn't be able to look even half that good, yet she did. Dark, wraparound shades—with electric yellow frames of course—and she actually looked like one of those fashion magazine nymphs. She was sure doing a job of selling it to Christian.

He made one final token protest that DeMille's Tweety Bird mode instantly quashed. When the Frenchman caved to the inevitable and conceded that maybe a short drive was possible, DeMille pulled him down to her and kissed him on both cheeks.

Not on the lips, Luke was pleased to see.

Then DeMille winked at Luke.

For the life of him he still didn't know why.

9

*C*ompletely aside from her new plan, Zoe itched to find out just what the car could do.

The engine's throaty rumble begged to be allowed out to play. It ran smoothly, in perfect tune, but it had so much power she could feel it vibrating the car right through the seat and the steering wheel. It was a vehicle that begged to move super-fast.

And they were crawling behind a horse cart. The two-wheel cart had been piled high with someone's household belongings: a dresser, bed, some bags of clothes. And the woman sat atop a pile of pillows, clutching a small houseplant to her chest and chatting with the drover as he shushed the horse along. Moving day.

The delay was actually a good thing, even if it was making her crazy. It gave her time to familiarize herself with the cockpit. It was unlike anything she'd ever driven. She'd been in stripped-down vehicles before with no pretty trim and an exposed roll cage—that wasn't the problem. But this dash and the controls weren't stripped down at all.

In front of the passenger seat were two screens the size of tablet computers, though thankfully their screens were dark at the moment—she didn't need more distractions. There were several other instruments including a large compass. Rally racing was as much about navigation as anything. No GPS, no satellite images or ultra-hi-res maps, or even a cell phone was allowed. Old-school navigation. She knew The Dakar used a GPS monitor for the race officials, but it was very specifically crippled so that it couldn't be used for long-range navigation.

The center of the dash was filled with rows of switches. Each time she was trapped in traffic, waiting for pedestrians or a truck to get out of the way—they thought nothing of stopping in the middle of a one-lane road to make a delivery —she studied the panel. Lights, instrument power, yada, yada. There was a jacks switch, which must mean there were hydraulic jacks underneath in case a quick tire change was needed. CTIS she'd read about, but never used. It allowed the inflation/deflation of the tires while driving: softer for sand, harder for rocks or road. She tinkered with the settings until she could do it without looking.

Most of the dash's center was taken up with a very simple display that showed compass heading and speed. Speed was critical. Going even one kph over the limit on any Road Sections of the course could have disastrous penalties of time and money.

In front of the driver's seat, she was facing a wholly daunting change from the typical car or dune buggy. The driver's console had a massive digital display for speed, but it also had dials for engine revs, gearing, oil pressure, temperature, transmission fluid pressure and temperature, vacuum pressure, voltage, even altitude and fuel/air mixture ratio. It took her most of the way through the city to get them locked in her head, including the ranges that meant okay versus "oh crap!"

Christian had, of course, showed her how to start the car and shift—asking three separate times if she knew how to work a clutch. Looking studiously fascinated by his droll insults had been a challenge, but she'd managed.

A rally car's display was so much easier to interpret than flying her RPA. Each gauge was only single-layered—a dial or a number—without additional tactical overlays. The center of the steering wheel was covered in fingertip controls from wipers to engine responsiveness. Where she'd expected a stick shift, there was a towering lever that was a handbrake. The shifters were small paddles on the back of the steering wheel.

They'd eased out of the garage onto the sun-scorched street, away from the staring construction workers, away from the dark garage with its shadowed corners. At the blue-and-red tree with its musicians, they turned right and started winding their way out of the city as the flute music shifted and changed to echo the rumbling of their two big engines. And then a long, slow mile behind the horse cart and the woman clutching her house plant. Hard to get a feel for an off-road vehicle on city streets.

The suspension was abominably stiff; she could practically feel every tiny pebble they rolled over, every discarded flip-flop. Every grain of sand.

The clutch was high and tight, just the way she liked. The paddle shifters on the back of the steering wheel let her shift gears without taking her hands off the wheel. It only felt clunky for the first few shifts. Even though she hadn't gotten into third but once or twice as they'd crossed Dakar, she wondered what it would cost to retrofit them to her Mini Cooper at home.

Then she pictured Luke climbing into her Mini. Now that would be a sight. Maybe next time they were both on base she'd try to talk him into trying it just for fun. His shoulders were so broad that they'd probably rub against hers. It would take nothing for him to reach out and rest his hand on her thigh as she drove along.

She wanted someone who couldn't stop touching her. Not for the sex, but just for the contact. If that made her a hopeless romantic, let it. Actually, she preferred the line from *Romancing the Stone:* "A hope*ful* romantic."

Of course not with Lieutenant Commander Luke Altman. But with another man it could be nice. As she'd cleaned up the disaster that was her personal life—mostly by joining the Army and burying the past—she'd started dreaming of what a good man might be like. She had definite ideas, but wasn't having much luck locating a man who could fulfil them.

She trailed the Citroën quietly in the wake of Luke driving Christian's Renault until they passed beyond the north edge of the city. They rolled off the end of the last sandy road as it devolved into beach sand. To the south lay the grand sweep of Dakar's peninsula. The few tall buildings of beachside resorts and the tiny financial district stood like a dust-fogged child's game. The beach, which had been thick with fisherman skiffs, had emptied as they'd eased north around them, finally reaching an abrupt end to the city.

Christian had Luke stop and she rolled up beside him. She'd wanted the sexy red Renault, but her persona had to take the lemon-yellow Citroën. It matched her clothes, her hair, her social media banners, even her Mini Cooper. Truth be told she was getting a little tired of that color in her life, but not enough to disappoint her fans.

Something in her appearance had to change soon to keep her fans entertained. Usually she could plan before she was ready to change it, but this time it was apparently going to be a total surprise when it arrived.

She could see through his rolled-down window that Christian was contemplating some way to switch over to her Citroën, but she cut him off.

"You have the camera ready, Christian?"

He held up his brand new Nikon Z7, now sporting a big zoom lens. It would shoot 4K video—about a hundred times what she needed for a couple of quick posts. His toy and all of its lenses cost more than her monthly salary. Almost more than her Army pay combined with the revenue from the few select ads she allowed on her site.

Fine.

She waited until they'd all donned helmets, though Christian had been hard pressed to find one small enough for her head…or big enough for Luke's. Luke had let her tease him about that, so maybe he'd finally accepted her earlier apology.

If not, tough!

"How far can we go?" She laid on her sexy, let's-go-jump-a-truck tone.

Christian's eyes went wide, and beyond him at the wheel, Luke's narrowed. Ticked off by who knew what? Studying her? What? They really needed to talk about him using more words.

Christian managed to choke out around a woman-eating smile, "Two hundred kilometers to Saint Louis. There are a few streams, but no rivers or roads. Only one or two tiny villages. We can go as far as you'd like, my darling Zoe." Even his smooth French accent wasn't going to get him where he was thinking this was going.

Wearing his normal silence like a cloak, Luke continued leaning forward with his hands clutched around the wheel so that he could see her around Christian.

Watching me a little too intently to pretend you don't care. But that was the only clue she had for interpreting his thoughts. She could *always* tell what men were thinking—pretty simple equation actually: male thoughts about a woman equaled sex. The math was a lot easier than fuel loads and weapon ballistics for her Avenger drone.

Luke was intriguingly enigmatic.

To hell with him.

She wasn't Sofia, dating a married man no matter how pretty he was.

"I've got one more question."

Christian and Luke both watched her in anticipation, awaiting sex for the former and something impossible to interpret for the latter.

"Yes, my darling Zoe?"

As if.

She hammered down on the gas and popped the clutch.

The Citroën leapt like a rabbit, spewing a rooster tail of sand all over the still-parked Renault. This was *definitely* no Huckfest truck. The Citroën was five hundred horsepower of a girl's best friend.

She hit third gear and the first beach berm at the same time, catching air on all four tires. Rather than bracing for the hard jar of the landing—a real beginner's mistake—she let her body go loose with the floating sensation.

Airy float…

Airy float…

Splat!

The heavy suspension ate it up, smoothed out the ride.

A street vehicle would have bottomed out or perhaps busted the suspension. In a Huckfest truck, that would have been a hard slap. But it didn't even limit out the springs on the Citroën's seat, never mind the suspension.

Up into fourth, she flew over a washboard area as if she was only touching the very tops of the bumps and skipping the potholes entirely.

Around a curve in the dunes, she slammed into a stream —axle deep and two car-lengths across. Water arced in a massive plume like she was parting the Red Sea. It felt as if she was. Escaping the darkness. If she could only race fast enough, maybe it would never catch her. Maybe she could fly beyond it as she did when linked to her RPA.

Back into third to recover her speed, then fourth and fifth as she headed down for harder sand along the tide line.

A flash of red in her mirror was the only warning she had before Luke took her on the high side with Christian cheering from the passenger seat—not that she could hear him over both engines' roar.

That would definitely never do.

She dropped back to fourth for more power, but every time she tried to get by him, Luke slid the Renault over, closing the gap with the waves. Up the beach was speed-robbing deep sand. The advantage lay down on the hard sand, but she couldn't risk more than a couple inches of water or it would rob her as badly as the sand. A slap by a big wave could completely dislodge her—a dangerous proposition going a hundred kilometers an hour.

Tired of the game, she poked twice at going past him on the low side.

Both times he blocked her.

Then she saw the beach swinging out toward the ocean, followed by a curve inland to make a new cove. It wasn't much, but hopefully it was all she needed.

LUKE BLOCKED HER AGAIN.

DeMille might have spit sand all over him once, but she wasn't going to get away with that twice. She was good, but she wasn't a SEAL. Girl had no idea what she was dealing with.

This time she fell way back, then came racing toward him with an alarming suddenness. He could see her once again lift up a rooster tail of sand several times higher than her car.

Rooster tail? Chicken tail. She was one of those fancy birds with bright feathers in constant need of tending and preening. Damned cute…and flighty—unpredictable from one second to the next.

He didn't understand how he'd missed the cute before. *Because you like your women with breasts built to make a grown man weep.* True, but then why couldn't he erase the image of DeMille as she'd zipped herself into the yellow leather jacket and climbed into a racecar?

Suddenly, the feel of how his palm had fit the curve of her lower back while running the steps at the African Renaissance Monument took on new meaning. It burned where it rested on the steering wheel. He'd felt every muscle, felt the softness and warmth of her skin through the thin moisture-wicking material, far more than he felt the heartbeat of the Renault's engine.

She was—

Catching up fast.

He squeezed over.

"Make her eat surf," Christian called from passenger seat. Whatever his other shortcomings, Christian was mad about racing. He kept giving Luke little tips. Some Luke knew from racing bikes, but others were new, unique to getting the most out of a world rally car.

If Christian was fine with Luke putting his other car into the surf, then DeMille was in for a hell of a ride.

Just as she pulled close behind his bumper, he veered down the sand toward the ocean.

He checked the rearview to watch the splashdown.

DeMille wasn't there.

"Where the—"

Christian was shouting out in surprise, and looking the other way.

DeMille hadn't merely come around his other side. She shot high and hot across the beach and up into the soft sand. Even over his own engine, he could hear her take another gear.

Then she lifted off. Where one cove had ended to bend into the next, the sand had built up high.

Using it like a stunt ramp, she was airborne.

Her massive catch-up speed hadn't been about overtaking him at all. She'd been gathering speed specifically for this jump.

He could only watch in awe.

For a long second, she flew down the beach as if she was

her damned drone brought to life. He half expected wings to slash out sideways. Hang time like he'd never seen.

The car twisted slowly, leaning more and more to the right.

If she hit like that, she was going to roll. Bad!

"*Merde!*" Christian managed in a voice that made the same assessment.

Moments before she hit, she turned the front wheels to a new alignment. Then revved the engine hard enough for it to cry out. But it also applied a twisting force that killed the sideways roll just before she touched down.

The tires caught and bit at the perfect angle, jerking her brutally to the left before a brief fishtail that left her aimed straight down the next beach and well out in front. He couldn't have done it better. And maybe not as well.

"Holy mother—" this time Christian wasn't staring at Zoe racing away to the right, but instead straight ahead.

Luke looked, then jolted.

He jammed down a gear for more power and cut the wheel hard. They were up on two wheels, riding the hairy edge of a roll themselves.

One cove's beach had swept outward—and the curve of the next had swept in.

While Zoe was jumping the divide between them, he'd distractedly continued driving out the curve of the disappearing cove. He was now aimed straight for the ocean while the beach swung away in a new direction.

They were slammed hard when they hit the water, but he managed to continue the turn as the deepening sea slowed them. Still he might have gone over if a wave hadn't caught him halfway up his door and slammed him down onto all four wheels again. He sliced for the harder sand of the beach before the wave could drag him out to sea in the undertow.

Four-wheel drive, a powerful engine, and perhaps more luck than he deserved—after watching Zoe when he should have been driving—were all that kept him from unexpectedly setting sail in a Renault racing car.

Once clear of the water, he jammed to a halt on the beach.

He and Christian looked at each other, then in unison turned to stare down the beach.

Zoe's car was a tiny spark of yellow sunshine far down the stretch of beige sand.

"Tell me you got that on video," Luke could only hold onto the wheel and squint against the brilliant sunlight.

Christian's voice sounded as if he'd just had amazing sex and hadn't recovered yet.

"I got it."

10

*L*uke had tried, but though he'd caught up to her—eventually—no way had she let him pass. A few times she'd had to abandon the beach and race between the massive baobab trees like slalom poles. Or perhaps like a pinball dodging between the massive gray pillars of the wide trunks with a major tilt penalty if she clipped one.

Once or twice, while racing through the brush, Zoe found a dirt track, but those were usually so rutted that it was less hazardous going overland among the scattered thorn scrub. At least being in front, she only ate a little dust…the Renault in her rearview was coated rust-brown rather than lipstick-red. In the lead, she got to breathe ocean salt and fresh palm breezes when they jogged inland. On the occasions when she managed to reach sixth gear—often topping two hundred kph, over one-twenty miles an hour—even the morning's heat couldn't catch up with her.

Christian obviously knew the route well and several times directed Luke to turn aside. Perhaps in hopes of passing her by in the process. But she'd flown hundreds of drone missions where her job was to go in first, often providing guidance to the manned aircraft behind her. She'd developed a sixth sense that had managed to anticipate each time Luke gave the slightest twitch out of her rearview mirrors.

"Not getting by me that easily, Luke."

He too had answered her every move with a countermove —he couldn't pass her, but neither could she lose him. He drove the same way he ran, with an unexpected smoothness of flow. As if his hand was forever placed at the small of her back, she could feel herself driving more cleanly with each moment they vied for the lead.

Twice he got close enough beside her that she could see him watching her as much as where he was driving. It wasn't a greedy look like Christian's, wanting all that any man ever wanted from her. No, Luke's assessing gaze wasn't quite a smile but it spoke of the joy of the challenge. He was a warrior for SEAL Team 6, of course he was competitive.

Well, she hadn't become a Night Stalker by slouching along.

Half the time she could have jumped a truck better than the Huckfesters she flew with. She and her father often took the trucks and dune buggies he'd built out onto the sand for testing. Her favorite times had been when he had a pair of them ready at the same time.

Side-by-side family races had ranged up and down the dunes.

Lines of attack.

Jostling for the best angle to take the big dune slopes.

Backsliding in the sand from a misjudged climb.

Punching through the flow of Oso Flaco Creek where it drained deeply across the beach.

Bobbing and weaving to shake out the armature and run in the gearbox so that everything ran tight and smooth. By twelve, she could match most other racers on the dunes. By sixteen, no one could touch her—not even her dad.

Those had been her favorite times growing up. She'd always been much more her father's daughter than her mother's even before—

Nope! Not going there!

Zoe jammed down a gear and almost ran Luke into the waves. She hadn't even realized he was there, but he backed off fast to save himself. Too bad there was no one to save her.

It was the last time Luke came close to seriously challenging her lead.

She was ten car-lengths in the lead on a long sandy stretch of the beach when the first sign of Saint-Louis appeared. It was a magnificent ten-meter fishing boat pulled up onto the sand—right across her path. It was such a surprise that she almost slammed into it broadside. Thankfully a receding wave left her a low-side gap that she was able to slip through, ducking below the proudly jutting prow. Luke missed the timing as the next wave rolled in and had to take the longer route around the stern through the deeper sand—stretching her lead to fifteen lengths.

The boat was like a canoe with pointed ends that someone had put on a torture rack until it was shockingly slender—almost elegant in how it stretched out to twice the length that seemed proper. A whole line of the long boats were perched upon the beach with their prows aimed out to sea. Dark bottomed, they had white upper sides. Each boat's name—or maybe it was each family's—had been painted down the length of the sides. The entire prow was elaborately decorated with orange, red, and blue images that might be blessings offered to the gods of fishing, or perhaps were simply each fisherman's expression of art.

In the midday heat, the fishermen were sitting in the shade of their boats, mending nets or chatting. Maybe they'd been out for the morning fishing and were now waiting for an evening cast.

She was so busy admiring the boats that she missed when Luke was no longer visible in the gaps between them.

Zoe spun the wheel, sliced up the beach in the narrow alleyway between two boats—barely missed snarling her tires in a piled-up fishnet—and prepared to gun off in hot pursuit before she spotted the red Renault. It was parked high on the beach in front of a single-story beige concrete block building. She eased up through the thick sand and parked alongside it as Christian and Luke climbed out.

Luke smiled at her over the roof of his car. He actually smiled. It was like a gut punch. No, bad analogy. It was like a gut punch by a comfy pillow. It said, *You done good.*

Coming from a Team 6 SEAL officer, it didn't need to say a single word more than that. She couldn't tell if it did say more because it made her look away. Luke Altman smiling was just...wrong. And smiling at her was downright confusing. It hadn't taken a genius to read what he thought of her at the airport.

The Many Grimaces of Lieutenant Commander Luke Altman. They had all too frequently been aimed at her in the past. Even on the Honduras mission where she'd thought she was doing important work, she could now see that he'd barely tolerated her presence.

Fine. After this mission she'd swear to never have a good idea again.

Except he was smiling at her.

Why did the man have to be so damn confusing? If he would only remain a mere macho jerk, she'd know what to do with him.

Speaking of which…Christian opened her door as she killed the engine and shed her helmet. At least he was a smooth and well-mannered macho jerk. That she *absolutely* knew how to deal with. He was close enough that she could see the look in his eyes. Except rather than avaricious desire, it was…pain.

"Are you okay, Christian?"

"I am fine. Fine!" He brushed it off but she didn't quite believe him. "The way you drive, my darling Zoe. *Incroyable!*"

"Christian?"

"It was a fantastic drive. You have the gift. Your assistant is surprisingly good as well…"

Luke had come up beside Christian and was actually grinning again. Or still. Or something.

"…and with a little practice, he could be almost as good as me."

Luke's smile grew. He remained half a step behind Christian and she knew that Luke's ego was really enjoying this.

"But you Zoe. The way you flew," he slapped one hand off the other and arced it to the sky, but winced hard and didn't complete the gesture, drawing his arm back slowly.

Luke had noticed it too, his smile turning off like a light switch. He caught Christian's arm as he stumbled and helped him to stand upright once more. Then he probed Christian's back with his other hand. It earned him a spectrum of winces and one deep grunt.

"Doc was right. You screwed your back, my friend," Luke rumbled out.

"It was during your recovery after Zoe's first jump. Not your fault; I don't know how you saved it."

"Almost didn't," Luke continued in a surprisingly friendly tone as he massaged Christian's lower back.

Zoe had been certain that Luke utterly despised Christian. Guy bonding must have happened in the car—like a cloud of shared testosterone or something. If they were bonding over her, she was going to take them both down. She didn't care if they both towered over her.

"Might not have saved us from a swim except for some of that advice you gave me when we first started out," Luke was turning downright loquacious. Maybe he was the one who needed to go see a doctor.

Nikita would never believe it. Zoe wished she'd taped the moment so that she could prove it had happened.

"Let us sit and eat and drink. Then my back will be better."

Zoe looked around and didn't see where they would go.

Christian pointed. "Mama Odette makes the best *ceebu jen* in Senegal."

An old woman sat out on a patio overlooking the beach. She was wizened in a country where fifty was old and sixty was ancient. In her hand was a heavy, meter-long stick and she was beating it into a large wooden bowl placed between her feet with the energy of a twenty-year-old. It took a moment for Zoe to figure out that it was a giant mortar and pestle.

"See? She is already grinding the spices for our meal." It was more the right size for grinding an entire pumpkin than the scant quarter-cup of spices she scooped out of the bowl as they settled in the cool shade of the tin-roofed awning. As a young servant girl served them tiny glasses of mango juice, Zoe could only look out at the strangeness of it all.

Close by her chair, Mama Odette was cooking on a small propane tank—smaller than for most BBQ grills at home—with a single burner fitted directly on top of it. The large steel wok there appeared to be her only cooking vessel.

In front of them was a line of traditional fishing boats baked in the midday sun, looking as if they'd been little changed in centuries.

And off to the side were parked two vehicles at the peak of exotic motor sports—world rally cars.

It was a land of such sharp contrasts.

LUKE WONDERED what had happened to him.

Actually, he knew the answer: Zoe DeMille had happened to him. But that didn't make the feeling any more familiar.

This morning the flighty girl in her lemon-yellow jogging clothes had proved that she had stamina and skills. Six times up ten stories of stairs, he'd been able to see that she improved rather than flagged the more she ran. He had to respect that—even if it was so unexpected that he wondered if he was remembering it wrong. No, her athleticism couldn't be denied. Just because a SEAL's mission field pack could weigh more than DeMille herself didn't change how fit she was.

Next he tried to discount how the small of her back had fit against his palm, but it had preoccupied too much of his thoughts since then to question that either.

In the garage she'd been playing Miss Sexy Airhead, which had been news on its own—the sexy part. The blonde airhead part he'd already known about—or had always assumed before. Christian certainly believed it.

He kept an eye on Zoe and Christian sitting at either end of a small, battered sofa, talking about racing. It was a technical conversation of car handling that he could barely follow, yet he knew that Christian still only saw his Tweety Bird target.

But the way she'd driven.

Luke had initially wondered if she could even navigate the streets of Dakar. The Renault that he'd been driving was an eager car, severely hot to trot. It wanted to dig in and go like a woman in her prime. He'd kept waiting for DeMille to be overpowered by the car and crash it into some banana stand or cream a faded-orange taxi.

But Zoe hadn't just tamed the Citroën, she'd dusted his ass with it!

That jump hadn't been the final trigger for him. Not that it wasn't about the sexiest thing he'd ever seen a woman do—it was. But as she'd outsmarted him for kilometer after kilometer, he'd learned to respect her as well.

He could count the number of people who'd done that to him on a single hand—with most of his fingers folded.

Zoe DeMille had outmaneuvered him at the juncture of the two coves—then kept doing it for two hundred kilometers. Even Nikita couldn't do that. She was an awesome SEAL, but to be so endlessly creative—that wasn't skill, it was a gift.

Some of it was driving skill; Zoe had clearly driven these kinds of vehicles before. But it didn't matter how much of a feel he got for the car—or how many underhanded plans Christian cooked up for him because Christian knew the terrain—Luke couldn't get past Zoe's guard.

The woman who climbed out of the car on the beach of Saint-Louis wasn't the same one who'd settled behind the wheel in the dim Dakar garage. Her hair was matted with sweat from the helmet she'd worn. She'd unzipped that leather jacket, again revealing the tightly clinging shirt beneath, sweaty and dusty now. The immaculate Zoe DeMille looked slightly disheveled for the first time since he'd met her. Even when they'd crash-landed a helicopter into that jungle river in Honduras, she'd surfaced more like a cartoon mermaid than anything else.

Sitting beneath the tin-metal awning, her eyes hidden by her yellow-framed dark wraparounds, she looked stunning. Her easy confidence as those slender hands arced like a bird in flight when she was describing her approach to a jump. The heat-heavy midday breeze managing to tease her hair into soft ripples as she leaned forward and slammed back to imitate a hard-landing, punctuated by a happy laugh.

She might be entertaining Christian, but now she stood tall in his mind. The woman had skills—real world skills that he understood. Escape and evasion tactics that had never been taught by any SEAL course, she'd displayed at the wheel of her car. No wonder she was a top RPA pilot. If she could fly like that when bound by the restrictions of terrain and gravity, what she could do aloft must be seriously next-level shit.

It was only looking at her, shining in the sun as she fluffed her hair with her fingers, that he finally figured out what she was doing.

She actually *had* a new plan. A Plan B.

Plan A she'd cooked up while he was standing in Hathyaron's Pakistani compound. And its death notice was the question she'd asked in the garage: *Why aren't your cars on the way to the Dakar Rally in South America?*

He'd caught that she'd hoped to attach herself to Christian's team. It would have been a great chance to hide in plain sight while they hunted for Hathyaron.

But when that got shot down because of Christian's screwed-up back, he'd thought she wanted to go for a drive just for her social media thing.

Then, when he saw her drive, he'd decided it was a joy ride. He'd rarely had as much fun in a car—front or back seat —as chasing after DeMille. Maybe it was chasing the pretty woman—

Whoa! Had his head really gone there?

It had.

Except that wasn't what she'd been up to at all.

It wasn't the jump that gave away her Plan B—something she might have mentioned that she had, rather than leaving it to him to figure out.

He watched her bend and twist to work out the kinks from two hard hours of driving. Fantastic flexibility that was a joy to watch.

But after racing her for two hundred kilometers over incredibly challenging terrain, her Plan B was so goddamn obvious she could have posted a billboard along Maine Route 1.

It was also brilliant. With all of the cues she'd given, he didn't need to ask what it was—now that he'd gotten his head out of his ass.

If they could convince Christian to take a car to the Dakar Rally and let Luke drive it, he could still chase after Hathyaron. She'd gone out of her way to force Christian into the car with him so that Luke had the opportunity to demonstrate that he had the skills.

Her ploy also forced him to look at DeMille in a new way. She wasn't some overbuilt bitch like Marva. Her apology this morning had sounded sincere and heartfelt—even if she hadn't really done anything wrong except slash open a scar so old that he'd forgotten it was there.

And she had Christian eating out of her palm—he was positively lapping up the crap DeMille dished out. Maybe in addition to being smart, she was also reliable. Novel idea.

She'd slid so smoothly from Plan A to Plan B back at the garage that he could still barely see the transition in memory —not a chance that Christian Vehrs had caught on.

Not going to The Dakar? Can we please take the cars out anyway? Then that whole frenetic pitch where she hadn't given Christian time to refuse.

She made Luke feel slow.

No one did that! But DeMille had.

They *needed* Christian's willing cooperation. And she'd seen how to get it from the very first second.

How could he help but smile at her. A great driver, funny, cute as hell, and smart to boot. Climbing out of that car and fluffing her hair in the sunlight, what wasn't there to smile about.

She'd befriended Christian. No problem for DeMille— apparently every person with a Y chromosome was her instant friend. No, that wasn't it. Nikita also liked her, as had DeMille's commander. He and Sofia had spent much of their abortive date talking about DeMille. And her flock of rabid fans were mostly women—plus at least one very essential guy named Christian Vehrs.

Luke had better do the same. Being nice to a man who

deserved a sharp slap upside the head for how he thought about Zoe wasn't easy, but Luke had found a way there when Christian's back had acted up. He had done plenty of missions with guys who'd screwed up their backs on the infiltration and completed the mission anyway.

Doing a second undercover assignment with DeMille was shaping up to be very interesting.

*a*fter dinner, Christian's back was so bad that he could barely get up from the battered sofa. With Mama Odette's guidance, Zoe had raced to a local pharmacy and then dosed Christian with prescription strength codeine, which apparently didn't require a prescription in Senegal.

"Sure! Anything you need: Schedule II narcotics, Cipro antibiotic, cough drops. No problem. All at the pharmacy. Doctors in Senegal are only for when you break something. You go to the hospital if your only other option is dying, otherwise we don't waste the time. And most times, if it is time to die, people just do that rather than fighting it. Let's go! I'll race you back, dearest Zoe. This time I will drive."

"Christian. Your back?"

"Pfft!" he waved his hand airily as if dismissing the concern. Then he tripped on a crack in the sidewalk and would have gone down if Luke hadn't caught his arm. Christian yelped as the motion pulled at his back hard enough to punch through the painkiller.

"A taxi, my friend," Luke kept an arm around Christian's

shoulders, looking supportive, but also effectively trapping the man.

As far as she could tell, Luke was being sincere with his kindness. She still needed to find out what that was about. If he was being sincere about that, had he been sincere with his smile as well? As they'd eaten their triangular areas of the *ceebu jen* platter, she kept catching him watching her. A few times he was looking at her body—in such a thoughtful way that she could feel the heat rippling through her, and not as a blush to her cheeks.

But mostly he was looking at *her* as if he'd never seen her before. Sure he had—he'd simply looked through her, not at her. Luke's new state of observation was decidedly unnerving.

"It will be a much smoother ride in a taxi," she assured Christian. It would, but some part of her wanted Christian out of the way, and not just because of his habit of only looking at her body rather than at her.

She decided to trust the instinct, even if she didn't know the cause.

"We'll take the rally cars back to Dakar for you."

Christian's protests didn't alter Luke's actions in the slightest. Christian was soon tucked into the back of an orangish cab and was most of the way to asleep in the back seat by the time Luke had given the driver the address. The four-hour drive would cost him under a hundred bucks and he'd be thankful for it later. At least Zoe hoped so.

The cab had pulled away after Mama Odette gave the driver a lengthy lecture about this being a good friend of hers and she'd know if he wasn't treated well or if he was ripped off or... That's where Zoe's high school French gave up the ghost.

Then Mama Odette had waved and headed inside her

house without another word, leaving Luke looming over her until Zoe found herself shuffling her feet on the hot sand.

She tried looking up into Luke's eyes, but the sun was close behind his head, blinding in the bright sky. Looking toward the house felt as if she was trying to stare at their hostess who had apparently had enough of them…or perhaps had enough sense to snooze through the midday heat. Looking at the sea felt like she was avoiding looking at Luke. And shifting so that she could look at him clear of the sun still left her blinded by the sight of him. He'd always been handsome in a rugged, rough-and-ready way, but now he was…

Zoe was losing her mind. This was Lieutenant Commander Luke Altman and she was—

"What's the prize?" He folded his arms over his beautiful chest and looked down at her with those equally lovely blue eyes.

"The prize?"

"If I beat you on the drive back?"

Zoe laughed, "You couldn't even catch me getting here."

"I'm light one passenger now."

"Still won't help you catch me."

"What will?"

"Not being married, for one." Zoe had no idea why she'd said that. That so couldn't be what he was asking.

"Not married." And by the thousand-and-first grimace of Lieutenant Commander Luke Altman she now knew exactly what button she'd hit this morning at the top of the African Renaissance Monument steps.

"But you were… And…" Zoe started piecing it together. "And she called you an asshole. And I said—" Suddenly the fish and rice that had tasted so good before twisted in her stomach like it had come back to life. "I'm so sorry, Luke. I'd never— I didn't— I—"

"Not your fault, DeMille. I don't talk about it much. Try not to remember it much."

"You don't talk much at all."

He scoffed—maybe that was his version of a laugh, but he didn't say anything else, and Zoe again found that she was shuffling her feet.

"Is it something you want to talk about?"

His face didn't change, but she could see his arms tightening.

"I'll take that as a big fat no."

"Smart," he nodded his approval and she felt fantastically tall…at least five-five.

And if he wasn't married? And he'd smiled at her? Then he was thinking… "Whoa!"

He gave her another dose of silence. Maybe he'd meant the double entendre, *What* will *let him catch me?* Nope. Not answering that one. She'd stick with racing cars. Those she understood.

Cars.

"I'll prove you can't catch me."

Instead of a grimace, he raised his eyebrows.

"You take the Citroën." She'd still beat him even if she drove the Renault. She crossed to the Citroën to fetch her helmet and jacket.

"You got a red outfit to wear with the Renault? Not sure it's legal for you to drive it if you don't." There was something sly in his voice. Teasing her about her suitcase? Teasing her at all? That would be an absolute first for him.

In answer, she grabbed her shirt's zipper at her throat and tugged it down far enough to expose the front strap of her bright red bra. She'd long since learned that even being lightly built, a girl needed support when off-road racing.

"Is that red enough?"

Luke's eyes went dark. He didn't move an inch as she made a show of putting on her jacket and zipping it all of the way up without zipping up her shirt first. He hadn't moved when she'd donned her sunglasses and helmet.

It was the first time she'd ever gotten a "male" reaction out of him and it felt like someone had just kicked on her body's turbocharger. Chance had led her hand to grabbing the red bra when she was changing. Which had left her wondering just how desperate she was to get Christian to lend them his cars.

Enough to…?

No! She'd decided that before she'd even returned to the garage. Even pretending just wasn't going to happen. But to have it work so well on Luke Altman—the *unmarried* SEAL Lieutenant Commander Luke Altman—that was a different matter entirely.

She stepped around him, climbed into the Renault, and fired off the engine. Plucking Luke's helmet off the seat, she held it out to him. He took it autonomically but made no move to put it on.

"You got to catch me to get the prize." By which time she hoped that she knew if she wanted him to.

"I—"

She never heard "I—" *what* because she gunned the engine and popped the clutch.

In the rearview she could see him trying to bat the sand she'd sprayed off his face and out of his hair.

LUKE SPIT out more sand as he yanked on his helmet and jumped into the Citroën. By the time he'd strapped in, she was a kilometer down the beach—well clear of the fishing boats and accelerating hard.

The shore lay south-southwest, almost straight into the sun. And there was a tiny shining star redder than Mercury far down the beach. He'd be damned if he didn't catch it.

To hell with behaving. Most of the fishing fleet had pushed back out to sea while they ate...much of the beach emptying. He opened up the Citroën.

"Come on, baby. Show me what you can do!"

And the car leapt. They were twenty klicks down the beach before he caught up with her. The Citroën was awesomely powerful. Though catching up to DeMille had seemed a little too easy as if she'd been waiting for—

DeMille slashed up the beach. The tide had come in, so the beach was narrower and all the sand they had to run on was soft. What was she up to this time?

She started carving S-turns in front of him, up and down the beach. Soon, he was enveloped in a cloud of dust and had to slow to make sure he didn't end up in the ocean or wrapped around a baobab. When he finally broke through into clear air, DeMille was again well down the beach.

"Gonna play hard to get, DeMille? Well, two can play at that game."

This time he waited for a long straight stretch that he could see was clear before he attacked. He jounced and rocketed over the lumpy sand, carved by wind and water into knee-high humped dunes. The car was jumping every other one.

Launch...slam! Launch...slam!

He hoped he wasn't about to shatter the car. That would piss Christian off but good.

Luke was almost upon her. Close enough to imagine that he could feel the heat of her. Smell her over the Senegal sea and iron dust. Could almost touch—

And she jolted ahead.

She'd been holding a gear in reserve. Now she was taking the dunes in groups of three. He tried, but he couldn't get the Citroën to fly the way she was lofting the Renault.

No, she wasn't lofting it. She was racing low and fast, as if she'd found the flow of running up the steps and now he was the one who was clumsy like some midshipman jouncing up a ship's ladder.

How?

He tried changing gears and engine power.

No better.

Then he remembered something Christian had said about the suspension. He angled across the dune tops ever so slightly. Not a big obvious zig-zag as she'd done earlier to raise the dust cloud, but an angular attack, up and down the beach. The ride smoothed out and he began keeping pace with her.

Now that he thought of it, he saw that Zoe was doing the same.

Damn but she was incredible, hurling three tons of racing machine over rough ground at two hundred kilometers an hour.

He managed to pull even, but he couldn't get by her. He knew that she was toying with him, but he wasn't going to let her get away with it this time.

For twenty kilometers neither of them could get more than a few meters of advantage. Waves breaking in a white blur to the right. Palm trees close on the left, but the bright sun far enough into afternoon to pound relentlessly against the car. No sound but the engine's roar. No feeling except the twitching of the wheel in his hand and the impact of tires on sand transmitted to his butt.

Ahead by a nose, the length of the front end...

Then catching a bad patch of sand, and suddenly he was staring at her rear bumper, again clawing to keep up.

He was just about to—

Zoe cut over hard in front of his nose. She didn't clip him, but it was a close thing.

His rear end broke free—she'd forced him to brake at a bad moment on a swell of sand, and probably knew that. It took everything he had not to roll or flip. Dumping speed. Handbrake on, then back off. Down two gears and gun it while counter-steering.

The dust and sand was a cloud around him as he finally spun end for end. Running backward down the beach for a moment, then snapping around to aim forward once more.

Finally back under control, he prepared to gun after her. Paybacks were gonna be hell.

Except she wasn't down the beach.

Instead, she'd parked the Renault sideways across the sand like a road block.

DeMille simply sat at the wheel, looking at him out the side window.

He rolled up until his front bumper stopped a single meter from her door.

Never in his life had he needed a woman the way he needed Zoe DeMille. Not Marva. Not the head cheerleader who'd taken his cherry at sixteen—Susan? Cindy? He didn't know. It didn't matter.

He needed DeMille.

But still neither of them moved.

They finally shut off their engines at the same moment.

Shed helmets.

Stepped out onto the hot sand.

Closed car doors.

Zoe didn't move away from the Renault, outlined in yellow against the red.

He couldn't stop moving.

1 2

*Z*oe couldn't move. Pinned in place by…what?

Not like the shocked disbelief that such a thing couldn't be happening, like so long ago.

Simply unable to set her body into motion. It waited for something. Waited somewhere outside her control. All she managed was to remain standing.

Luke didn't hesitate. By some superhuman strength, he approached her. Not puzzled by her inaction. Not even hesitant.

He stepped to her and lifted her as if she weighed nothing. Lifted her and placed her back against the driver's door. His hand scooped her butt as her legs wound about his hips of their own accord.

She groaned as she tightened her legs to pull them closer together.

This was what she needed. She needed a man. It had been a long time and she needed him so badly that it actually hurt. Zoe needed someone to want her. One who saw her. Who…

His kiss seared thoughts out of her brain faster than the heat of the afternoon sun. His heat reflected her own as she clung and held and bit and beat her fists against his shoulders.

There was no undressing. No time for that.

No pause allowed in this race. Too much need.

He pushed against her, pressing hard between her legs exactly where she needed him. Their first time was going to be fully clothed.

Luke drove against her. Slammed her back harder against the car as he raked his teeth down the side of her throat.

Against the car.

The...*car!*

All she could remember was the car against her back, her own helplessness, and—

Zoe screamed!

It ripped out of her.

Her body's uncontrolled flailing found a target.

She doubled her fists together and slammed them at her attacker. She heard a grunt of pain.

Again, fists joined and raised.

Slam down!

Something caught her fists before they found their target. She fought. She squirmed.

Her body was still pinned to the car.

The *car!*

She couldn't escape. She couldn't free her arms. Couldn't free her body.

Her knife. If only she could reach her knife, she could—

But her hands were trapped. She couldn't break free. Couldn't—

"DeMille! Stop!"

She screamed again, but there was no help. No one to save her.

No one on the lonely stretch of empty beach.

No one to—

Beach?

She was on a beach?

The next cry caught in her throat.

Not in a dark garage that reeked of motor oil and grease? Pinned against a car by...

"Luke?"

"Welcome back," his voice was no more than a low growl.

"Let me go," Zoe couldn't catch her breath. Each attempt stuck in her throat. A throat that hurt as if she'd screamed until... *"Please* let me go," the helpless pleading tone hurt almost as much as the scream had.

Luke eased back, lowering her to stand on the sand. The last thing he released was her hands—he'd caught her joined fists easily in one mighty hand.

When he finally released her, her knees let go and she slid the rest of way to the sand. Pulling up her knees, she buried her face against them.

After a long moment, she heard Luke slide down to sit with his back against the car too, but she couldn't look at him.

"What happened?" Why did she even ask? She remembered, but wished she didn't. Maybe Luke would be kind and not answer the question. She felt unaccountably chilled in the shadow of the car despite the hot afternoon and the scorching sand.

"I was hoping you could tell me."

She could, but it would kill her to open the door on that piece of her past. All she could do was shake her head. She barely knew Luke, and there were places she wasn't ready to go with anyone, especially not some SEAL Team 6 superhero.

Luke remained silent for a long time. Long enough that she was afraid she was going to have to speak first. Even if she couldn't look up at him. Even if she couldn't face…

"I'm guessing there's someone I need to kill. Very slowly and very painfully."

That forced her to look up at him.

He was staring at the Citroën's front end, parked just out of reach, not at her. His jaw was set in a grim line. There was already a bruise forming on his chin and cheek.

Had she— Yes, she'd done that.

"Who?" Luke's voice was still rough with anger when he asked.

"He's already dead."

"Do I tell you *Well done?*"

She shook her head. "Dead, though not my doing."

"You do this thing every time?"

Again she could only shake her head. "First time ever."

"Well, ain't I the lucky guy."

She buried her face back on her knees. For one glorious moment, she'd had exactly what she wanted. Exactly what her body craved. And then— He was never going to touch her again; not unless he was a total idiot. Lieutenant commander wasn't a rank awarded to idiots. At least not very often and never in SEAL Team 6.

"I'm not pissed at you, Zoe."

"No. Don't call me that," she held her knees tighter. "You've never called me by my first name before."

"Considering what I was about to do to you, using your first name seems about right."

"Screw my brains out?"

"Yeah," Luke sounded pretty grumpy about not getting to do that. Or maybe embarrassed at having seen more than she'd ever shown anyone.

"I was looking forward to that, too."

"Then…why?" There were a lot of long pauses when talking with Luke. She supposed that she'd rarely left him big enough gaps to speak. Not that he used all that many words even around the long pauses.

"The car. Being pressed up against—" she shuddered.

Luke grunted.

"It felt…amazing." Now she was doing the pause thing.

"For about six seconds."

"You were counting?"

"Not likely." His soft chuckle actually made her feel a tiny bit better about the whole disastrous mess.

"Do you still want to…?" She couldn't finish the sentence. She couldn't believe that he was even here beside her still. That he hadn't simply driven away in disgust.

"What? An apology fuck for trying to crack my jaw?" It was purpling more brightly with each passing moment.

"No. I mean…" No, it was too humiliating to ask. "Never mind. Maybe we should just drive back to Dakar and pretend none of this ever happened."

"Zoe… DeMille… Shit! Whoever you are, you dizzy broad. Yes I want to. I'm not the sort who is going to hold a rape against a woman. I only hold it against the bastard who deserved to die."

"That's not what I mean."

Luke dug his hands through the sand for a bit before answering. "Better explain yourself then. I'm just a local boy from the Maine woods, not some New Age, sensitive hipster-type." That almost earned him a smile, but she couldn't quite find it yet.

"How can you want me after I..." she nodded behind her toward the car. The car where he'd almost done exactly what she'd wanted before she'd totally lost it.

Luke rose to his feet and held out a hand. He helped her to her feet, but didn't let go of her hand.

"DeMille—no, to hell with that. Zoe, when you're ready, I'm your man. Yeah, the heat right then was pretty hot. But you're my favorite fantasy of the moment." He shrugged. "Kind of sounds like shit coming out that way, but it's true."

"*I'm* your fantasy? Despite being a screwed up mess?"

He shrugged a yes.

A superhero, Special Operations Forces SEAL wanted...*her?* More than the heat of the moment? That was certainly unexpected.

The slutty part of herself, the one she'd tried to leave behind with the Huckfest truck jumpers, wanted to jump Luke right here and now. Ten years ago she'd buried that desperate girl, even holding a ceremony out in the dunes and burning that damned photo that just happened to include every single guy she'd fucked during that year's event.

The sensible military girl knew that guys like Luke Altman weren't for women like her. He should be with...

"What happened with you and Sofia?" She regretted the question the moment she asked it.

Luke offered her a half smile. As if he could see everything behind her question. The nerves about her own slender and short physique. Wanting to have sex with the man who'd already slept with her commander. Being so much less of a woman that—

"Nothing," Luke interrupted the crazed stream of her thoughts.

"What?" Is that how he treated women? Insipient rage was blasting the last of the fear out of her system. "You can call doing it with her *nothing?*"

"No, I mean literally nothing. It was weird. Drinks. A little talk. I even liked her by that point. Not just her body."

"Which looks awesome," And so unlike her own.

"Which *looks* awesome," Luke agreed without the least hint of embarrassment.

She couldn't believe she was discussing her commander's body with a man who had just said he wanted to make love to her. Was she trying to talk him out of it? No, even she wasn't that stupid about men.

"Wasn't enough. Should have been." He looked out to sea for a long moment, then shook his head. "It wasn't. We even tried a kiss, but…" Luke shrugged as if he talked about women with other women all the time. "It wasn't like kissing my sister or anything weird, it was just…nothing."

"Did I mention that you're an asshole?"

His smile slowly reappeared as he looked down at her once more. "You might have."

"Asshole." She went up on her toes and kissed his unbattered cheek.

Not once since he'd helped her to her feet had he let go of her hand. Maybe having sex with Luke wouldn't be slutty, because she didn't want a man between her legs—she wanted *this* man between her legs.

LUKE SCANNED the beach for potential threats as he

constantly had during the drive to Saint-Louis. On the drive back he'd had other things on his mind.

Miles of empty in both directions. Christian had said that that the nearest road here was four or five klicks back into the bush. The only living things that came here would be the seagulls and the occasional rally car. There weren't even any of the former at the moment.

Just the two of them, the sea, and a whole lot of sunshine. He hadn't wanted Sofia Gracie, but something about Zoe was electrifying his body. And he didn't think it was just the idyllic setting.

He turned back to face her at the unzipping sound.

Zoe shrugged out of the jacket. Then, without looking away from him, did the same with the blouse and finally the red bra.

He knew he should move. Knew this was his cue. But all he could do was look at her. She was strangely perfect. Her small size had nothing to do with the size of the person inside the body. Moments ago she'd had a panic attack. And now she was… Or was she?

"Said I didn't want an apology fuck."

She nodded. Her hair slid across her bare shoulders in a soft cascade as she leaned down to untie her shoes. Once again he was staring down at the dark part in her hair.

"How about sex?" Her head remained down as she shucked her pants. "Consensual sex, Lieutenant Commander Altman. How about that?"

"Why?" What the hell was suddenly wrong with him? A cute-as-hell chick was offering her body. His own body was rapidly making its vote loud and clear.

She stood up and looked at him. Not a scrap of clothing

and utterly beautiful. She belonged back in her coffin wearing a flight suit. She didn't belong…he looked around…out here. Palm and baobab trees offered shade along the beach. The Atlantic Ocean rolled practically to their feet. A pair of fantastic race cars parked beside them—ones she'd proven that she could drive more competently than he could fully comprehend.

And this slender beauty stood waiting for him. Not fifteen minutes ago she'd been screaming in terror. Had she stuffed that away? Where? When would it lash out again? If she hit him on the same side of the face, it might fall off. Her blow had been fantastic for someone her size—for a person any size.

She knelt over one of those very nice legs and unstrapped an ankle sheath. Boker Plus Anti-Grav knife with carbon fiber handle and ceramic blade. He supposed he was lucky her legs had been locked around his waist and she hadn't been able to reach it during her panic.

Zoe tossed it atop the rest of her clothes and rose back to stand before him, naked and glorious.

"Where?" He didn't have a blanket and had learned the hard way that sand wasn't great for the guy and totally sucked for the woman when you were having sex.

In answer she leaned back against the driver's door of the Renault.

"You sure?"

She nodded.

No hesitation.

No sign of fear.

Those blue eyes showed nothing but absolute certainty. Was it that she wanted him to purge her past? Or had her panic attack already done that? Or was Zoe DeMille simply that damn fearless? Maybe she'd hypnotized him and this was all an illusion.

Luke brushed his fingertips over her breastbone, tracing the line between those small, perfect breasts. He could feel her heart beating. It wasn't racing wildly.

How was she so strong?

WHEN LUKE KNELT before her and kissed her between the breasts, Zoe didn't know whether she wanted to laugh, cry, or scream again. Except this time the scream would be from contact shock.

Her father had taught her to love cars. Driving the beach and dunes today—the first time she'd been on sand since the final long-ago Huckfest—had brought all of it back. The bad, the horror, but also the good.

Luke was definitely from the last of those. She'd hurt him and he'd done nothing in return. He'd listened. He'd understood.

Who was the last man to understand her? Had there ever been one?

Christian Vehrs thought she was just some object of lust for him to conquer. Luke moved his hands up her legs, started by rubbing a thumb back and forth where her ankle sheath had been strapped, acknowledging the soldier. Knowing an ankle sheath always left a little irritation, like a wristwatch worn too tightly, he massaged it for a moment. His rough, powerful hands, gracing over her skin like warm water sluicing away the remnants of fear. Of a past she'd make sure never took control of her again.

She fisted her hands in his hair as he tasted her. Breast, belly, hip—each place purged.

And behind her was the rock, the bastion of her young life—a fine car. The metal and glass so warm against her skin it was like coming home. The strength engineered into the car and held there, waiting for a driver who understood how to unleash all of that power. How to see beyond the machine and become bonded with it. To let it drive her as much as she drove it.

She'd loved to drive.

Somewhere she'd lost that, flown instead. If not for the horrors she'd been confronted with in her father's garage, might she have entered The Dakar years ago? Or gone Formula 1?

Luke drove her body the way she drove a car. One moment coaxing her to open to him, to give over control, and the next moment bypassing the obvious to trace the line where butt met thigh.

When she would have begged him to plow straight ahead, he drew a gentle spiral that circled her breast five times or perhaps a hundred from the outer edges to the aching center. And he almost killed her with pleasure when the final contact was not with his fingers, but with lips, tongue, and teeth. His touch convinced her that she was shaped just as she should be. Not like her commander. Not like the curvaceous women who had always plagued her thoughts, but rather exactly as she should be.

This time, when he rose to his feet and lifted her, there was no protest in her. She was so ready to fly.

She hadn't noticed when he undressed. Didn't care that he'd been carrying a condom somewhere—didn't care if it was presumptuous or just practical.

It didn't matter. She gave him complete control and let him steer the course. Let him control her body just as she'd controlled the Citroën. When he took her and pressed into her and drove her hard against the Renault's driver-side door this time, she no longer had the power to protest or accept.

She was past functioning as anything more than a body for Luke to take and use. She wrapped her arms around his neck, buried her face against his throat, and breathed him in. The tears that mixed with his own salty sweat as his body bucked and rolled against hers were not joy, but neither were they sadness.

They were just tears of release. A release that rolled through her time and again until nothing else remained.

Afterward, when she could, she planted a kiss on his collarbone to let him know she was okay—she could do no more. In answer, his arms slid more tightly around her and they remained a long time together leaning against the car as close as two bodies could be.

13

"*Y*ou bastard," Christian sounded more impressed than angry. "How is it that you get Zoe and I do not?"

Luke had no idea. It was like a DeMille-sized bomb had been dropped on his position and he still hadn't recovered. Taking her against the car parked a hundred kilometers from anywhere was a tropical-beach fantasy that still didn't seem real. Going down on her last night in her bed had simply been downright awesome.

Christian, who they should have easily beaten back to Dakar, had returned and been put to bed by his wife hours before he and Zoe returned.

He hadn't remembered holding her for so long in his lap after they'd made love, but when he'd sat down in the sand and she'd curled up there, it was hard to complain. She made no attempt at explaining or apologizing for her crying. Maybe he should have asked, but she'd stopped soon enough and simply remained in his arms. There were also no words about the sex they'd just had. He liked sex, knew he was good at it

—which didn't begin to describe what had just happened between them. The warm day and the soft woman had made the passage of time meaningless.

It had gone dark as they'd wound through the streets of Dakar. Leola had greeted their return in a transparently sheer nightgown of purest white that offset her dark skin and hid absolutely none of her exceptional assets. Despite the stunning display, Luke had barely looked at her, which hadn't pleased their hostess in the slightest.

Instead he was watching every single motion Zoe made, all the while wondering what it would be like to touch her ass as she climbed the stairs ahead of him—turned out it was exceptional. Or to once more have his hand at the small of her back as she arched against him—even better. Some day he *had* to see how she would look in a nightgown as sheer as Leola's, but black to offset her light complexion.

She teased, but it was always a cheery banter, not games.

Or maybe it was games with others, but not between them. He didn't think that games of that kind would be possible between them after her past had unraveled on her in his arms. There had been no grand confessions afterward. He'd no more mentioned Marva's betrayal than she'd explained her past. But there were no games. No woman had ever given herself to him so completely.

Zoe in the morning had turned out to be much as he'd guessed—not an ounce of coy in her trim body.

She'd woken like a soldier, one moment asleep and the next wide awake. From curled up against his shoulder, where she'd spent the night, to lying full on his chest and humming happily in a single move as fast as most women might flutter their eyelashes.

Thank God he always kept a couple condoms in his med

kit, because it wasn't long before she was arched over him and had finished waking them with awesome morning sex.

If she'd been any bigger, they'd never have fit in the shower together, but they had. While his body didn't recover *that* fast, hers did and he'd made the most of it. Devouring her cries with a kiss as her body jolted against his palm. Even the delicious Marva had never responded the way Zoe DeMille did in his arms. Vibrantly alive and completely frank in her approach to sex. For her, sex wasn't something that was to be withheld, twisted, manipulated until he went mad. No, with her it was simply about using each other's bodies in glorious ways.

Zoe placed a phone call he couldn't quite hear over the buzzing in his ears as he dressed. Then when she had bent over at the waist until she was head down to run a dryer over her hanging hair, he decided he'd better get out of there. If he looked at that fine ass pointed aloft much longer, he was going to be getting undressed again double-time.

Christian was there when he made it out of the bedroom and down to the outdoor courtyard breakfast table.

"You bastard," Christian repeated. "How do *you* be the one to get her? You must explain this."

Not a chance, even if he had a damned clue.

Christian looks so comfortable in his personal kingdom. The large home wrapped around him, the collection of very expensive racing toys in the garage, and the elegant garden. Christian sat at the head of the table that could easily seat twenty guests in the garden; Luke sat to his right. Rather than the heat of the morning sun, they were in the dappled shade of thick palm and fruit trees. Blooms the size of his head covered one tree and as many dusky red mangos hung from another.

Hawks circled high above. A pied crow, darkest black with his proud white necklace and breastplate landed at the far end of the table with a harsh ar-ar-ar-ar. Christian tossed it a chunk that he tore from a baguette and the massive bird flitted away with it. A trio of mourning doves were bathing in the small puddles on the concrete around the swimming pool. A flock of small yellow birds flitted onto a blooming hibiscus. Bright yellow. Zoe's color.

Luke could still taste the strong red *bissap* juice that Mama Odette had served with the *ceebu jen*. And the milder but richer taste of Zoe that lingered on his tongue from their last lingering kiss in the shower.

He was definitely losing it if a flock of birds had him thinking about Zoe in ways to give him a serious arousal. Time for a subject change.

"Great pair of cars you've built," Luke offered as a maid brought hot coffee.

"Ah," Christian nodded his head. "Yes, you drive very well. So, *you* win her with *my* car. I think this is very unfair, but *c'est la guerre.*"

"*Guerre?* What does that mean?" French had never been one of Luke's languages. He knew *C'est la vie,* "such is life," but not—

"*Guerre* is 'war' in French," Zoe explained as she breezed out the French doors and up to the table with her blonde hair floating gloriously off her shoulders. Six-foot-tall runway models didn't look so poised as she did when she sat down at the table across from him. "Are we at war?"

"A war it seems I have lost," Christian admitted defeat with a smile and shrug.

The way that Zoe glanced up at him, Luke definitely felt as if he'd won. It wasn't as if they were in any kind of relationship. Like all his forays with women, they'd fade away when he was called up on another mission. Except this time he was already *on* a mission. He'd done it with women soldiers before, but always between assignments, never during one. It was his "way out" of any female trap, "Duty calls. Been great, babe. I'll call ya." Without a single chance that he would.

But Zoe…

"You know, Christian…" Zoe had that tone again. Luke suspected that Christian was about to have the hammer dropped on his head and that he wouldn't see it coming.

"If you were to start The Dakar, even just the first hour of the initial stage, you could capture your 'Legend' status for entering your tenth Dakar Rally."

"But who would drive for me then? Even I must accept I cannot run the whole of The Dakar this year. I already let my navigator go and join another team because I could not race."

Luke felt the blood drain from his head and go straight to his groin. Zoe DeMille was far more than a fantastic driver with a seriously sex-kitten body. He wanted to drag her off into the thick foliage of Christian's garden to show her just what he thought of her. It wasn't just a brilliant plan; it was genius. And she'd found a way to sell it that he knew Christian could never resist.

Zoe rested her chin on her palm and her elbow on the table as she leaned toward Christian. She was wearing a loose top like the one she'd worn on her arrival at the airport. This one was Renault red and from his angle he could see the strap of her bra—lemon-yellow.

Luke wasn't sure whether she was trying to slay him or Christian. He definitely no longer begrudged her the weight of her suitcase. He looked forward to taking that scrap of yellow off her at the first opportunity. Or better yet, leave it on—it and nothing else. Then he'd—

"You, my dear Zoe? You would drive my car for me?" Christian's voice was caught up in the wonder of it. Luke had to admit it was a hell of an image.

But… *What!* It was supposed to be him doing the driving, not—

"And after you *have* to drop out to save your back…"

"Ah, your assistant would be your co-driver. Yes, he is very good, even if not as good as you or me."

Luke would show Christian just how goddamn good he was. And Zoe too… Except, as hard as it was to swallow, Zoe was a better driver than he was. Someday he'd get her out on a pair of motorcycles and see how she did. Zoe DeMille in full body leathers? Oh, he definitely had to see that in real life.

"But how to get my support truck and my car to The Dakar in time? The ship from Europe left weeks ago and is already there."

"I hoped you'd be willing. I already called a friend. He has a transport plane that must pick up a delivery in Buenos Aires. We'll just take your vehicles to the airport with us and I'll have my friend fly them to Mar del Plata for the start—it's barely out of his way. You just buy us the plane tickets on the very next flight out."

Luke now understood the phone call that Zoe had made. He imagined that a C-130 Hercules cargo jet was already en route and would be gathering up Christian's vehicles shortly after they themselves were safely gone.

"Which—"

"Oh, we must take the Citroën, Christian. She and I match as if it was destiny."

The guy never stood a chance.

While Christian pulled out his phone, Zoe looked over at him. Luke couldn't help but smile.

She blushed and looked away. Beyond cute.

"I wasn't sure if you'd be angry," Zoe whispered to him when Christian had gone forward to use the 787's bathroom and stayed to flirt with the waitress under the guise of having to stretch his legs.

"About what?" Luke had taken advantage of an overlap of their lap blankets to slide his hand across under the blankets. He ticked his nails lightly along the inner seam of her jeans. It sent a shiver of anticipation along her skin.

"About me arranging for the C-130 without consulting with you. It just made sense and I was sure Christian would agree." She did what she could to keep her voice level, but Luke's lightest touch, even his smile, was doing strange things to her.

He ran his fingers up along her inner thigh until the heel of his hand rubbed against her. She clamped her legs together, trapping his touch there. She'd done it instinctively to block him, but now that she'd pinned his hand there, she didn't want him to move it away. Her wanton past was her past. Since reaching the rational age of eighteen, she'd chosen lovers with care and typically enjoyed her time with them. They invariably made love to *The Soldier of Style* rather than to Zoe DeMille, but she'd learned to live with that.

She didn't know how Luke saw her, never mind *what* he

saw in her, but it certainly wasn't her online self. It made every touch of his have more meaning, be more important than it should be.

She never, ever cried having sex. And she'd wept on his shoulder, unable to stop for an embarrassingly long time. And still he hadn't walked away from her in disgust. Instead he'd sat down on the sand and shifted her so that she could stay in his lap, curl up against his SEAL-broad chest, and simply weep.

Afterward, he'd made a point of dressing her himself, which was good because her body was still warring between numb and tingling with the aftershocks of him wanting her at all and the incredible releases he'd delivered. When the first piece of clothing he'd put on her had been her knife's ankle sheath, her heart had made a strange flip. She had no idea what it meant, but it was undeniably there. He wanted to protect her. Being a man, it was a gift he would never understand the magnitude of to a woman—ten-fold to one who'd been violated before.

Once fully clothed, he'd actually lifted her into the Renault before planting a deep kiss and copping a feel that had left her breathless. This time they'd lined up side by side for the start. They'd run the last hundred kilometers in perfect sync, neither pulling ahead for more than a moment even though they were pushing the cars' limits the whole way.

Last night he offered equally synchronized sex.

Zoe had barely made it through the door of her room without laughing in Leola's face. She'd briefly imagined that being naked beneath a two-thousand-dollar Kiki de Montparnasse negligee robe was how all sexy Senegalese women greeted their guests. All the closed doors of

Senegalese homes, each with a nearly naked Leola behind it was so unlikely that it was funny.

Leola and Christian were a perfect match—both in it for whatever they could get. Instead Zoe remembered the people at the beach or out by the tree having tea, simply glad to be together. Real friends. Normal people, belonging. She could see herself with them and that made her like the city.

Realizing that Leola's greeting was intended just for Luke had almost killed her sense of amusement.

Until, unimaginably, it was Zoe's ass he'd grabbed as soon as they'd turned the landing. Her desire to ask if Luke was out of his mind, wanting her over the gorgeous Leola, was short-circuited when Luke brushed her hair behind her ear and then traced his fingertips along her jaw the moment they'd safely escaped to her bedroom.

She'd answered his silent question with just as many words by simply stepping into his arms. This time he'd undressed her and she him. She'd been right about the Sig Sauer compact sidearm he'd acquired in the handoff at the airport; wrong about him having a knife. He wore two.

Always a light sleeper, she'd collapsed onto his shoulder afterward and not had a single thought until she woke in the morning. And that first thought, just as it was now on the plane, had been very simple: *More!*

Luke's hand didn't press harder against her beneath the airline blanket. Instead, he started a slow, circular massage with the heel of his hand, sending successive shock waves of turbulence rushing through her system.

Did he enjoy sending her flying like some RPA pilot? Did he get off on having such complete control over her body that she was utterly helpless? Remote piloting was her job, but his lightest touch stole her breath and mind. She felt she should complain, but her body won that argument before it even started.

"You arranging the C-130?" Luke whispered from somewhere close by.

Zoe had closed her eyes to revel in the sensations that were shifting from full throttle to wide-open turbocharger as well. She managed an "uh-huh" sound, but she wasn't sure what she was acknowledging other than asking him not to stop. Oh, her apology for ordering the plane without involving him first. Maybe that was her form of remote piloting him. Did that make what he was doing to her body more or less manipulat—

He nibbled on her ear and elicited another "uh-huh" that prayed he wouldn't stop.

"Almost as sexy as the way you drive." His whisper, barely louder than the plane engine's roar, sounded so close to her ear that it would have tickled if it didn't feel so good.

So he thought she was sexy because of how she drove? Why wasn't that a surprise? Even as her body continued responding to his touch, Zoe knew it couldn't be about *her*. That would have been too much to ask.

Was this being about her driving better than it being about her online persona? She supposed it was. Driving a race car *was* closer to her true self.

Did that make it okay even if it *still* wasn't about her?

Luke leaned close enough to brush a kiss across her lips. She'd expected a SEAL to be a masterful lover—they were good at so many things—but she'd never expected him to be a gentle one. It was an electrifying contrast. She let her body's acceleration drive her deeper into the seat cushions. At least if it wasn't *about* her, it *felt* as if it was.

Thirty-six hours in Dakar and they were flying to South

America. Not just as some "pretend" support team, but in the race where they'd have a far better chance at finding Hathyaron. She still didn't doubt for a second after seeing that garage in his Pakistan compound that he would be racing at The Dakar.

In the last thirty-six hours she'd also gained a lover against whom she had no resistance. And she didn't want any.

She opened her legs beneath the blanket and let him take her the rest of the way aloft.

If this was flying, maybe she'd never come down.

14

Luke rubbed his thumb across the FIA driver license bearing his picture.

International Competition Authorization.
Authorization is given to this license holder
to enter and/or drive in any event
inscribed on the FIA Calendar National Race.

What favors had Zoe called in with the Fédération Internationale de l'Automobile to get these? Or maybe he didn't want to know.

Think, Luke. She hadn't sold herself. She'd called SOCOM and told them what she needed. Then Special Operations Command had taken care of all of the details while their plane was en route. She and Luke would now both be fully registered with FIA including any fees and required qualifications—faked but on record. Exactly as he would have called for, if it had been his op.

His op. Up until this moment, some part of him had thought it was. Assumed it was.

Not so much.

This op had been completely in the control of Zoe.

He was…her personal assistant. As stupid as that sign she'd made for him to hold at the airport might seem, it was exactly what he'd become. Not a position he was comfortable with.

Looking around didn't make him feel any better.

He, Zoe, and Christian were queued up in a hangar-sized shed in the Argentine seaside town of Mar del Plata. Of which he'd seen nothing after the thirty-hour flight had landed at midnight. The cars had been waiting as promised, with the keys left at the Avis rental counter—after four hours passed out in a hotel and then straight into the "scrutineering" shed by dawn with nothing but coffee and a chocolate croissant to ease the pain.

His eyes hadn't even focused until they were inside so he'd missed his first look at Argentina. Other than the Spanish and the Latinate complexion of at least some of the locals, they could have been in a steel barn in Brussels. Along this side of the building were dozens of desks manned by clerks who were checking over everyone's documents to make sure they were in valid.

"Scrutineering" was the in-depth inspection of both the drivers and their vehicles to make sure everything was in order. Christian's vehicles (the Citroën and the support truck) —which had made their direct flight in half the time of their own route through Dulles, Panama, and Buenos Aires—were being inspected for compliance with The Dakar Rally's safety and outfitting regulations. He hated flying civilian for that reason, but it wouldn't have done to let Christian see the military C-130 that had delivered his vehicles. That would raise far too many questions.

In the shed they were checking everything from tire size to engine horsepower to making sure that no unsanctioned navigation equipment had been installed. There were a dozen vehicles ahead of them in the long queue and a dozen more waiting to get in. Male drivers were standing near the desks, laughing and joking over past races and hot women, while they awaited their own inspection.

Any of them could be Hathyaron. Hoping to spot someone of Punjabi, Pathan, or Sindhi descent—which constituted seventy-five percent of Pakistan's population—was probably fruitless, but he kept an eye out.

There were a few women competitors in the queue besides Zoe, a very few. A pair were over in motorcycles—tall, powerful-looking women who looked ready to wrestle the heavy machines through two weeks of sand.

A tiny Japanese woman was clambering up into the cab of one of the massive Hino racing trucks along with two barely taller men. The ten-ton trucks took a crew of three: driver, navigator, and engineer. The three of them looked almost comical in the immaculate matching racing suits in front of their gigantic machine. Most folks in the scrutineering shed wore t-shirts and shorts because of the heat.

Then he turned around and nearly rapped noses with a tall flaxen-blonde.

"Hi," she offered in one of those smooth Texas accents that always seemed to add extra syllables to the simplest words. She held out a hand, which he shook while he was busy looking. Tall, with a men's plaid work shirt unbuttoned low enough to allow her breasts to make a fine statement above, with the tails tied off to reveal flat abs and shapely jean-clad hips below. She was a treat all the way from her alligator skin boots to her straw cowboy hat.

"Hi," he managed in his Maine-flat mono-syllabic tone.

"I'm Tammy Hall. And this must be your first Dakar Rally."

Luke nodded and managed to retrieve his hand. He recognized her type. Liked the type; had enjoyed its benefits any number of times. But he could feel the look Zoe was burning into his back.

"Well, if you need any tips, you just feel free to come find me, honey." Then one of the clerks called her name and she moved off with a feline smile (the sort worn by hungry lions) and a toss of her hair that floated half down her back.

"Gonna be an interesting race," he muttered.

"What's that?" Zoe hadn't been glaring at him, instead she'd been cozying up to Christian.

Luke thought about Tammy as he ran his thumb over the license again, so new he imagined that he could feel the heat of the plastic fresh out of the machine. Did the woman actually know she was trying to sell it so hard? He supposed she did, because he knew in retrospect that it had worked on him any number of times. He looked down at Zoe, again speaking intently with Christian and some other guy who stood the way a macho version of Tammy might.

Had Zoe fallen prey to such games? He'd certainly never seen her play them. She teased and flirted, but she never did the flinging-her-body thing. She had to know how cute she was and how easy that would be to do.

When the clerk called for his packet, not sure what else to do, he handed the entire stack over: license, passport, insurance, and whatever other cards SOCOM had determined he'd need to enter.

There must be some way to get back control of the situation, but he didn't see that happening anytime soon. He looked over the barricade at the Citroën. Now they were checking what was stowed in the narrow cargo space behind the driver's and navigator's seats: water, seat belt cutter, thermal survival blankets, flares, a horn, reflective triangle, spare tires, and the like.

For the moment, Luke was merely "support crew." He and Christian's mechanic, the towering, soft-spoken Ahmed, were to drive the support truck. The clerk asked him several questions that he had no idea how to answer, but Christian stepped in and soon they were through the line. He noted that Zoe was asked far less.

Not gender bias. She simply exuded that she belonged. He knew how to do that, but Zoe had unbalanced his world somehow. Being constantly a step behind had to end soon. Zoe'd had her days of fun, but she worked in a coffin and he worked in the real world. Enough already.

They exited the far end of the queue to await the car's clearance. A phalanx of reporters with cameras and microphones were lined up. Behind them, the parking lot was filled with ranks of inspected motorcycles, cars, and racing trucks. All were covered with bright stickers of team and race sponsors. He figured out that these were the ones successfully through scrutineering because large black-and-white racing numbers had been plastered on them. The magnetic decals were on both doors (both sides on the motorcycles), front bumpers, and the rear of every vehicle. It was a far cry from him and a couple buddies running dirt bikes in the Maine woods, or even a SEAL team doing offensive and defensive training in a line of Hummers.

A woman jumped forward and snapped Zoe's picture.

"*The Soldier of Style,*" she gasped excitedly. "You're racing The Dakar?"

Luke was going to shoot himself. This couldn't be happening.

Zoe offered one of those light-up-the-world smiles that she'd used so lethally on Christian.

"I am," she matched the reporter's own breathless speech. Tweety Bird DeMille was back in full force. "I've raced before, of course, but never anything as grand as The Dakar. My good friend Christian Vehrs needed a co-driver on short notice and offered me the slot." She pulled a beaming Christian into the shot. One of these days, after they didn't need him so much, he'd earn himself a bloody stump for the way he wrapped his arm so possessively around Zoe's shoulders and pulled her hard against him. Or maybe Luke wouldn't wait that long. It was one way to get Christian out of the car—make him bleed.

Luke already knew he wasn't the starting co-driver, but now he was completely sidelined, not even in the image. Not that he'd have let himself be photographed. And it wasn't like he cared. Not a chance. Actually, it could be an advantage, now that he thought about it. Lurking in Zoe's shadow might not be such a bad idea. Besides, she threw one easily as large as the far more obvious Tammy Hall without even trying. Letting Zoe *think* she was the one in control wouldn't hurt his ego any. In the meantime, he could get it done.

They all bubbled at each other about the amazing opportunity and the exciting route. The reporter was drawing obvious conclusions that Luke didn't like at all. Zoe wasn't *his.*

He'd never even really cared if he had exclusive use of a woman while it lasted—after his ex-wife it never seemed to matter. Yet he wanted to slowly and painfully snap off each one of Christian's fingers where they'd shifted to around Zoe's waist.

The reporter was worth watching. Hot German with cutely short, mid-blonde hair offset by a dark suntan, blue eyes, and nice curves—not quite the eye-poppers of Tammy Hall's. And not a single distracting thought crossed his mind when he looked at her. Whereas looking at Zoe...

Unable to stand watching Christian try to assert his claim on Zoe, Luke looked around again. Theirs was far from the only interview going on. There were lone reporters like this woman "Liesl Franks—freelance," but most were TV cameraman and interviewer-with-a-mike pairs. Interviews were happening in half a dozen languages: Italian, French, and Spanish were most common. But he again spotted the Japanese team that was being interviewed by a crew with a kanji logo on their camera.

Fifteen or twenty interviews were going on simultaneously and he could see the other drivers eating it up just like Christian.

Behind them, rope lines held back a mass of fans stacked at least five deep down the whole line. Before or after interviews, drivers were going over to the line to sign programs, photos, jackets, even across the top of a woman's breasts with a magic marker—one woman had already collected enough signatures there that she was running out of room for others to sign despite her hefty build.

The major drivers stood out because they had a hired entourage of pretty local girls behind them, most wearing sexy tops and straw cowboy hats. There were more cowboy hats in Argentina than at a Texas rodeo. The girls were handing the drivers eight-by-ten color glossies and signing pens, snapping photos for the fans' cameras, and whatever else it was that sexy entourage girls were paid to do.

It was definitely wild.

There was a flow to it though, that their party was disrupting. More drivers came out of the administrative queue, but Zoe was hanging tough with the Liesl woman, forcing other drivers to move around them. Zoe must be eating up her own hype. Sad.

Three hundred and fifty-four vehicles were entered this year with an average of two drivers. Motorcycles only had one driver, but the massive trucks had driver, navigator, and engineer, so the count averaged out. Double that for two support personnel and another transport for each entry. That meant approximately fourteen hundred individuals and six hundred vehicles were involved in the race, not counting the race officials, media, entourage gals, and other hangers-on.

And Hathyaron the arms dealer was one of them. Somewhere.

Let Christian and Zoe bubble along; he hadn't forgotten their target.

It would help if they knew what he looked like. The Activity hadn't been able to even confirm his nationality.

"He's probably a Legend," Zoe spoke from close by his elbow. "Those are the ones who've done at least ten Dakars. It just seems likely after seeing that garage—it represents someone who has invested a great deal of time and learning to prepare for this. Christian will know all of them. Liesl has also covered the last six Dakars and is writing a book about the Legends."

Relieved and without thinking, he wrapped an arm

around her shoulders and kissed her on top of the head, causing her to make a happy hum. Zoe hadn't lost track of the target for a single second. She hadn't bought into Liesl's hype, Zoe had convinced the reporter to buy into hers. Any of his teammates, even Nikita, he'd have chucked on the shoulder or given them his "well done" nod. So why did he grab and kiss Zoe?

Liesl hadn't gone away—she prepared to snap his picture.

And he prepared to reach out to grab her camera and smash it.

Zoe simply held up a hand to stop her, then shook her head.

"But—" Liesl protested as she lowered her camera.

Luke absolutely didn't want to be noticed. There was enough of that shit going on in the SEAL community and he certainly didn't want anything else to do with it. The number of "Tell All" books was disgusting.

There were also far too many news articles about ST6 operations. Actually, there'd been a spate of articles on missions that he knew for a fact hadn't been run by ST6, but had been very vocally credited to them—probably by those assholes over in Delta Force. Maybe turnabout was fair play. He liked that idea. Not this mission, but after some future one; he'd definitely be dropping Delta's name. For this one, an embedded-civilian style scenario, he wanted to remain as anonymous as possible.

"He doesn't like to have his picture taken," Zoe tried offering.

"But *The Soldier of Style* has two men vying for her attention. The story. *Es ist wunderbar.*" Liesl tried to raise the camera again.

"Please, no," Zoe already had control of the reporter without her even realizing it.

Luke *did* still have his arm around Zoe's shoulders. He gave a small squeeze of thanks and let her go to remove the temptation for the reporter.

"No pictures at all, *ja?*" The reporter asked unhappily.

"*Nein,*" Luke confirmed—finally they'd hit German, which *was* one of his languages. And somehow that was a mistake.

Liesl eyed him speculatively before a slow smile crossed her face. "Does Christian know?"

"Know what?" Luke offered his best scare-the-crap-out-of-recruits look. Somehow she'd figured out that he was military and that belief—no matter how accurate—couldn't be allowed to persist.

Liesl's smile didn't falter for a moment. It worked on his men without fail. What was it with these women that it didn't even leave a graze on them?

"Nope! He hasn't a clue," Zoe offered cheerfully, totally spoiling his play—not that it had worked any better on her. "Another thing we'd like to keep that way."

"*We?*" Liesl's eyes widened for only an instant before that smile returned two-fold. "*The Soldier of Style.* You really *do* serve!" Liesl had a merry laugh. Whereas Zoe's... *Huh!* He hadn't heard her laugh much. Wasn't sure if he ever had.

Luke just hoped the reporter knew how to keep her damned mouth shut. A reporter? Good luck with that.

15

*S*omehow Zoe had survived the two days leading up to The Dakar.

Now she lay face down, alone on her hotel room bed, and didn't know if she could make it to the starting line.

Sitting at home on her social media feed had kept everything at arm's-length. She put on a show and the fans gave her their love. She never held real-life fan events of any sort. Her need to keep the two worlds of her life completely separate in real life and internally was absolute. Now the blurring of those lines was letting the darkness she kept locked in her past slide to the fore at unexpected moments. Fighting to keep that back was even more exhausting than the constant pressure of the pre-race social obligations.

Between Christian's post from Senegal and now Liesl Franks' stories, her life was rapidly spinning out of control. Liesl knew she had a hot story and had worked out a three-way deal that made Zoe's head hurt worse than her early training days as an RPA pilot.

First, Luke would be left in the background as much as

possible—though she'd almost tossed him to the wolves that first day for how he'd been checking out that Texas blonde's cleavage. With him hiding in plain view to search for Hathyaron, it threw herself and Christian together into the foreground. Thankfully Christian was kept distracted by the other Legends, but she had to be constantly at his side to meet and greet.

Not a single one of whom was Pakistani or Afghani this year. There wasn't even a listing of any vehicle from a country between the Arabian Peninsula and Australia except for a lone motorcyclist from India. If she didn't know the nationality of who they were looking for, how was she ever supposed to find them?

Second, there was no exclusivity allowed when giving interviews at The Dakar—publicity was part of the deal. Section 47P of the regulations—the penalties section—stated there was a five hundred euro fine for not stopping in an interview zone. Even worse for being otherwise uncivil—the fine *plus* possible disqualification. Liesl had tacitly understood that she might never be told the real reason the military had inserted a team into the race. Instead, she'd negotiated that she'd have an exclusive on *The Soldier of Style's* inside story.

Anyone else got only the public story: she'd met Legend Christian Vehrs through her fan group and they discovered their mutual love of rally racing. And it stopped there—though most services had blithely ignored that last bit of information. Christian had certainly worked to give them, and himself, the impression they were also a couple.

Liesl got as much of the inside story as *The Soldier of Style* was willing to tell.

The third part of Liesl's deal—that Zoe absolutely hadn't counted on—was that Liesl set out to make her famous. She'd upsold the story to Reuters news service, who had flown in a videographer, and they were both now following her every move. Another thing that thrilled Christian.

Luke occasionally deigned to scoff at her. Or maybe he was trying to make fun of the lunatic situation, but she didn't feel much like laughing. For the most part she hadn't seen him in the last forty-eight hours even though they were sharing a bed.

That definitely wasn't thrilling her so much. The first knock on the door both mornings had been Liesl, even before room service could be begged for coffee. And by the time she'd chased out Liesl, Christian, and whatever other Legends happened to be hanging out in the suite drinking beer or wine (always French) each night, she was too tired to do more than collapse beside Luke.

That was becoming a major problem. At least she'd assumed that was the problem. Yesterday morning Luke had already been gone when she woke up, and she hadn't heard him come in. For a relationship that was only four days old, not seeing him for the entire fourth day wasn't good.

And now she was waking alone again.

It was a bad sign that left her even less interested in getting out of bed. Having had his fun with her, he was done and moving on.

The Dakar Rally was a spectacle and the city of Mar del Plata was doing its damnedest to make it one of grand proportion. The elegant Teatro Auditorium had run highlights of prior Dakar rallies on its large screen— accompanied by lots of teasing of racers with spectacular crashes, flips, rollovers, or simply getting lost. The Casino Central had thrown a massive bash. And the lobby of the side-by-side Hotel NH Gran Hotel and the Hotel NH Gran Provincial had hosted massive parties.

The lobbies had also been thick with hundreds of vendors from Toyo Tires to Oakley sunglasses, each one doing their best to attract the attention of every driver or crew member. It was a good time for hot Argentine women—hired to dazzle the ninety-nine percent of racers with a dick for a brain as they hawked their rep's wares.

The Dakar was far bigger than just the race or even the vendors—it was an excuse for a massive celebration, South American style. Outdoors had included band concerts, dance troupes, and open-air bars along the seawall and the prime beach of the city. Plenty of "good time" girls working those venues.

Had Luke shifted his attention to one of them?

Or that sexy, built blonde?

Or one of the women on motorcycles? He mentioned motorcycles in almost every other sentence. Of course he spoke so little, that still wasn't very often.

Wherever Luke had gone, Zoe sure hadn't seen him in their bed.

Once again she'd been absolutely right about her attractions as a woman. She'd been born for an era of five-seven Tom Cruise and five-four Michael J. Fox as heroes. The problem was she'd grown up into a world built for the likes of six-foot Chris Pine and six-two Ryan Reynolds.

And six-four Luke Altman.

Nobody ever stuck—not that she cared.

Except this time she did, not that it helped her at all. Maybe Luke was off with Liesl? If so, that definitely wasn't part of any deal Zoe had meant to make, even if Liesl was much more his type. A tall, willowy blonde with a nice, if not dramatic, figure. Zoe had seen them side by side enough to know they made a lovely couple, instead of a goofy one that had people tilting their heads strangely when they deigned to notice her beside him.

If it was over, then—

"Still in bed?"

She managed to flop her head the other way on the pillow and open one eye. That, at least, *was* worth the effort. She felt too tired to take advantage of it, but a naked and still-damp-from-the-shower Luke Altman was formidable motivation to change the direction of her thoughts. If she hadn't been worn out, she might have noticed the shower running and taken some hope there. Was it enough to get her moving? Would it matter if she did? He was already gone, wasn't he?

He smiled at her.

So what if he was done with her. Maybe they could have one last tussle between the sheets anyway. She'd certainly never had a lover of Luke's skill before and wouldn't mind a final encore before he completely drifted out of her life.

Maybe it *was* worth waking up today.

If she did, would he—

There was a sharp rap on the door.

"Go away, Liesl. I'm about to be busy." Hopefully.

"Race day. We must now be moving." Christian called through the door.

Crap!

"Yes, Zoe. *Ein sehr* important day." Liesl, too.

Double crap!

Luke shrugged.

Giving in to the evil plan of the twisty, sadistic Fates (*so not my sisters in spirit)*, she clambered out of bed. On her way to the bathroom, she kissed Luke quickly because he was so very pretty standing naked in the middle of their bedroom. She did her best not to groan at what she was losing because even a brief kiss with Luke was a complete toe-curler.

She came away with her t-shirt only a little wet. Her attempts to sleep in one of Luke's hadn't worked. It never stayed on both shoulders, the sleeves reached her elbows, and it fit her like an old lady's house dress practically down to her knees. Real attractive. All it did was remind her of all the reasons Luke shouldn't want her. And since she wasn't getting any sex at the moment, it was a place in her brain she really didn't want to go.

Grabbing the towel out of his hands, she headed for a quick shower. Passing the front door, she popped the handle and called out, "So come in already."

Then she ducked into the bathroom door, leaving a naked Luke on the other side to scramble for cover as Christian and the camera crew walked in.

RATHER THAN STANDING NAKED in a hotel suite, Luke felt as if he was melting beneath the midsummer sun in a full-body fire-resistant Nomex racing suit. For lack of better cover, he reached for a throw pillow from the small couch, but was far too slow to really hide anything. Besides, the pillow he'd grabbed was about the size of a dinner plate.

Zoe certainly generated heat in him.

Curled up in their bed with the covers pulled up to her nose so that she was little more than a floof of blonde hair on a pillow, she was about the cutest damn thing he'd ever seen. In one of her tight t-shirts and very brief panties, she was a total turn-on. He should be pissed about her leaving him standing naked as everyone barged into the room; instead he wanted to laugh aloud at the joke.

She teased everyone a little bit, but he now understood that she'd always particularly targeted him. Standing outside Hathyaron's garage building and forcing him to ask for what he wanted when she damn well knew what he meant. The way they'd raced together. Every time she...

Now that he thought of it, he could see it was a pattern that held right back to the start of the Honduras mission. She had teased Nikita and Drake on that mission...somewhat. But she'd never given him a moment of peace.

He stood there naked in the middle of their hotel room, except for the tiny pillow that didn't hide squat.

Then a mental lightbulb went off, one that froze him in place.

Did she understand how much she liked him?

Did he?

It wasn't just having her in his bed. Since when had he been content to just lie down beside a sleeping woman without waking her to screw her brains out? Never. But he had done just that last night beside Zoe—moving especially carefully so as not to wake her. He'd drifted off happily just listening to her quiet breathing as she snuggled up against him in her sleep. Not that her contact had let him fall asleep very quickly.

It had left him plenty of time to think about her unexpected skills. He particularly appreciated the way her mind worked: seeing a solution and jumping right in with both feet because she knew it was right and to hell with the consequences. Differently built, she'd have made a good SEAL.

"Hi, boss," Nikita and Drake had followed Christian, Liesl, and her cameraman into the room. She smiled when she looked at him, such a rare thing that it momentarily dazzled him. He was impressed they'd made it down here so fast since he'd called them only last night.

"Nice outfit, Mr. Emperor," Drake smirked.

He offered them a nod of greeting. Problem was, his clothes were on the far side of the room and the one pillow wasn't going to get him there across the crowded room.

"Who are you?" Christian stepped up and got in Nikita's and Drake's faces.

Luke used the distraction to ease along the wall to his pack. He rummaged through it and began dressing.

Nikita moved up beside him while Drake was busy not answering Christian. "You treating her well?"

He started to answer, but there was something in her tone that made him finish pulling on his t-shirt to look her in the face. In this moment, she wasn't Nikita Hayward. Instead she was a SEAL so lethal that he'd promoted her to his Number Two on the team.

"Because if you hurt Zoe, I'll goddamn kill you, sir. And yes, it will be *completely* personal." Then she offered one of her most pleasant smiles—one that didn't reach her eyes at all this time—before moving back to her husband's side. She was supremely competent, one of the reasons he'd called for her to come join them. She'd also married a former Night Stalkers crew chief, which meant he was an amazing mechanic—the other reason he'd called the pair.

But dangerous, to *him?* That was new.

Luke finished dressing, including the racing suit and boots —Zoe had ordered them in electric yellow, of course. He rejoined the group but kept his own counsel.

Christian was still ranting (probably didn't like finding Luke naked in Zoe's bedroom either). Luke promised himself to never sleep apart from her for the duration of the mission, just for the Christian Vehrs-irritation aspect of it. He supposed that knowing Luke was here with Zoe and seeing proof were two different things. Or maybe it was that he knew he'd only get to drive Stage One. Perhaps he could feel control slipping out of his fingers. Luke felt empathy for Christian, but it didn't mean he was going like the man anytime soon.

Nikita and Drake were doing a fine job of being SEAL silent.

Liesl smiled like she knew too damn much.

Then Zoe came out of the bathroom.

It was the first time he'd seen her in her racing suit. Because he'd seen her drive, he knew it wasn't just his imagination that made it fit her so well. In her own way, she was as powerful as—

"Nikita!" Zoe screamed, raced across the room, and slammed into the woman's embrace, fitting neatly under Nikita's chin. They held onto each other like long-lost sisters. "Oh. My. Gawd! Luke didn't tell me he'd been able to reach you."

He'd never seen Nikita quite like that. Not even when she'd been falling for Drake had she looked so…soft. There was some bond between the two women that he'd never noticed and, seeing it, didn't understand—but it looked plenty real. It was the way he was learning that Zoe approached everything: with her entire heart.

Nikita understood that. That would explain why she'd become so protective.

And that Zoe was sharing a piece of that with him was a

gift he was only starting to understand.

She shot Luke a grin that held only a little bit of surprise. She'd been calling the shots enough on this mission and he'd felt it was time to call some of his own—he'd started by mobilizing Nikita and Drake to come join them.

Luke opened his mouth to explain, but never had a chance as Zoe turned to Christian and plunged right in.

"Christian!" with that impossible level of excitement of hers. Except it wasn't impossible from Zoe DeMille, merely irresistible. Joy seemed to pour out of her every single moment of every day.

Something else he hadn't had a lot of experience with.

"I know, because of the short notice, that you were having trouble getting another good mechanic. Nikita and Drake aren't racing mechanics, but they're absolutely amazing and can help Ahmed, your lead man, with anything we need."

Luke should have known that Zoe would understand the plan without being told.

For the two days between the scrutineering check-in and the race itself, Zoe and Christian had been off in the social whirl of drivers and race organizers. He'd stuck for a little while, then realized that he was a third wheel in more ways than one.

Sure, once he dragged himself away from the stewardesses, Christian had spent much of the long flight from Africa drilling him and Zoe on how to read the Dakar Road Book. The Road Book was the turn-by-turn guide to the race and the only navigation tool allowed in the car.

"One mistake can send you many kilometers off course before you realize it. You will have no choice except to retrace to your last known good point and try again. All the GPS will do is turn on when you get within several hundred meters of a check-in point to guide you in the last bit of the way. Everywhere else, you are on your own with only the Road Book and a compass."

Christian had truly feared that Luke couldn't navigate well enough, but that was only because he didn't know who he was dealing with. The Road Book was far better information than he usually had while swimming or hiking to a mission target. There were only a hundred symbols in the entire map coding system—most of which were pretty damn obvious. One exclamation point meant caution, two meant danger, three meant "Holy crap! Slow down and be careful."

Much of rally racing was about orienteering and land navigation, bread and butter to a Team 6 SEAL—or someone from Maine. From one peninsula along the Maine coast to the next might be a hundred meters across the water, but it could be a thirty-kilometer drive to get back to where they connected by land. And the logging roads he used to run on his motorcycle weren't exactly signposted.

But he stuck out in this crowd because he didn't have a lot of rally stories to share—as in none. And hanging with Christian, it was expected that he did. The guy was a Dakar Legend after all.

The only attention he was getting was pissing off Zoe. Between the various "cute girl" squads and Tammy Hall's occasional strafing runs, he was getting a lot of the kind of attention he always got and he could see Zoe taking it hard.

So instead, he'd gone on the prowl and stumbled on the Malles Motos class, or MM guys—everyone was ignoring the new "The Original by Motul" label except when the sponsor was around. In French, *Malles Motos* meant "Trunks Motorcycles." These guys raced with no support trucks and teams, no camper vans, not even a mechanic. The MM competitors showed up with a motorcycle, a box of spare parts, and a tent. The race only allowed thirty competitors in the class. The trunk box was the size of a SEAL team field pack and was transported from bivouac to bivouac by a semi-truck along with all of the other MMs' gear.

He sat and talked with them for hours.

They told Luke about single-track conditions, climbing the slip face of dunes, high altitude techniques (there were places in the Andes where they lost twenty percent of their power due to thin air), water holes, *fesh fesh* sand so loose and fine that it could mire a bike wheel-deep without warning. If they fell off their bikes in *fesh fesh*, which was almost a given, it was possible for your bike to disappear from view even though it was only a few feet deep. The dry stuff almost flowed like water.

At first he'd thought they were the misfits of the race, taking on The Dakar with no support and no team. But the more time he spent with them, the more he respected them. There was a purity of adventure with them that seemed to be lacking elsewhere. Just rider, machine, and terrain. It also sounded absolutely brutal, which fit right in with his training and career. In a way, they were the hardcores—the Spec Ops guys of The Dakar.

And at this moment, he'd take a ride with the MMs if it got him out of this hotel room.

Nikita threatening him. Drake probably glad to back her up. Zoe collecting staunch defenders right and left as she was fast becoming world famous. Next thing he knew she'd be dropping out of the military and be gone into whatever the hell her civilian world was. Probably end up with some asshole like Christian Vehrs with his smooth French accent and enough capital to front a Dakar Rally car of his very own.

Nope, Luke wouldn't like that image one bit.

"Can we get a move on?" His growl sliced through all the dynamics ricocheting around the hotel suite.

There was an awkward silence as he killed a half dozen conversations, which was a good trick as there were only about that many people in the room.

"C'mon!" Zoe still had an arm around Nikita's waist. "I'll introduce you to Ahmed. He's Christian's lead mechanic from Senegal and he'll put you to work. Actually, he'll totally flip over you. You look so amazing, Nikita."

Nikita was dressed in her usual civilian—jeans and a black t-shirt. Her brunette hair back in its typical ponytail. She maintained the peak level of fitness that was necessary to be a DEVGRU SEAL. He supposed that she did look amazing.

Marriage also agreed with her. When she'd joined ST6, there'd been a sadness that he figured nothing could ever erase. In fact, he'd assumed that it was a key element of her success because that sadness fed a deep-rooted anger that had seen her through the entire DEVGRU selection process—the first woman to pull that off.

When Drake Roman had showed up and started messing with that sadness and anger, Luke had threatened to kill him if he screwed up one of his best operators.

But he hadn't.

Nikita had become even more driven, more impressive, but the sadness and anger no longer drove her. He blinked as he watched her go out with Zoe and Christian. Nikita of old had worn a force field around her that repulsed all boarders.

Yet she'd greeted Zoe with a welcoming hug in which he could detect no hesitancy.

Was that another of Zoe's gifts? She'd certainly slid past *his* guard.

"You heard about Pakistan?" Drake was the only one who'd hung back when all of the others had left.

"No, what?"

"Hathyaron's compound doesn't exist anymore."

"What do you mean?"

"About twelve hours after you left, it was bombed by a pair of Chengdu F-7s owned by the Pakistan government. Obliterated the place."

Luke shrugged. "Pakistanis have followed us in enough times."

"Word on the ground is that it was a personal favor requested by Hathyaron—made *after* we were there. Also, an airport security team at Bacha Khan in Peshawar broke into a hangar. They found several vehicles, including the truck-trailer that left his compound—tire prints match what you sent in."

"Any other clues on the vehicles?"

"You mean before the Pakistan Special Services Group seized them?"

Luke grunted. The SSG was Pakistan's form of Spec Ops and the guys weren't half bad. If they too were doing personal favors for Hathyaron by erasing evidence, that wasn't good news.

"Yeah. Four vehicle drivers, still in their seats. But nobody's talking…in fact, last I heard they still hadn't found the poor bastard's heads or hands. No way to identify them."

"Erasing his trail," Luke nodded.

"The on-duty air traffic controller—the only one who

might have identified the plane that had been near that hangar—was found at home, in bed. His head was still there, but a machete had chopped him and his wife into six separate pieces. No rape. No robbery."

It made sense. Brutal, but not stupid.

Would Hathyaron's ego still bring him to The Dakar? Yes, it would. It didn't even have to be ego. If there were any last minute dropouts—there weren't—it would have made him too easy to find and he'd know that. Luke thumped a job-well-done fist down on Drake's shoulder.

Drake shifted from reporting sailor to his normal casual himself. "Funny when it happens to you, isn't it?"

"When what happens?"

Drake was generally mild-mannered. He was the easy-going one, always glad to do what he was told—though fully capable of taking the initiative when necessary. A lot of SEALs wanted to lead; Drake just wanted to be on the team and had proved he had the skills to be.

He started to get angry, which Luke knew how to deal with. But before he needed to react, Drake stopped, then shook his head.

"You don't see it?"

"See what?"

"Shit, Altman, you were never stupid."

"Still not."

Drake made a point of looking over at the bed that was still all rumpled. Luke could see the impression of Zoe's head on *his* pillow, hers still exactly as the hotel had plumped it. She'd already been on the edge of his pillow when he finally dragged himself back to the suite last night. And she'd stayed there.

"Shit, Roman. You talking about what's between me and some woman?"

"No, asshole." The heat suddenly flashed back to life, sharply enough to have Luke stepping back in surprise. "I'm talking about what's between you and Zoe DeMille, who happens to be my wife's best friend. A woman who also saved our asses any number of times back when I still flew with the Night Stalkers." Drake had backed him up against a wall without his even noticing. Drake didn't have Luke's broad build and was an inch or so shorter, but that didn't seem to matter.

"I'm not talking about this." Luke went to push Drake aside, but Drake shoved him back against the wall.

"This isn't from chief petty officer to lieutenant commander, Luke. This is me and you. Just like aboard ship in Honduras. What the *hell* are you up to?"

Luke hit Drake with a palm strike against his sternum hard enough to knock him backward. The bed caught the back of his knees and he collapsed onto the mattress.

"I'm not talking about this with you or with anybody."

Drake sat up partway, rubbing his palm against his breastbone. "You goddamn better talk about it with Zoe. I can see it in her, even if you can't. Like you once told me about Nikita, she's dealing with some next-level shit and if you don't respect that, it's going to blow up in your goddamn face." Then he pushed to his feet and strode out the still-open hotel door without looking back.

Luke looked at the mirror. "Has everybody lost their goddamn mind?"

He was almost out the door when he realized that this *was* the first race day. Tonight they'd be sleeping seven hundred kilometers away. He packed his duffle in about thirty seconds.

It took him another ten minutes to locate and pack all of Zoe's stuff.

"Personal, goddamn assistant, my ass."

Hair dryer and brush, makeup, toothbrush, other girl products. From the dresser came underwear, shirts, slacks, and all the rest of it. He found sunglasses, lemon-yellow hair clips, lemon-yellow shoes, and...shit! Too damn many reminders that Zoe was someone he didn't begin to understand.

On his final sweep he found the t-shirt she'd slept in. It was black and worn almost wordless. He twisted it in the light to read: DeMille Dune Buggy and Auto Service.

After what had been done to her there—for he had no doubt about exactly what had gone down—how could she wear that?

It smelled of her. He didn't know what it was, but it was absolutely her. How could something so damn small encompass such a woman? Rumpled together, it barely filled his palm. He rolled it up and tucked it into his own pack.

Luke Altman, personal assistant, hefted his duffle and her suitcase out of the room. For two nights they'd slept here together, just slept. Was it already ending?

The mission would really be kicking into gear now. Was it the relationship-ending signal he was so familiar with?

For the first time ever, he truly hoped not.

Yeah! That and "Don't let the door hit you on the way out" would win him a kewpie doll at the county fair.

Last out the door and all on his own.

16

Z oe'd been sitting beside Christian in the Citroën
for almost an hour. Breakfast of *medialuna* crescent
rolls had been eaten while watching Ahmed lead Nikita and
Drake over the car. She had a thousand things she wanted to
ask Drake, about how a guy's mind worked around women.
She wanted to cry on Nikita's shoulder that it was already
over before it began. And she didn't want to talk to anybody
for fear she couldn't hold it together.

But there hadn't been a chance for any of that before it
was time for them to line up for the start. The motos and
quads had started leaving shortly after sunrise. The cars were
up next and they'd been in line by midmorning.

They sat along the resort waterfront between the two
sprawling, four-story brick buildings of the Hotel NH and
Hotel NH Gran Provincial. Ahead of them lay the boardwalk
and the sea, behind them stood dozens of ten-story
apartment and office buildings like a forest wall. She'd had no
opportunity to explore, or even stop long enough to breathe
the air.

The Dakar was "the event" and touching "the natives" just didn't happen. Were her vlogs—video logs—and feeds like that? Zoe DeMille is the event. Don't associate with the fans directly. Keep everything remote, then it will never affect you? What an utterly depressing thought, she really had to cut that out.

One by one, vehicles rolled up onto the podium at the Stage One start. It had a big ramp up, a car-long flat spot over a story in the air, then a slope down the other side. A great arch spanned over the top to support a massive big-screen projection television.

On the screen were close-ups of what was happening on the podium. It let the passive crowd assembled along the waterfront see and hear everything.

Each racer drove up onto the flat and parked. Motorcyclists dismounted, drivers climbed out of their cars, trucks pulled up beside the ramp and their drivers clambered up to the flat spot. While cameras zoomed in, the emcee announced their names and vital racing stats. The crowd, which numbered in the thousands, cheered and applauded just as strongly for the latest car as they had for the first motorcycle hours earlier. The drivers waved to the fans, blew kisses, and shot a thumb's up before getting back in their vehicles.

Once they were helmeted and ready, the timekeeper stepped forward and counted down the seconds to their official start window. At the crucial moment—*Three fingers... Two...One!*—the engine roared to life and they rolled down the front ramp and onto the seaside plaza. A sharp left around the front of the hotel, then out the other side onto Maritime Boulevard to head north. Every two minutes, another team started the race.

The real race wouldn't start until they had wound through the city and reached the end of the roads. There was a fifty kilometer "Road Section" along normal roads where speed limits and other rules of the road had to be maintained. Road Sections weren't race timed, though there was a precise time limit to complete them—no stopping for burgers along the way—and arriving early incurred the same time penalties as arriving late. Road Sections were about exactness of navigation, not speed.

"Selective Sections" were almost entirely about speed. That was where every second counted as the racers left roads and headed off into the wild on beaches, tracks, dunes, or wilderness as the Road Book commanded.

The emcee announced the next driver's name. Even if he hadn't been parked directly in front of them for the last hour, she'd have known all his vital stats. She recited them along with the announcer: Sergey Kanski, Poland, five Dakar starts, three finishes (best two years earlier in twenty-third place), driving for Toyota (one of the biggest teams). His co-driver…

Zoe had memorized every single thing Christian had told her about every single driver. (For example, Sergey was very good to his wife—both the one in Warsaw and the one where he trained half the year in Morocco.) She'd chatted up each driver she came in contact with. Not one had mentioned anything about Pakistan. Nor had one been kind enough to offer a simple, "Hello, I am the Taliban arms dealer you are hunting for. Please may I give you the names and addresses of my Al-Qaeda contacts as well so that you can target them with missiles from your stealth RPA."

Each hour of this mission was more exhausting than the one before. Each night she'd been tortured by the idea that she'd read something wrong. The beautiful service garage at

Hathyaron's compound. The poster of the Dakar Rally in the place of honor on the wall. They *had* to lead here...didn't they?

She didn't dare admit her fears to Luke. What would he think of her for having led him here, especially if here was nowhere near his target? He'd think that she had seduced him because she wanted to race. Not because she...

Because she...

Her brain felt as if it was stuttering.

She hadn't seduced Luke. *No, you just stripped naked in front of him on a deserted tropical beach in the middle of an impromptu car race.*

If her four-point harness didn't have her so effectively pinned to the Citroën's passenger seat, she'd be pounding her head on the dashboard. Except that wouldn't really count as she was wearing her helmet.

Kanski got his start signal and rolled off the podium. In moments he was gone down the street—probably well cheered on by both his wives.

They started the introduction for Christian up on the big screen.

"Finally reaching Legend status, Christian Vehrs is starting his tenth Dakar," the emcee shouted out to the crowd who broke into a big round of cheers.

"Christian?" He wasn't moving forward. He'd started the Citroën's engine, but he didn't drive up on the podium.

"Watch this, my darling Zoe. You will see what makes a great driver of The Dakar."

Her own face flashed up on the screen. "His navigator, Zoe DeMille, *The Soldier of Style*, is starting her very first Dakar. We must wonder what is going on there."

The crowd roared its approval of the question though

they were craning their necks searching for her in the shadows behind the podium. More than a few lemon-yellow flags were waved over people's heads. Would her commanders think she'd done this because Christian was her lover? A foreign national of uncertain allegiances? Or for her own self-aggrandizement? The numbers on her social media connections had jumped twenty-four percent in the last three days and the race hadn't even begun yet.

Still Christian waited.

"And now…" The timer stepped forward and flashed out ten seconds.

There were penalties for late starts. Christian must know that.

At five seconds, Christian punched in the clutch and shifted into first gear.

"Christian. What are you doing?"

At two seconds, the emcee and the timekeeper both backed up to the very edge of the podium. They'd been warned that something was going to happen. Christian popped the clutch and gunned the Citroën.

Like the good Dakar Rally car that it was, it didn't jolt forward, it leapt.

In just the few dozen meters from their hold position to the ramp's base, it was moving fast and clean.

Christian hit the rear ramp of the podium. The sudden angle slammed her into her seat and elicited a deep grunt from Christian. By the top of the ramp they had enough speed to jump completely over the flat section of the podium, arcing through the air, then slamming down onto the forward exit ramp.

The crowd went wild—the roar so loud that it was a palpable wave.

And Christian screamed!

The end of the front exit ramp dumped them onto twenty meters of paved plaza. A path had been cleared to the north. If they missed turning onto that route, they'd plunge across the plaza, through the packed-solid beach crowd, and then into the sea.

Christian was still screaming in agony, both hands clamped on the wheel.

But he wasn't turning. She had no doubt that his back hurt so much that he couldn't think or react, because his scream still pierced her ears despite her helmet.

Zoe reached out her left hand, managed to grab one of the spokes of the steering wheel and yanked it as hard as she could. It forced Christian to let go and she made another half turn, aiming them down the route.

"Brake! Christian! The brake!"

When he didn't react, she remember the tall handbrake and slapped it back. The hydraulic cylinders slammed the rear brake pads full on. Because they were in still in first gear and the clutch was still in, the engine stalled hard and slammed her sharply against the harness. Her breasts might be small, but they were going to really hurt as soon as the adrenaline let go.

Too bad. She'd been looking forward to Luke fondling her breasts. Or would have been if they were still... Not anymore.

Stopped in the middle of the plaza, she couldn't seem to let go of the wheel.

Christian was grunting. Hurting so bad that every time he even raised his hands to take the wheel, she saw him flinch at the pull on his lower back.

Luke and a pair of medics sprinted up to them at the same time.

They extracted Christian and got him on a backboard.

Somewhere in the background she could hear the emcee talking about Christian's accident last year. A glance showed that some technician was astute enough to have a clip of the disaster on hand and the spectacular end-over-end crash splashed across the big screen above the starting podium. The crowd groaned in sympathy.

"You've got to move this car," a race official was right in her face. "You're blocking the starting lane."

"Drive, Zoe. Drive!" Christian called out as they rolled his stretcher toward the waiting ambulance.

Luke looked at her from outside the car, across the empty driver's seat. She hadn't even released her seatbelt and she still clutched the steering wheel in some haze of desperation that this wasn't happening. Luke didn't climb in through the open driver's door that his hands rested on.

"Move your ass over, DeMille. You're a better driver than I am." Then he slammed the door and was racing around the car to the passenger side as he pulled on his own helmet.

"Get this car out of here. Now!" The official shouted.

"We're both on his team, both entered and licensed. Can we legally take over?"

"Honey, thirty meters from the Stage One podium? It's all yours, just go!"

She threw off her four-point harness and crawled over the console between the seats, then pretzeled herself around until she was in the driver's seat.

Luke slid into the passenger seat almost as fast as she was out of it. "Damn but that's a cute ass you've got there, DeMille."

"Shut up!" If he was done with her, she sure didn't need to be hearing that kind of crap. But if he *wasn't* done with her —he had been naked in their hotel room just an hour ago— which must mean something. Too bad she didn't have time to think about what.

But *cute?* She was so goddamn sick of being *cute* she could spit kittens—which would be even cuter!

Rather than making herself more crazy—if that was possible—she moved the seat all the way forward, snapped on her harness, and started the engine. She was careful not to look at Luke—she didn't want him to see how much she was smiling.

"THE TURNS, Luke! The turns. I only memorized the first six."

Luke was still trying to get his harness clipped. It was set so small, he could barely get his hands around to the adjustment straps. "Follow the previous guy."

"Hello, two minutes, now more like three ahead of us. Got nobody to follow."

He glanced down at the Road Book, then up at the trip odometer. "Sweep left in seventy meters. Then you have a straight run of three hundred meters."

"Great, Luke. At eighty kph, that's my next eight seconds." Her first turn slammed him painfully into the passenger door.

"I didn't learn Stage One—Christian was supposed to do all of it."

"Well, he didn't!"

"Left then a tight right." He risked releasing one hand

from his safety harness to advance the Road Book readout. A glance out the windshield showed a line of policemen directing traffic. "Zoe!"

"What?"

"Take a goddamn breath, then follow the line of policemen. In the city, they'll be our best signposts." He finally got the harness set properly, the seat moved back enough that his knees weren't in his chest, and began calling the turns *before* she reached them.

"His scream, Luke. I've never heard anything like it," her breathing was still far closer to hyperventilation than normal.

"Yeah, I could hear it over the crowd. It happens."

"Not to me. Okay, Mr. Super Soldier? I work in a very quiet world. Radio calls from command and helicopters. I listen to ground teams only occasionally. So, I'm not used to people screaming in agony right next to me."

"Zoe…" He knew what to do with a soldier in the field. Dose him down and patch him up until the medic showed up or you needed a body bag. That took care of the injured.

But how long since he'd dealt with someone who hadn't already lived through that harsh dose of a mission turned ugly? Years. What did he do with a woman racing along a city street and beginning to freak?

"Whatever made me think I could do this?"

"You can outdrive a Team 6 SEAL—and trust me, we get serious driver's training. And based on Christian's curses as we raced along the Senegalese beach, I'm guessing you could outdrive him as well."

"I know how to drive, Luke," her voice climbed higher and tighter rather than easing. "That's not the damned issue."

She slammed through the next five turns as he called

them out—barely in time. The next one he called too early and she almost blew into an alley through a sidewalk crowd. They should have driven together over some terrain. Their timing was off.

He had studied the Road Book until he could read the directions without hesitation, but she'd been the one to ride with Christian, to practice with him. There was no synchronicity in what they were doing. And when they got away from the city center and the traffic police, he hadn't called out a red light and she'd almost raced into crossing traffic—leaving black rubber on the pavement that they could ill afford to lose. Christian had said they'd go through several sets of tires over the two-week race and the number of spares were limited by the rules.

The time he'd spent with the Malles Motos guys had taught him how to ride the course if he was alone on a motorcycle. It hadn't taught him anything about how to help another driver.

They both needed to breathe.

He slowly got a handle on the call timing. Then he started feeding her information on speed limits, traffic, and other obstacles. Once they had that down, he checked their overall timing on the route—surprisingly, they were right in the slot. Night Stalkers missions, both drop-off and extraction, were planned to plus or minus thirty seconds. So that part of the challenge was nothing new to either of them. Another bonus.

"You feeling any better?" he asked on a long straightaway that carried them out through Mar del Plata's suburbs that looked no different from any Mexican town he'd ever been through. One story buildings, mostly white with brightly colored doors and the occasional man-tall graffiti littered the roadside. No hovels of the desperately poor, at least not along this route. Just typical—

"Go to hell, Altman." Zoe didn't even glance in his direction. Her hands were clenched so tightly about the wheel, he didn't know how she could steer.

"Sure, if that's what you want, DeMille." He tried to make it funny, but she didn't seem to take it that way. The guys on his team would have at least given him a pity chuckle. Not Zoe.

Fifteen minutes away from the podium, another seventy to the start of the Selective Section.

"You really *are* an asshole." She didn't make it sound like a joke this time.

He considered lashing out at her, pointing out that she was really a bitch when she was driving, no matter how cute her ass was. It sounded funny in his head that way, but he didn't think it would play well.

"So, what's the damned problem, sailor?"

"I'm a soldier, not a sailor. An Army aviator. Okay? That's all I know. For three days I've swallowed Christian's shit and been the chirpy little Girl Friday and 'Oh, isn't he so sweet to let me drive with him?' until I'm ready to gag on it. I've spent hour upon hour at his parties getting my breasts stared at and my butt patted. And—"

"You've *what?*" Imagining someone touching Zoe without permission was—

"Give me a break, Altman. What hole do you live in that you don't know that's how women get treated. Don't believe me? Ask Nikita."

Luke tried to imagine someone doing that to Nikita, a Team 6 SEAL, and not winding up bloody and mangled.

"*And* I still don't know anything!" Zoe hunched over the

steering wheel as if it had just been stabbed into her chest. "Is Hathyaron even here? That's the worst of it, Luke, I don't know. I've totally screwed up. All I want to do is crawl back into my coffin, do my job, and never come back out."

ZOE COULD FEEL the hot tears running down her cheeks and soaking into the helmet padding to either side of her face.

And that wasn't even the worst of it.

Move your cute ass!

And that's how Luke saw her as well. He was already done with her and still calling her cute. She'd show him goddamn cute! When they hit the Selective Section, she'd pound the car to pieces until he was screaming just like Christian.

She'd never heard a sound like that in her life. Except inside her own head as her virginity, as her girlhood, as her unforgivable innocence was ripped away in a single instant of never-ending torture. And not just once. Repeatedly over years. At first she'd avoided her father's garage for all the good it did her. Toward the end, she'd sought it out just to prove—

"Zoe. Zoe! *DeMille!*"

"*What?*" She shouted back at him.

"*Stop!*"

Her eyes focused and she was almost the one to scream. Slamming hard on the brakes, the Citroën squealed all four tires. When they stopped, the nose of the car rested only a breath from slamming into the undercarriage of a parked truck. It would have shredded their car if she'd hit it.

"Are you okay?"

"Do I *seem* like I'm okay?" Her heart was pounding so hard she couldn't breathe.

"Uh, no."

Zoe hung her head between her arms.

"Want me to drive?"

No. She wanted him to go to hell along with all the other memories. If he was now in her past, fine let him. She was *so* done with it.

Luke gave her silence. He didn't push. He didn't insist. And at the moment, silence was a true gift.

"Where's my next turn?" It practically tore her throat apart to grind out the question.

"Eighty meters back."

She nodded, but couldn't raise her head yet. Breathe. Just breathe. That's how she got through these moments when they slammed her unexpectedly. An RPA was far more forgiving though. If she flew in the wrong direction for three seconds, no one knew or cared. She cracked open the small triangular window at the leading edge of the window—the only part of the car's glass that opened—to get even a little more air and stared at the parked delivery truck. Its driver came around the far side and startled in surprise when he found a Dakar WRC car blocking his door.

"Zoe DeMille?" It wasn't Luke, but the truck driver. Then he rushed to her window holding out his clipboard and a pen. "Please sign this for me. Oh, lovely style, senorita. I will cherish it forever." He continued on in racing Spanish.

She managed to ask his name, then reached a hand out through the small opening to write his name and sign it with a flourish that she'd stupidly practiced for hours, right down to the heart-shaped o in Zoe. She wasn't even going to think about how sad her life was.

A glance at Luke. Still doing his SEAL waiting thing. She was really going to miss him.

Shifting into reverse, she rolled backward until Luke indicated the turn she'd missed. In her rearview mirror she could see the next driver: Pierre Manot, Switzerland, three Dakars, just celebrated his fifth anniversary of marriage to his high school sweetheart, driving for…

She took the turn. Except for turns and warnings, Luke didn't say a word for the next forty kilometers. For forty kilometers she slowly pulled back her dignity piece by piece. No one had ever seen her have an episode that bad. No one. And now he'd seen two of them.

"Who is she?" The first non-racing words between them in half an hour.

"Who is who?"

"The woman you're with." Though why she decided she needed to torture herself with that, she didn't know.

LUKE THOUGHT ABOUT that as he called the next several turns.

Rally racing used to mean getting away with whatever you could in between checkpoints. The checkpoints were never known, so you had to simply make sure that you matched the ideal course timing as closely as possible. And if that meant going double the speed limit to catch back up to the plan after a delay, that's what you did.

Now, with the GPS tracking their every move, speeding was prohibited and it all came down to precision—thankfully something Zoe specialized in. Her flying, her driving, her brain were incredibly precise. Even her *The Soldier of Style*

persona—which he'd initially assessed as flighty and inane—
he now understood was meticulously planned and
maintained. Though he'd still tag it as inane. The only time
he'd seen her let go was in his arms.

Who was the woman he was with?

He stole a moment to look over at her, but couldn't think
of how to describe her. Words weren't exactly his best play, he
was far better at doing and showing. However, taking her out
into the low bushes they were presently driving past outside
of town wasn't really an option. The scattered one- and two-
story homes were no longer crowded wall against wall.
Patches of green stood between the house of tan stone
or brick.

What was she asking? Was she asking for help in
understanding herself? How was he supposed to—

"Fine. Never mind," her growl was worthy of a ticked-off
Rear Admiral.

He concentrated on the Road Book for a moment as they
were turned south with five extra turns that the course
designers must have put in just to be irritating.

"She's..." How was he supposed to describe Zoe?
"Surprisingly sexy and—"

"I take it back, I don't want to know." Zoe picked up
three more seconds on their laggard time by slaloming neatly
around an overloaded bus before an oncoming hay truck
threatened their existence.

Starting with sexy probably hadn't been the best choice.

"She makes me laugh."

"Hard to picture you laughing," Zoe's tone was still
acerbic. Okay, maybe he didn't, but she made him feel as if
he wanted to. He hadn't had a whole lot of laughter in his
life. A mom who bugged out when he was two. A drunken

father, with a lobsterman's powerful fists, who thought that beating on his son would help mold his character. They'd both been black-and-blue the day he left for the Navy.

What had he just been thinking about her moments before? Oh, right. "The way she thinks is stunning. And I'd say that your assessment about Hathyaron being at The Dakar is plenty sharp enough to continue the mission. Even before Drake heard—"

"The way she *thinks?* You've got some strange criteria, Altman."

He wasn't quite sure why Zoe kept talking about herself in the third person, but maybe after whatever that episode had been, it was more comfortable for her.

Perhaps she was asking him to help her define who she was.

That happened all the time during the sixteen months of SEAL selection and training. That was how he'd figured out who he was. That level of endurance couldn't be done without coming to terms with who you were. Was this Zoe's "Hell Week"? Maybe it was. Seven days ago, he'd been standing in Hathyaron's compound in the middle of winter in Pakistan. Now it was the morning of the seventh day—midsummer in South America.

"She's someone who does her best to make others *not* notice her," Tweety Bird DeMille all dressed in yellow was a highly engineered distraction from the real Zoe DeMille, who he was only starting to understand. "And utterly fails because of who she really is." Nikita, he knew, was notoriously hard to impress, yet Zoe certainly had.

"Great," Zoe's tone could dry out burnt toast. "When do I get to meet this perfect bitch?"

"Got a mirror handy?"

Zoe was passing a line of cars and almost clipped the nose of the last one when she jerked back into the lane—not quite squealing the tires.

"Wait." She set herself solidly in the lane. They were now on a nominally two-lane paved road—paved as in the potholes had sharply defined edges where the pavement had cracked off and broken.

Luke held on, but she managed to veer around a particularly deep hole at the last second.

"Who are you talking about?" He could practically hear her teeth grinding.

"What do you mean?" The road was getting rougher, jouncing them harder with each passing mile. He guessed they were reaching the end of the city…and the roads.

"Who are you *sleeping* with, Luke?"

"*You.* Or hadn't you noticed?" Again she made him want to laugh. She had the strangest sense of humor and it just tickled him.

"Not so much these last few days. Who were you with?"

"The Malles Motos."

"The Motorcycle's Trunks? Is that a strip club?"

This time the laugh actually came out before he could stop it.

"In a way. They've certainly stripped away all their support."

"Everything just hanging out there," Zoe's tone still had an odd bitterness he couldn't pin down.

"Yep. Those guys—"

"Guys?"

"—are very attractive."

"Guys?" Did she think he was being like sexually

attracted to guys? No, she was just teasing him again. He wanted to hoot aloud, but decided to play it up instead.

"Awesome dudes. They're running bare bones."

"You mean bare-assed, don't you?"

"Ouch! That'd be an uncomfortable way to run the Dakar."

The GPS flashed on, indicating they were within three kilometers of the timing zone at the end of the Road Section. The arrow indicated that it was well off to their right. He scrolled the Road Book and saw that there was a deceptive turn farther ahead that would send them that way. An earlier turn would probably get them lost deep in some farmer's field. Tricky bastards. They were still on course no matter what the GPS said.

He fooled with the trip computer for a moment, double-checking their odometer reading against their scheduled arrival time. They should hit the check-in station to the minute. A hard jounce rocked the car. If the potholes got much deeper, they'd need alpinist's climbing gear to get out of the next one.

"What are you talking about, Luke?"

"I'm talking about the Malles Motos. Supposed to call it The Original by Motul."

"The French engine oil provider?"

"Yeah. Those guys run with no support except for a small trunk of parts. Do their own service, their own camping, their own route planning, and they ride without a support team. Really impressive." He called out the final turn and he could see the white tents of the check-in point not far ahead.

"That's where you've been these last two nights is hanging out with motorcycle racers?"

"Sure. What did you think I was doing?"

"Being off with someone like one of those Argentine dancers or Liesl or the blonde with the major front-end armature or something?"

"Couldn't get to Liesl even if I wanted to, not with the way she's bolted to your side. Besides, do are you crazy enough to think I'd be with anyone else when I've got you?"

"Apparently, yes, I'm that crazy."

Zoe rolled up to the time check-in and pulled the time card out of the special dash holder that Christian had tucked it in.

Had she thought that he'd lost interest in her? Was that why she'd almost crashed them early in the course? Not overwhelmed by the driving, but by their...relationship?

He'd admit they'd left fling somewhere back on the road and he hadn't even noticed. Since Marva had cheated on him and blown up their marriage, he'd only ever had flings. A few of those had lasted as long as month or two, but weren't involved enough to call them anything more.

For fuck's sake, how had he ended up in a *relationship* after seven days?

Luke decided that it was a good thing he wasn't the one driving.

$\mathcal{Z}$oe waited through the five-minute hold at the timing station. All she knew about the next stage from the Road Book was that there was no mention of dunes. In fact, most of today's Selective Section was technically on roads because the course markers didn't have the dashed line of off-road. But neither was their route going to be even marginally paved. It was technically marked "track," which probably meant just as little as it sounded.

Luke was still with her? What did that mean? (*Means you're still together, you goofball.*)

Actually, it didn't. But if he thought so, maybe they still were.

And if they were, the things he'd said about who he was with…were about her?

He liked the way she *thought?*

The way she made him laugh (even if she'd only ever heard it as a smile)? Except he actually had laughed at her just a moment ago. *At* her, not *with* her, but maybe it was a start.

And…sexy? That was the first thing he'd said—as if such a delusion was possible.

With a roar, Kanski's Toyota leapt out of the holding station beside her.

She checked over the car. She left the tire pressure set to high. On dunes she'd deflate the tires for better traction, but "track" probably meant dirt roads. She dialed the shock absorbers to a stronger response—there'd be no way to dodge the potholes on a track as it was probably more pothole than road. Fuel status was still good—they had to be able to go the entire route on a single tank—no en route refueling allowed. She changed the engine setting from "1," which meant no turbo and very fuel conservative, used for road driving, to the max responsiveness of "4"—all out power. Oil temperature and pressure were—

Their timer handed them a new time card. She double-checked that it was their car number and it was stamped with the next minute before tucking it carefully in the dash holder —losing a timecard incurred a major penalty.

At thirty seconds, she shoved in the clutch and shifted into first gear.

At fifteen, she slid her little side window closed but no longer felt stifled for air. No longer felt the choking oppression of all her doubts. They were still there, but their chokehold had eased from imminent death to mild strangulation. No prob! She was used to that.

The timekeeper started the ten-second countdown.

"Luke?"

"Yeah?"

Five seconds.

She didn't know what she wanted to say, but once the racing started, there wouldn't be a chance for stray thoughts.

Four.

"This woman you're with?" Unbelievably herself.

Three.

"Uh-huh."

Two.

"Um… Please don't give up on her too quickly."

One.

"If you say so." Zoe swore that she could hear the laugh in his voice and that encouraged her more than anything.

She punched the gas and popped out the clutch. The Citroën roared to life. Five hundred horsepower launched them from zero to a hundred kph in less than two seconds. First, second, third, fourth—a four-wheel drift through the first corner—and she launched down the track.

What she could have done at Huckfest with a car like this almost hurt her heart. Well, she'd had enough of that.

Luke wanted her.

That was the present and she'd be damned if the past was going to come between them again. It was so hard for her to trust, but if she wasn't going to trust a Team 6 SEAL lieutenant commander, she'd better get her head fixed.

Third gear, second through a tight corner that Luke had warned her about. Out of the turn: third, fourth, fifth…then the world opened up in front of them.

Zoe hadn't been ready for it.

At Huckfest there was a starting dune. Jumpers started from its wide flat top to take advantage of the sharp downslope to build speed. Opposite, there was a high dune to climb, then a single jump over the backside. A momentary sensation of flying, with a view over successive dunes and the Pacific Ocean, then the hard slam like one burst of a sexual release as you came back to earth.

On the race from Dakar, Senegal, to Saint-Louis, they'd been entirely on the beach. The Atlantic had rarely been more than a few car lengths away and their highest altitude might have been the moment she'd made that jump to pass Luke and Christian.

Here, the track led to the Argentine oceanside south of Mar del Plata. It was a strip of dirt atop a cliff. To her right was arid brush—far denser than Senegal's, though that wasn't saying much. To her left was a five-story cliff down to the Atlantic. Senegal was in her past, all the way there across the ocean. She'd do her best to leave her doubts over there.

And if she didn't pay attention, she might well end up there—as a floating wreck.

The track wove back and forth atop the cliff, sometimes mere feet from the drop-off to the beach. Each hummock that she jumped had to include a dose of faith that while she was in the air, the road and cliff wouldn't veer out from under her.

"Two exclamations in half a klick," Luke called out.

Fourth, third, second. She slowed perhaps more than she needed to, but she didn't have a feel for how cautious the course designers were. Three exclamations might be all the way to first gear.

Two exclamations was the sharp turn she'd feared, but it wasn't that sharp.

Zoe accelerated as she swept through the corner—

Then slammed on the brakes and the car jerked to a halt and died as she'd forgotten to drive in the clutch.

She looked out her side window at the face of a boulder larger than the delivery truck she'd almost hit earlier. Its rough face was so close that she could make out individual grains in the massive chunk of sandstone. In the sudden silence, a seagull began laughing off her feathered ass at them.

"Okay, now we know what a two is," Luke said calmly.

"Yeah," Zoe swallowed against a dry throat. She pulled back on the tall handbrake that stuck up from the middle of the console—the size of a baseball bat, there was no way to miss grabbing it in an emergency. She hit the Engine Start button on her steering wheel while holding the brake.

Giving it gas, she released the brake and was once more racing up the track, but no faster than her heart, which was still trying to throttle her. Ten minutes into her first Selective Section and she'd almost knocked them out of the race. What else was she going to run into over the next fourteen days that would try to kill her?

Other than a Pakistani arms dealer?

LUKE HUNG ON. The car danced and jerked like a living thing.

Its massive suspension smoothed out all except the very worst of the road's surface, but Zoe's control was shaking them hard.

She changed gears every few seconds: sometimes more frequently, but rarely longer. He now understood the characteristic sound of the videos he'd watched of previous Dakars.

Roar, roar, roar, ROAR! with the increasing pitch of increasing gears. *Bwaa, bwaa, bwaa* of downshifts. Then roaring up again.

She downshifted into turns and accelerated hard on the

straightaways, even when they were only a hundred meters long.

Each tiny change of the steering wheel twisted the highly reactive car. Cleaner landings off jumps, smoother slides around dirt corners, counter-steering against acceleration torque—Zoe's hands were in constant motion.

It was a challenge to watch the Road Book and not her.

He remembered that he'd once thought of her as blurred because of the way energy seemed to constantly vibrate off her. Here, in Christian's world rally car, she finally made sense. No Tweety Bird energy spent to distract or tease. Zoe was one hundred percent about milking the most out of the car over specific terrain.

She displayed a fearlessness. She took blind corners on faith. No exclamation marks warning of danger? She accelerated into corners—sliding through them in dramatic four-wheel drifts. Blind jump in the middle of a straightaway —she might slow for the angle of the jump, but not because she couldn't see what lay on the other side.

Then they descended a narrow notch through the cliff and down to the beach.

That was where Zoe shone. Fourth, fifth, sixth gear— wide open at over two hundred kph, a hundred and twenty miles per hour, she flew along. If there was one thing she understood, it was sand.

He didn't recognize what was happening at first. The motorcycles had all started before the cars and were long gone. Their single tracks had been obliterated by the thirty cars ahead of them, leaving their own sliding twin tracks.

But the air, which had been so clear, began misting up. The midday sun blurred by dust, then by sand thrown in the air. Sand thrown by what?

By...

Zoe was overtaking Kanski. A seasoned Dakar Rally driver, who had left the timing area two minutes ahead of them, and she was overtaking him. There wasn't a chance that their car was more capable than Kanski's, which meant that it was Zoe's driving.

As she came even with Kanski and began the battle to pass, Luke could feel his body heating up again.

The memory of just the two of them racing along the Senegalese beach. Of the way she'd felt as he took her against the side of the Renault. The second time she'd been true to her word, giving herself to him as much in joy as the first time had been in fear. She'd bared more than just her body—he'd never felt so connected to a woman than right after she'd first beat on him and then, when all was done, wept on him.

She hadn't done either one again, but it had given him insight into the woman. That there was a woman in there, not just a body for him to enjoy. Had he always been that shallow? Women were for... But Zoe wasn't like that. It wasn't like she had some pre-ordained purpose. She hurt and ached and felt joy and had a dark past that she confronted with towering strength. Were all woman like that? More complex than he'd ever bothered to think about?

Maybe he could ask Nikita.

He checked the odometer again, glanced at the Road Book, then began to smile.

"Zoe," he called to her over their helmet intercom.

"Uh-huh," she tried again to get by Kanski, but he wasn't having any of it on the narrow beach. It was high tide, and there just wasn't that much room to play with between the cliff face and waves.

"Really put the pressure on him. Distract him until he's only paying attention to you."

"Why?" But she was already accelerating hard on his passenger side.

"But don't try to actually pass him."

"Say *what?*"

Kanski came up close to the cliff edge to block her and she slid down toward the waves.

"In about six more seconds, there's a right turn that will take us back up the cliff. Distract him so much that he misses the turn."

In answer, Zoe dropped down a gear and thumped on the gas. A rooster tail of sand shot out the back of the Citroën as she weaved side to side behind Kanski like a maniac, mere inches off his bumper. In the lower gear, there was no doubt that Kanski would hear the Citroën engine's roar like the wrath of the gods on his tail.

He could feel Kanski and his co-driver glancing at each other and thinking, *No way!* Or perhaps, *What the hell?*

Three.

Two.

Zoe had gotten so close to the water that she had two wheels in the backwash of the waves and Kanski was right down there with her, to block. The Citroën's windshield was blasted nearly blind with sand and water despite the wipers being on high.

But Luke sat on the dry side of the car and kept watching ahead for the turn.

There.

"Now! Hard right!"

Zoe sliced from left to right, so close to Kanski's bumper

she could have flattened a taco between them. She shot blind across the beach on his word.

Then the wiper managed to clear the windshield and she corrected a few degrees as she punched for more power.

Luke glanced back.

Kanski was in an arcing four-wheel slide as he tried to recover.

"Too little, too late, dude," Luke called out with a whoop.

They sliced into the narrow cleft in the cliffs three car-lengths ahead of Kanski.

"And that's how we do it in Maine!" Luke shouted rearward before he faced forward and scrolled the Road Book for the next set of instructions.

"Ma-ine?" Zoe managed on a bounce as they jumped clear of the arroyo and landed once more on a clifftop track.

"Ay-uh," Luke confirmed happily.

"*Too little, too late, dude* is what they say in Maine?"

"Sure…" Except it wasn't.

"It sounds like you're from *Bill and Ted's Excellent Adventure.*"

"What's wrong with that? I like that movie."

Zoe actually spared him a glance during her latest drifting turn.

"What?"

"I'm just trying not to admit that I like it to. Most people think it makes me weird."

"Idiots. It *was…*"

And they both shouted, "Excellent!" together which left them both laughing.

"Well, I'm not going to start calling you dude. You're a girl-type person."

"So, what *are* you going to call me?"

They passed a lone tree. Luke twisted around and began counting seconds. Kanski was five or six seconds back now. *Most* excellent.

"A lovely, smart, sexy woman who drives like a god and enjoys goofy movies? Damn, I don't know, Zoe. Dudette doesn't seem to cover it."

"That's goddess to you. I drive like a god*dess!*"

The track slashed down toward a stream a dozen meters across. There was nothing to indicate how deep it might be.

Zoe drove through it at speed, blasting water aside, and actually shifted up another gear as she climbed out the far side.

Goddess Zoe? She wasn't going to get any argument from him.

"*E*ight hundred and twenty-three kilometers," Luke announced as they rolled into the bivouac.

And Zoe could feel every single one of them tramping through her body like a centipede army bent on her destruction. Only a hundred and fifty klicks had been on a Selective Section, because Stage One was the easy one—six hundred something had been timing challenges on roads. *This* was the easy one? Someone shoot her now, please.

She and Luke hadn't talked much through the rest of the drive beyond what was needed for the racing itself. But it wasn't an uncomfortable silence, she hoped. They'd simply focused on the task at hand like the good soldiers they were.

On a couple of the longer straightaways, they talked over the import of Drake's news about what had happened in Pakistan. While it was chilling, it didn't shed any more light on what was happening at The Dakar. That conclusion had also cast its own pall over further conversation.

After the emotional drain of the start and the first Road Section followed by the pounding exhilaration of the

Selective Section, the long Road Section to the end of Stage One became a timing challenge that ultimately consumed all of their lagging energy, despite drinking water and eating a couple of energy gels. Maybe the gels had energy, but she certainly didn't.

The bivouac had been set up by the assistance vehicles that had hurried ahead—doing their own timed rally race, but only on Road Sections. There existed no Selective Section for the assistance crews.

Santa Rosa de la Pampa might be a city of a hundred thousand, but they weren't in it. Instead, the bivouac was on a tabletop-flat farmer's field far enough out of town to make the tall city buildings no more than a heat shimmer in the distance.

The area was a fenced-off rectangle covering many acres —a one-night-only pop-up city of nearly two thousand people: five hundred competitors, an equal number (at least) of assistance personnel, the same again in media, officials, vendors, caterers and… It was a wild scene, not counting the fans who'd come out from the city.

Then she eased around a corner looking for her lane—tall banners with car numbers flew to indicate where to go—and almost plowed into a dance troupe. A great number of women were moving in two circling lines, one facing each way. Attire ranged from jeans with loose white blouses (the kind that looked silly on flat-chested women but fantastic on the Argentines) to elegant rawhide skirts and vests topped with (what she assumed were traditional) flat-topped, flat-brimmed Old West hats. They all looked like they were having such fun.

And they made her want to hide. For nine hours, her world had become the inside of the Citroën. Her heavy helmet buffered, but my no means blocked, the roar of barely muffled racing engines. Her seat vibrating to that basso rumbled, when it wasn't being slammed and jarred by rough surfaces and hard turns—which was continuously. The only breaks had been the two timing breaks at either end of the Selective Section and the fastest rest stop ever made by a woman in a full racing suit.

These dancing women were a shock to her world. Over the low growl of her idling engine, she could hear their festive band, the rumble of other cars, the harsh *burrrr-ap!* of a pneumatic impact wrench as someone had their tires changed —or perhaps more dire repairs.

The scent of hot metal and dust had been replaced by hot dust and cooling metal.

She really needed to get out of this car and her gear. Easing around the dance troupe, which was now doing something between a man-eating shimmy and a groin-wrenching hula, Zoe decided it would be a good thing to get Luke well away from them quickly no matter what claims he made.

With only a little direction, she wound her way through the sprawling camp to where Ahmed, Nikita, and Drake had set up. It was only late afternoon, but they had big floodlights rigged in a shop area made of a large pop-up canopy. The rest of their base was a big camper van and a well-stocked service truck.

She rolled up and parked the car where Ahmed directed her beneath the blinding lights.

Liesl greeted her two steps from the car with a videographer and an ice cold Coca-Cola. Because of the latter, it was hard to be angry about the former.

"We're with Zoe DeMille, *The Soldier of Style.* How was your first-ever Dakar Rally stage?"

"Long," Zoe had to reach deep for the bright laugh, but she found it. She was intensely aware of Luke as he swung wide around the camera's field of view and came up behind Liesl and the videographer to watch her. Yellow racing suit unzipped far enough to reveal his black t-shirt like a deep cleavage on his SEAL-awesome chest. His eyes hidden behind mirrored shades. He crossed his arms over his chest and looked absolutely gorgeous. So male and powerful. Unlike the wilting mess she knew she was presenting to the camera.

"What part did you like the best?" Liesl didn't even give her a chance to catch her breath.

The best part? *Finding out that Luke still wanted to be with me.* "I've always enjoyed racing on sand. There were only twenty kilometers on the beach today, but it made me hungry to tackle the dunes." Sand was also the only kind of racing she'd ever done, so that easily counted as the best part of the driving.

"Twenty kilometers that did not go well for Sergey Kanski of Team Toyota," Liesl informed the camera. "He finished seven minutes off the best time."

"He's a fine racer, even if I did manage to get by him on the beach. I used a trick I doubt he'll ever fall for again." Only seven minutes off the lead? She hadn't seen him pass her again. Maybe on the Road Section…though she didn't see how.

She herself had passed several drivers out on the track. Two in racing, one mired in a mudhole, and another car that had gone nose down into a deep ditch and had turtled onto its back on the far side. The two drivers had been standing to one side watching anxiously as a racing truck used a long strap to flip the car upright. She wondered if it was still drivable after it was righted or if they were out of the race in Stage One.

"Zoe? You do not know?" Liesl looked at her in surprise.

"Know what? I only just arrived."

Liesl looked like she'd just swallowed the sweetest chocolate in the world. Zoe wondered where she could get some. Or anything else that wasn't an energy gel.

"What would you say if I told you that out of ninety-three entries in the car category, you are currently standing third, only forty-two seconds off the lead?"

"What do you get if you multiply six by nine?" Zoe replied with the exact quote from *The Hitchhiker's Guide to the Galaxy*. After all, forty-two was the answer to "life, the universe, and everything," according to Douglas Adams. Even if it no longer felt that way.

Luke's bark of laughter and Liesl's puzzled expression was Zoe's excuse to escape. Only Luke understood that nothing was truly important other than finding Hathyaron and the answer to everything else, including the race, might just as well be forty-two. *Hathyaron* was the real question and they were no closer than they'd been nine hours ago.

Then she stumbled to a halt as she spotted Christian sitting in the shade of the canopy.

"How did you get here?"

"I hitched a ride on one of the helicopters."

Zoe hadn't paid much attention to them—which was a major mind warp as her entire job was all about tracking the helicopters of the 5E. It was like a part of her had gone missing. The Dakar's helos—eight Airbus helos so she only knew them by their specs—floated overhead doing camera work, rescuing crashed drivers, and transporting race officials. Also, apparently, severely injured Legends.

"What about your back?"

He shrugged, then winced. After a sigh, he explained. "I have a back brace on under this shirt and enough painkillers in me to not care. But I cannot drive. They say I'm lucky I didn't make myself paralyzed." He sighed again, expressing exactly what he thought of his doctors. "You did very well today, Zoe, so you must keep driving. But this was the easiest stage with the shortest Selective Section, so you must step up your playing. Come. I have videos. I can show you some things you can do better. Then we must prepare your Road Book."

Apparently reaching the end of the race had nothing to do with the end of racing. God but she was tired. Even the Coke, which was now empty without her noticing, hadn't done a thing. Normally, that much caffeine and sugar would hyper her straight into space: don't pass the stratosphere, don't collect two hundred dollars.

She looked for Luke but he was nowhere to be seen. At least she knew he wasn't off with Liesl—because she and her videographer were still hovering just as if they too had been manufactured by Airbus rotorcraft. She was asking questions about her thoughts during the transition moment after Christian had blown his back jumping the podium.

How was she supposed to remember something that long ago?

Almost eight hours.

"Just let me shower first," she headed to the camper. She was slow to get there.

First, Ahmed wanted to discuss all of the details of how the car was performing. Was it pulling left or right, or was it running true? Any adjustments for the suspension that might improve cornering? Was the acceleration strong enough or did the turbocharger need tuning?

"It's already strong enough to give me whiplash every time I need it," appeared to satisfy him. It certainly earned her a brilliantly white smile. Moments later, he was pulling out air filters, checking oil, and all the rest of the things that the geeky part of her wanted to watch and the rest of her couldn't care about at all until it got a shower.

Then Nikita pulled her aside and congratulated her on the stage.

"We need to find Hathyaron," Zoe went for one of the questions that was plaguing her after Nikita had led her away from the others.

"Drake is out circulating with the crews right now. He's listening for Pashto- or Urdu-speaking teams, even their accents. No luck so far."

"Good idea," Zoe wavered on her feet, then realized she was slowly being cooked alive. Nikita had led her out of the busy tent and back into the sunshine. Finally tracing the problem, Zoe unzipped the flame-retardant racing suit right down to her shorts. The hot afternoon air was a cool balm in comparison.

"You need a shower," Nikita took a step back and pretended to hold her nose.

"Duh!"

"The shower in the camper isn't very big, but you can try."

"Try what?"

"To shower with Luke, of course. Though I still can't picture him with a woman."

"I'd have thought you could picture him with too many

women." Neither Zoe nor her imagination needed help imagining Luke Altman with a long line of shapely women.

"They don't count," Nikita shook her head. "My commander used to have lifelong bachelor stamped on his dog tags. Now not so much."

"Whoa, Nikita. We're sleeping together. That's all. Using each other for sex," then she sighed, "and not much of that lately."

"Lately? You've been together six days and you're already sleeping together without sex?"

"That doesn't mean anything." But it did. None of her relationships had ever lasted to the point where sex wasn't a nearly nightly (*and* morningly) mandatory event. The problem had been that when the sex calmed down from dating heat to relationship pleasure, her relationships had invariably faded with them. If she understood what was going on, she and Luke had already made the transition due to circumstances beyond their control. And they'd done it without everything falling apart.

"What are you two ladies talking about?" Luke stepped up to them.

"You, of course," Zoe riposted, then wished she hadn't.

Luke's eyebrows raised above his mirrored shades.

"Don't worry, boss, none of it was good," Nikita patted his arm, then walked away. Luke didn't even turn to watch her go.

"Here," he held out a paper plate.

Zoe's body kicked in all at once like her engine dial had just been set to Four—full power. On the plate were two long kebab skewers of grilled steak chunks, with scallions and cherry tomatoes interspersed between chunks. Beside it was a large bread roll and a chimichurri dipping sauce. The feast for her eyes was assessed by her nose as exactly what she needed—together they transmitted their doubly reinforced data stream directly to her stomach, which growled loudly enough to make Luke chuckle.

"Speaking of gods…" She grabbed a skewer, dipped it into the sauce, and slid off the first chunk between her teeth. The outer char and inner marinade combined to make a small piece of heaven. The peppery meat accented by the cool cilantro and sharp vinegar of the sauce made her want to eat slowly to appreciate every bite—and to scarf the whole thing down in a flurry of greed.

Luke rustled up a pair of camp chairs and set them in the shade as far from the bustle as possible.

Definitely speaking of gods, Luke looked as delicious as their meal as he slouched down and sighed happily.

"Any thoughts?"

His leer answered that well enough. She needed a temporary subject change if there was a chance she was going to finish her dinner rather than dragging Luke into the trailer and ripping his clothes off.

"Other than that?" She told him what Drake was listening for out among the other teams.

He nodded that it was a good idea, but grimaced on its chances of success.

"Yeah, my thoughts too. I'm starting to think he isn't Pakistani at all. If he's a foreigner, he could be anyone."

Luke grunted agreement.

"So how do we find him?" She voiced the question for both of them. Their shared silence lasted long enough for her to start on the second skewer.

"Shit!" Luke's final assessment on the situation matched her own.

IT SEEMED to take the fun out of the evening.

Zoe had looked so small out of the car. The contrast from Zoe the driver to Zoe standing so much shorter than everyone else was almost surreal. So powerful when wrapped in steel, and so petite when standing beside it. Even the car was taller than she was.

Yet she was the one they all mobbed. Liesl, Christian, Nikita, Ahmed: they all wanted a piece of her. Well, so did he. The long silence of racing fit him well. He'd enjoyed the task of a single focus instead of the normal twenty that a mission required. Turns, speed, timing were all he could control while in the car. No phones or radios were allowed for the Dakar teams except for an emergency satellite phone—with massive penalties for calling anyone other than the race officials to report a breakdown or accident.

Being cut off had let him shed the mission from his high-priority task list.

He'd stuck with that upon their arrival: listening to Zoe spar happily with Liesl. The woman never ran out of energy. And he didn't want to be running out of energy when they got off alone somewhere—so he'd followed his nose to the catering area just two rows over. He even ran into the Malles Motos crowd, but declined their invitation to join in, apologizing by holding up the two plates of food he was already carrying.

A long day of racing, arriving in camp to good people and good food—life wasn't bad at all.

Except this wasn't his life, as Zoe had just reminded him.

Hathyaron the arms dealer simply had to be here. Zoe had been absolutely right in connecting the dots he'd missed of the heavy tire tracks in the Pakistani soil, the high-tech garage, and The Dakar Rally poster.

To date they'd been moving on the idea that he was Pakistani and that would make him stand out. Except it hadn't. No team from there. No flight that could be traced back.

"Definitely a foreigner." Luke nodded over Zoe's shoulder. She turned in time to see Drake talking to Nikita and shaking his head sadly. No luck on catching an Urdu-speaking mechanic.

She slumped lower in the chair, like all of her supports had just been pulled out.

"Something you need to know about SEALs, Zoe."

"Why doesn't this sound good?"

Luke wasn't sure what she meant, so he kept on anyway. "We train constantly. But there is a great deal of waiting as well. A sniper may lie in wait for days before they get their target in their sights. Patience is hard, but we have thirteen more stages. On this stage we learned he wasn't Pakistani. That's progress."

"That may be the longest speech I've ever heard you give, Luke."

"Huh." Maybe. But he liked talking to Zoe.

"You're right though. When I fly, there is always something I can be doing. We have our 'Road Sections,' flying from the airport of origin to the mission area, but during the 'Selective Section' of the mission itself, there is never any true pause. We're constantly reviewing details, shifting for different angles and better visuals, tracking our team and what situations they're headed into, relaying communications, and the like. Once we enter the battlespace, there's no moment for true rest."

Somehow, Zoe had reached deep and shifted back to her optimism. He could see it in her, sitting upright once more and resuming her dinner. Damn but he was a lucky bastard to have her on the team. Which wasn't the only place he was lucky to have her.

"No true rest here either," Luke leered at her.

The smile she returned as she suggestively slid the last piece of meat off the skewer with her teeth flash-heated his body. He was halfway to his feet to drag her into the camper when Christian hobbled up and handed him a small roll of paper—four inches wide and far too long. Tomorrow's Road Book.

Luke was at least pleased that Zoe's groan matched his own.

It meant that the next couple of hours would be spent sitting around a table together with Christian, reviewing the course and marking up the scroll. Christian liked lots of colors on his markups and had made Luke do that on today's: red for upcoming hazards, bright blue for particularly tricky navigation areas, green for places to make up time, fuchsia for timing waypoints (only a few of which were included; the rest were stealthy ones, hidden along the route at unexpected intervals, but couldn't be missed without penalties), and on and on. Luke had thought about making a color guide to go along with interpreting Christian's version of the Road Book route guide. He was going to go to one color: the bright blue had stood out best in the bright sunlight.

He looked at Zoe for a long moment, still holding the little roll.

She looked back at him, once again slumped in the chair.

"Showers first," he declared. "We'll start this in an hour."

Christian smirked. It took all of Luke's self-control to not put the man down and give him more than his bad back to think about.

He must have read Luke's mood, because the look disappeared quickly enough. Then he held out his hand, "At least I can start on marking the Road Book."

Luke tucked it into his pocket, earning him a slightly more cautious frown. Christian was starting to wise up. Luke wanted his own markings on the roll...and only his.

The shower did nothing to ease the heat of the day. It was too small to share, but the tiny stall had clear glass sides. Zoe had shoved him in first, then leaned against the door offering ribald suggestions as he took a combat shower: thirty seconds pre-soak, water off for shampoo and soap lather, one minute rinse.

While he was toweling off, Zoe slipped in. After some of the comments she'd made, he almost took her then and there without letting her shower first. She seemed to have tapped directly into his blood flow control, allowing none of it to go to his brain.

He leaned against the doorframe to watch her shower as he dried himself off. But he couldn't think of a word to say. He remembered the look of her naked body on the Senegalese beach, but that view had been very brief before they came together. He'd never simply looked at her naked form. Her hair darkening with the water changed her appearance dramatically. Instead of a cheery blonde fluff to her shoulders, it was a dark curtain down to her biceps that made her blue eyes shine forth each time she glanced his way.

When she stepped out of the shower, he couldn't wait another moment and grabbed her.

"I'm still all wet."

He tackled her with his towel. Squeezing all the water he

could out of her hair, he began working down her body. He'd backed up into the tiny hallway and she clung to the bathroom's doorframe for support as he worked her over. Her eyes slid shut and her breathing went short and sharp as he applied the soft towel to her lovely form.

Luke wanted to tease. To draw it out for her, but he couldn't. His slightest touch lit her up like a thermite reaction. Unable to help himself, he gave her what her body was clearly craving. Placing one hand to hold her sweet behind, he massaged her through the towel from the front.

When she came apart, he was almost envious. It was so fast and so powerful. She clung to the doorframe in desperation while the release slammed through her so hard he was half afraid that he'd hurt her.

"Now!" Zoe's whisper was fierce through clenched teeth with closed eyes.

Now, what?

"Hurry, Luke. I need you inside me now."

He pulled her from the doorframe. Her grip shifted from the panels to clench around his neck. Three steps later, he had her on the bed in the back of the camper.

"Hurry," she begged again as he struggled to sheath himself when she wouldn't let go.

He slid into her like he'd never been anywhere else. No one had ever fit around him the way Zoe did. It wasn't that he was entering a woman, it was that he was sliding into the best place he'd ever been.

She buried her face in the crook of his neck and together they went up again. As he drove her aloft, as he climbed right along with her, he knew this wasn't about the sex. Nor was it about fears or tears.

This was about him and Zoe. No one else who could ever

feel this way. This was connection at a level he'd never known existed. Being married to Marva—perhaps standing at the altar had been the very best part of the whole disaster—he'd admired her body and what she did with it.

Zoe didn't treat sex like an art form as the exceptionally skilled Marva had, but she also had no artifice. She simply gave so completely there was no questioning that she wanted to be with him in this moment more than anything and that made it all the more amazing.

He did what he could to delay crossing over the tipping point. It felt as if he perched on the precipice of some decision. He needed to pause, to hold off for a just a moment in order to understand what was happening to him.

But such thoughts were useless.

With Zoe in his arms, they were racing toward a finish line that allowed no turns or delays.

The release gutted him. It left her humming happily against his neck as he wondered what the hell had just happened. His body had no calibration for such a powerful release. It wasn't sex. It was filled with meaning. But his brain had been scrambled even more than his hormones and he had no idea what that meaning might be.

Zoe's body hummed.

She didn't mind Christian's sly comments as the three of them worked through the Road Book. Didn't care that the nine p.m. route briefing said they were in for even a rougher day than the Road Book implied. The Road Section would be short and the Selective Section horrendously long—the opposite of today. That was fine too.

This had to be just a hormone-fueled temporary euphoria. A mental aberration that she'd eventually recover from, but she hoped not.

It wasn't just her. Nikita, never one to be expressive, had offered no words. Instead, she'd merely hugged Zoe and held her for longer than even when the nerves had hit the bride as she'd been maid of honor at Nikita and Drake's wedding.

When she'd crawled into bed, exhaustion had threatened to take her. It certainly knocked Luke out of circulation.

Instead, she lay with her head on his shoulder and her leg thrown over his hips. The past she'd survived could never have been worth it, but the present certainly put it in perspective. With Luke she was simply Zoe and—she pressed herself against his hip, enjoying the deep heat that stirred to life—that was all he asked of her.

She worked hard to suppress the laugh that would surely wake Luke, because once it started coming out, she might not be able to stop it.

Luke only asked her to be Zoe.

But who in the name of all that was twisted and warped was that?

Chief Warrant 2 Zoe DeMille of the US Army's 160th Special Operations Aviation Regiment (airborne) ready for duty. *Yes sir, you betcha.*

The Soldier of Style: Living in the Cutey-Edgy Budget Battlespace. At least to a kajillion fans and most of her previous lovers, that's all she'd ever been.

The Rookie currently holding third place in the Dakar Rally. The officials had ruled that since Christian hadn't made if even fifty meters from the starting podium, she and Luke were eligible in the Rookie category—which they were leading by a huge margin.

Her Pismo Beach-based parents' daughter. A source of so much anger that in a sick way it was almost funny—in how it had twisted and twined its way through her life.

But most of all, she was a top pilot for Special Operations Command and her lover was a high-ranking SEAL Team 6 officer. And life simply didn't get any better than that.

*A*ny tiny hint of order that had occurred in the Stage One went right out the window in Stage Two.

He and Zoe had regrettably been woken by the alarm clock rather than their bodies, so there was no time for a rematch. But he certainly enjoyed waking up with Zoe curled up against him.

It was also not his standard mode of operations. He was typically gone from a woman's bed by two a.m. If she was in his bed, he'd become an expert at sliding out without waking her and going for a run—typically until she was long gone. Marva had slept well apart from him, sometimes in the other bedroom, claiming that her constant need for him made her too restless.

Zoe was snuggled so tightly against him that they might have made love in their sleep and not known it.

But they hadn't even grabbed a quickie because the alarm clock had electrified Zoe.

"C'mon, Luke. Stop dragging. Race day today."

Being a SEAL had whupped being a morning person or a

night owl out of his system—whenever he needed to be sharp, he was sharp. But when he wasn't out in the field on a dangerous mission, he liked to take a *few* moments to wake up. Zoe simply threw her internal On Switch, going from Sleeping Beauty to ballistic missile in two seconds flat. There wasn't even time to really admire her form as she dressed.

A standard Argentine breakfast had filled another thirty seconds of their morning: cream-filled *medialunas*—crescent rolls—with black coffee and a glass of orange juice. Their rank in the standings had placed them early in the starting lineup and had them hurrying to the timing start position just outside the bivouac gates.

The Road Section had proved uneventful.

One minute into the Second Stage, disaster had already struck. Two of the drivers of a Jeep were standing in the low swale between the third and fourth dune along the Selective Section. Brothers Andy and Jim Kyle, United States, seven Dakars each—two of the nine Americans in the race, including themselves. They were looking morosely at their vehicle from a distance. It was intensely on fire, the entire vehicle engulfed.

Zoe had slowed beside them, close enough for Luke to ask, "You guys okay?"

"Blown hydraulics line, we think. Maybe. Shit, I don't know," Jim managed while Andy simply stood there looking numb. And then there were seven Americans in the race.

"Need me to call—"

The guy held up a satellite phone to indicate he'd already placed a call.

"Sorry, man."

The poor guy didn't even manage a wave before turning back to stare at the burning remains of several hundred thousand dollars of race car. Once a carbon fiber body ignited, there wasn't much other than time that could put it out—certainly not the small handheld extinguisher they had aboard with their other supplies.

Zoe let go of the handbrake and opened up the engine with a roar to get up the next dune. Over that dune, a car was badly sand-bogged. Luke had only the briefest glimpse of two guys out in the heat with small shovels trying to dig in a couple of flat traction ramps just like the ones they had stowed in their own cargo area.

"Getting real," Zoe commented drily as she slid down a dune slip face, crabbing sideways around a particularly steep section.

"Seriously," Luke agreed. The GPS flashed on. "Way Point," he called out. Which meant they were within eight hundred meters of the point. They'd have to get within ninety meters before the GPS would mark them as validly reaching the electronic check-in represented by the Way Point.

"Which way?"

"Dead ahead or I would have told you."

"Some help you are," Zoe in race mode sounded pissed at him. No, ultra-intense driver *and* pissed.

Then he looked up and saw why. An insurmountable dune practically blanked out the world ahead of them. There was a low pass far to the left—far enough to add over a kilometer out and another back once through. He could see tracks that showed most racers had gone that way. Close to the right was a far higher pass. It looked as if only a single motorcycle had gone that way.

"Left?" he asked.

But Zoe was already slicing the other way, scooting

diagonally up the dune's slip face. He considered asking why, but even the intercom might not overcome the roar she was coaxing out of the engine. Besides, it might be better not to distract her as the car kept threatening to lose traction and roll over onto his side first. Each time, she did something that kept her crabbing upward rather than rolling down.

"Hang on," was the only warning he had as she reached the top. The steep approach had forced her down to second gear, the engine pumping at seven thousand RPM to keep them moving. Great rooster tails shot off the rear tires.

He grabbed the handle on the inside of the door and the other on the center console.

Just as the car reached the crest—and threatened to high-center atop the pass—she cut the wheel hard, slamming them through a nearly end-for-end turn. At one moment they were slicing right over the dune crest, at the next they were racing left along it. Now their left front tire was hooked on the edge of the ridge with the other three wheels having crossed over. She made it back up to third gear and powered up the ridgeline.

Now he was looking down a far steeper dune face than they'd just climbed. Had they crested directly over the ridge, they'd almost assuredly have done an end-over-end down the other side.

"How did you know?"

"Wind carves dunes in strange ways. I remembered one in Pismo when I was still fifteen that did that. I was out in a dune buggy and high-centered on a pass just like that one. Getting stuck was probably the only thing that kept me from really bunging up Dad's newest buggy. Even with the roll cage, I bet it would have really hurt."

By the end of her explanation, she'd reached the very

pinnacle of the dune that had blocked their way. Here, at the center of the dune, the back slope was much less steep— merely vicious rather than terrifying.

With a hard snap of the steering wheel, she managed to point them directly down the slope. Fourth gear, fifth, and they flashed through the Way Point several minutes ahead of the route through the lower pass.

"Next heading is 120 by the compass," he slashed a hand sharply to the right, "for five kilometers." He looked at the dunes across their path and knew it would probably take traveling ten kilometers in a zigzag pattern to cover those five.

Though with Zoe driving, maybe not.

GETTING REAL? Talk about the goddamn understatement of her life.

She hadn't remembered the dune that had almost battered her as a teenager until they were mere meters from the crest. This one wouldn't have battered them, it could have killed them. Ridge-running with one tire hooked over the top was a new one on her—it had been an act of desperation that had worked by pure chance. She'd meant to get two wheels on either side of that crest and high-center them to a safe stop. It was the only option left to her when she understood the steepness of the face they could never descend except in a tumble. But in only catching the one wheel, she'd learned a new technique. More importantly, it had been enough to save them from a very ugly descent.

It didn't help that one of The Dakar's official helicopters had been hovering only a few hundred meters away for her entire maneuver. She hadn't seen it behind them as she climbed the dune, but as she'd slewed around on the ridge crest, she'd spotted it flying lower than she was now driving. A cameraman leaning out the door had tracked her all the way up the crest. Luke wouldn't know, he had no way to see down where they'd come from because he'd been sitting in the passenger's seat tilted down the other side of the ridge.

She was used to looking down on helicopters—from sixty thousand feet. In the dead of night. Via remote feed from her RPA. But from two hundred feet away in broad daylight? Not so much. In the rearview mirror, she could see that it climbed aloft high enough to film her race down the dune face before peeling off to other tasks.

Near death experience. Wild-ass ridge running. ESPN at eleven.

Definitely *getting real.*

Zoe eyed the first dune of the next set and decided to go straight over it. With a long flat run, she was able to gather enough speed to take it while still in fourth gear. She eased off the gas as her front wheels left the crest, reaching out to pop the handbrake for just a moment. It made the rear wheels drag just enough at the crest that the car tipped from nose high to a level-flight jump. They fell almost three stories before they hit.

The car's suspension and the deep sand ate up the shock, and she was up in fifth gear as they hit to keep pulling them ahead rather than slower-spinning tires acting like an unintended brake that might flip them. The Citroën had taken it with less complaint than her Mini Cooper did when eating a pothole on the highway to Mobile.

"Go, DeMille!" Luke shouted loud enough to hurt her ears.

She slalomed for a low spot around the next dune. Her

lover was cheering her on. Since when did that happen? Lovers were always looking for a way to make themselves feel superior. Every relationship she'd ever been in had a built-in power dynamic of making the male feel even more male: the strong one, the teacher.

She was the one driving the race car.

—And Luke was cheering her on!

It wasn't her ears that were hurting, it was her heart. Her brain kept waiting for the subtle (or not so subtle) manipulation. For the wake-up call that said no matter what she did, she didn't really belong. Her heart had no idea what to do with what was happening between them.

Around the next dune wasn't another dune, instead there was a river—that she almost plowed straight into, not always the worst tactic. Except she spotted a head popping up out of the water, and another. Not trusting to brakes alone, she did a four-wheel drift to make sure she stopped before she drove into the river.

Then she realized that the heads were helmeted and on either side of a car that was flooded and floating downriver —driver and co-driver crawling out the windows of their sunken vehicle. She followed them for over a hundred meters, but neither one seemed hurt. She was about to turn around and figure out where to find the ford—and hopefully cross it with better luck than they had—when their car crunched up on a hidden shallow and its roof resurfaced before it stopped.

One of the big six-wheeled racing trucks pulled up to the river's edge and drove across easily—wetting about halfway up their monstrous wheels. As soon as it was completely across, it stopped and one of the crew climbed down.

Zoe had memorized most of the truck numbers as well,

though she'd only learned the drivers' names rather than the full crew.

This was Pierre Rousseau, France, seven Dakars, driving ten tons of Kamaz racing truck with a thousand horsepower.

He tossed a six-inch-wide strap out to the guys standing chest-deep in the river. One ducked underwater for a moment to hook it to his bumper, then gave a thumbs-up to the trucker. Rousseau's crewman hooked the other end of the strip to his rear hitch and in moments they had the car towed out of the water. As soon as they dropped the strap, the truck raced away, leaving the car's team to see if they could repair and restart their soggy vehicle.

Zoe looked at Luke. Halfway up the Kamaz's big tires would be near the top of theirs. Deep enough that the current might drag them away if it floated them before they crossed.

"You got this, Zoe. Do it!"

She could only look at him in amazement.

Zoe had lain awake for a long time this morning before the alarm went off, listening to Luke's heart and slow breathing. She'd slept in his arms with no thoughts to her own safety. No knife clandestinely slipped under the pillow—which had freaked out more than one lover who'd accidentally discovered it there. Not even on the nightstand. For all she knew, it was still in the bathroom where she'd stripped down while watching Luke shower yesterday. It might still be there now because she'd never thought to strap it back on. She'd worn a knife every day for over half her life, and suddenly she wasn't.

At his side, she'd gone to the driver's meeting without a thought of carrying her own weapon. When was the last time she'd felt for her missing sidearm—locked in her gun safe back at Fort Rucker? Hours? Maybe even days?

She lined up with the Kamaz's tracks, kicked the engine hard, then popped the clutch and plowed into the river. Her passage blew an arc of spray over Cid and Jabir, working frantically on their car—their second Dakar Rally, Ford car, United Arab Emirates, last year finished forty-seventh.

She stopped to apologize.

"Shit. Don't stress, Zoe. Like we weren't wet already. Just go," Cid turned back to his car. As far as she knew, she'd never actually met them, but they certainly knew who she was. They moved down several notches on her suspect list.

Dropping into first, she eased away to make sure she didn't blast a load of sand on them after the bath. Once away, she punched back up to racing speed.

Zoe looked at Luke, at perhaps the first lover she'd ever had who made her feel completely safe.

Without thought or comment. Without realizing quite how incredible he was, Luke was studying the Road Book to find their next destination.

Yeah, Zoe.

Getting *really* real.

"How could you do this to me?"

"What?"

"*What?*" Liesl raged at both of them the moment they climbed out of the car at the San Rafael bivouac. "Have you seen the footage? You are the new sensation of The Dakar... *Und es ist nicht mein Film!*"

Christian spun a laptop so that Luke and Zoe could see what he'd been watching.

Luke's stomach lurched as he saw the bright yellow Citroën clawing up an impossible dune face. Knowing what was going to happen didn't alter the sensation. Seeing it in perspective from the helo's vantage point almost made him nauseous. Down on the sand, it was simply what was happening. In the wider world? It looked terrifying.

They'd done *that?*

As the helo climbed and the wider view came into the frame, Zoe slipped an arm around his waist and held on. He pulled her tight against him and held on himself. It was an amazing sequence. Then, in a tapering telephoto, it followed her racing jump over the next dune and the flight down the far side.

"I take back what I said yesterday, Zoe," Christian turned from the replay as another scene unfolded. This time the camera was on the ground and had caught Cid's car failing to cross the upstream ford across the river and then slowly sinking as it washed downstream away from the camera (then a clip showing them back in motion—*Go guys!*). "Maybe I have nothing to teach you. Not many drivers would have dared to take the righthand course. So, until the next disaster or amazing feat, you are the media's darling."

Luke felt Zoe's shudder beneath his arm.

He looked down at her in surprise, but she was very carefully not looking up to meet his gaze. The air whooshed out of him as surely as if he'd been sucker punched in the solar plexus.

That amazing maneuver was pure luck? He wanted to ask, but decided that he definitely didn't want to know the answer. No, it was pure skill, but it certainly hadn't been with any planning.

How far out on the edge was she running this? That one he knew the answer to—about SEAL-on-a-mission far. Damn, the woman was amazing. He'd never met anyone like her.

The fact that he might not ever again was a startling thought that he didn't like at all.

"Go! Be famous for an hour or two." Christian had waved them away after they'd prepared the Road Book. Either his back was paining him too much— or he wanted some alone time with the hot Argentine brunette whom they passed as she sauntered down the lane toward Christian's camp site.

Zoe couldn't help but giggle.

"What is it with men and their little one-track minds?"

In answer Luke yanked her into the shadow of an Iveco truck. Marik Ebbers, Netherlands, Legend with seventeen Dakars, top finish was...

It was something she couldn't remember as Luke quickly proved where his "little one-track mind" was focused without question. For the length of perhaps thirty seconds, he locked his lips on hers and thoroughly manhandled her—one hand on her breast, the other down the back of her pants to haul them together. She managed to slip a hand over those six-pack abs and down the outside of his pants making him groan into their kiss until her head was spinning.

233

Then he released her all at once, forcing a gasp of need from her, and grinned down at her. "Having a woman like you around? Makes me very one-track."

If Luke really meant what he'd just said...

It wasn't that she doubted him. But until she was eighteen, she'd been just like Luke. And Christian. *Got a pulse? Let's do it.* She'd shed that idiocy at eighteen when she'd burned that awful Huckfest photo of her and the line of guys she'd fucked. Men never seemed to get past that. Christian certainly hadn't.

But if Luke really meant what he'd said, she remembered that transition herself. It had changed the course of her life in so many ways. She'd left men behind—at least random ones—and started working on fixing herself. She'd focused her energy on *The Soldier of Style* and joined the Air Force as an RPA flier.

Resting both hands on his chest and looking up into Luke's shadowed blue eyes, Zoe wondered—perhaps for the first time—*What if?*

Christian would never change. He was too much the privileged boy.

But Luke was a Spec Ops warrior of the highest caliber. What if he was changing? Was she ready for that? How—

"Okay, enough of that, you two."

―――――――

LUKE HAD SEEN Nikita and Drake coming up behind Zoe. The interesting thing was that Zoe didn't startle away. Instead she turned and leaned back against him as if it was the most natural thing on the planet. His hands had landed on her trim waist. In her turn, she'd laced her fingers into one of them and pulled it onto her so-soft belly as she turned so that she ended up inside his embrace.

It made him feel…like…an ST6 SEAL. When a mission wasn't totally in the shitter, being in SEAL Team 6 was the ultimate power drug. The best weapons, the toughest training, and the most dangerous missions.

Holding Zoe made him feel that kind of powerful, except it was a new kind as well. Strong and protective—that's what it was. As if holding her, he could do anything.

Felt like the old joke about two guys in Maine who get blown way off course in a hot-air balloon. As they were landing near a farmer working his field, they asked him, "Where are we?" The Mainer answered, in typical fashion, "You be in a balloon, you darn fools."

Zoe had certainly blown him way off course. *Where are you, Luke?* And the answer? *In a relationship with Zoe DeMille, you darn fool.* And he didn't want to be much of anywhere else either.

He looked at Drake and Nikita, chatting with Zoe as she continued to lie back in his arms. They were standing hip-to-hip, so close that they must…have their inside hands tucked in each other's back pockets. So close. So comfortable. It wasn't just that he saw that now. It was as if they'd always been that way and he could finally see it for the first time.

He glanced down at Zoe's black-and-blonde hair. What the *hell* had she done to him?

"Ahmed said he could handle everything the car needed, then shooed us away, too." Nikita's smile told Zoe so much that she needed to know.

235

Yes! This was how it felt when it was right.

Sure, she'd helped Nikita and Drake get together during the Honduran mission. But that heat, that rightness had been there for them from the very start. All she'd done was help Nikita get out of her own way. With the slightest shift, she was able to lay her head back against Luke's chest.

What if Zoe got out of *her* own way? Maybe she'd end up…exactly where she was. Being all wrapped up in Luke's arms was about the best place she'd ever been. It was no longer a question of how long would it last. It was now hoping that it didn't end. Ever.

And that was far too big a thought for the second night of The Dakar.

"Let's go dancing." She tipped her head back enough to look at Luke. "Can you dance?"

She could see where his eyes traveled down the front of her blouse. She hated when guys did that. But Luke? He'd earned a license to do it as often as he liked. It tickled her no end that he wanted to. The first time, when she'd caught him doing it as Christian drove them from the airport into the city of Dakar, had merely been surprising—and she remembered thinking, *How typically male.* Now she knew that nothing *typical* remained between the two of them. They'd left behind simply sex right along with mere lust and pure heat. She *wanted* to be with Luke. And she wanted him to *want* to be with her.

Apparently too mesmerized by her minimalist breasts to speak, Zoe looked back to Nikita, "Does he dance?"

"Not in my lifetime." Nikita almost laughed. Drake shook his head in agreement.

"Time to learn." She kept one of Luke's hands in hers,

grabbed Nikita's with the other, and together the four of them plunged into the social area of the camp.

They followed the sounds of pounding drums and blaring trumpets to the big open area out in front of the mess tent. There was definitely a party going on.

The San Rafael Guerra de Baile, the War of Dance troupe, had taken over the broad field. Men were dressed in clinging black slacks heavily embroidered in gold, and knee-high leather boots covered in bells that tinkled brightly with each leaping step. Their seafoam green, asymmetrical shirts and long black gloves were also beautifully embroidered. Their dance partners were just as colorful: gold heels, kicky little green skirts that poofed out with layers of equally tiny petticoats, which didn't even reach down to mid-thigh, their poofy-sleeved matching tops, and little straw hats trailing bright ribbons as long as their dark, flowing hair.

They were all working the crowd, and with each moment, more race drivers were enticed to join in. Zoe could already feel the beat in her toes and flowing up her body. It wasn't the rhythm of sex…quite. It was the rhythm of how good it felt in anticipation. And how good it felt afterward. The moment where a crow of pure joy wanted to sound out.

Luke gave her one of his, *Are you insane?* looks.

She took both his hands and pulled him down until she could shout in his ear over the driving beat of the band. "Do you think Hathyaron would dance or would refuse?"

His eyes flicked over her shoulder, assessing the crowd, then snapped back to hers in a moment. It had taken him under three seconds to see the pattern once she'd brought it up—he was just that astute. But had she just out-observed a SEAL? No, she'd dragged him into an environment that couldn't be more foreign to him if it was on Mars. She almost laughed at the comparison; he was the God of War after all, just like Mars—or at least close enough that she didn't care about the difference.

"My bet is he would," she shouted again. "He'd let loose because he'd think that The Dakar was the one place he was safe. That means that anyone who refuses is less likely to be a suspect." Then she started to dance backward toward the throng without releasing his hands.

A look of alarm shot across his face.

"You're not Hathyaron, are you?" Her tease got him moving, but it was a close thing. He might have balked if Drake and Nikita hadn't happened by in that moment, arm-in-arm with a male dancer between them trying to show them the steps.

She did her best to catalog who watched but wouldn't join. Some of them surprised her. The stern Russian motorcyclist, Roza Vilenko (two top-three finishes in nine Dakars), danced beautifully. She looked like the female badass from the next *Terminator* movie and moved as well as some of the professional dancers—of course she was doing the men's dance, not the women's. The women's seemed to be mostly about shaking their hips and making their tiny skirts flit up to reveal even more bare thigh.

Tammy Hall was in the middle of them, of course, with her blonde hair flying and her cowboy hat not looking out of place for once. Zoe was pleased when Tammy's attempt to peel Luke off Zoe's arm was rebuffed with utter disdain.

He did one of his who-the-hell-do-you-think-you-are looks and Tammy went away.

Being five-four, she'd never been able to wield that kind of look with any success. On Luke, it was terrifying—which was awesome.

Liesl and her camera showed up at some point. She gained another point in Zoe's estimation by mostly shooting her and Luke when Luke's back was to the camera—leaving him out of the picture as requested. She hoped that Liesl captured at least one with both of their faces so that she could have a copy.

The dance troupe was good. Once they had a driver in their crowd, they were very reluctant to let them out. It gave her enough time to memorize the thirty-six who wouldn't join in. As to the ones who did, out of six hundred drivers, at least a hundred of them were dancing. That left over four hundred who weren't here to change their suspect-likelihood. It was a long shot, but she knew that hunting a target was the accumulation of hundreds of tiny bits of data that just had to be correlated the right way to find an answer.

And while she was doing that, she was dancing with Luke.

It was an evening she was never going to forget.

21

$\mathcal{S}$tage Three was predominately on *piste*—on track. Dunes were definitely off *piste*—"HP" in the Road Book for the French *hors piste*.

Of course "track" was a strong word to describe the day's route. There was a dirt path that a road grader might have cut through the wilderness fifty years before. Or maybe a couple of ox-drawn carts had once come this way—when the world was even younger than she was.

Zoe could have measured the smooth spots in the road in meters—on a good stretch. The suspension was doing a dance that had nothing to do with a Michael Jackson moonwalk and a lot to do with a Metallica heavy metal show. The Senegalese beach had been so much smoother by comparison that the car had seemed to float while the suspension took the abuse. Not so much here.

Every turn was a slide, because at a hundred and fifty kph, the tires were only catching the tops of each road divot —too little traction to actually call it a turn. Places to accelerate strongly, like a run up to a dune, were replaced with a gear shift every second or so. Down, down, down, headed into a corner, then up, up, up before the next down, down on the twisting track.

The road grader—which hadn't been near this road since the Stone Age—had left low berms of dirt off to either side. As she was still in the top four—she'd dropped down a place but was still within a minute of the lead because Hermann Golschen (eight Dakars, Belgian, Peugeot) had moved up so strongly—she'd had an early start. By end of day, this track would be twice as pitted and even harder to run at speed. Despite how few cars had started ahead of her, every now and then a pair of tracks blew out over the berm. A pair of fresh tracks would shoot out of the middle of a turn. A new path would be plowed through the sparse bushes, then a new notch in the berm where the racer rejoined the road.

This was high desert and completely unpopulated. Definitely the land of Whatever Worked.

"Luke."

"Uh-huh."

"Any off-*piste* forbidden symbols in the Road Book?" In some of the environmentally fragile areas, or farmland, they were severely penalized for leaving the track.

"No."

She didn't need to say anything else. Luke began scrolling ahead in the Road Book. He made a pleased grunt.

"Okay, so, not this turn, but the next one. Straight off the middle."

In the second turn, she punched head-on through the berm and almost flipped. The berm was both softer and wider than it looked. *Have to remember that.* But she managed to keep the nose out of the dirt with a burst of power. Back in Pismo she'd gotten over the first instinct, which was to hit the brakes. Sudden deceleration would have nosed the car down and they'd have burrowed in.

"Ditch!" Luke had been looking ahead.

She gunned the engine and aimed for the highest ground she could see. It made a small lip of a jump—enough that she could fly nearly thirty feet. Looking down at the ditch as they flew over it said that maybe off-*piste* hadn't been the best idea —it was a rough, rocky defile that they never could have crossed on the ground. Landing on the far side in the middle of a massive acacia hedge sounded like a thousand fingernails being dragged across a chalkboard. All the thorns and woody stems certainly weren't doing anything good for Christian's paint job.

"Berm and a hard left."

Zoe jumped back onto the road and slid into a long drift to get lined up once more along the track. They did two more like that, surviving as much by chance as planning.

"Maybe going off-*piste* isn't the best idea."

Instead of answering, Luke shouted, "Dust!"

She raced the engine harder because her first thought was *fesh fesh*—dust so fine that it might as well be quicksand. This absolutely was the kind of country to expect it in.

Except this dust wasn't vast clouds of talcum powder fineness. Instead, it was a hazing of the air, especially on the outside of the turns where a sliding turn would particularly kick it up. Though the leaders had started two minutes apart, she had caught up to someone enough that his dust hadn't settled yet.

"No more turns for a while," Luke was looking straight ahead.

Zoe rarely looked beyond the next hundred meters of track, but she followed his gaze. The flat plains of the Dry

Pampas had climbed into the Andean foothills without her noticing. The track did indeed stretch out long and straight ahead of them. Even as she pushed up through fifth and into sixth gear—something she got to use far too rarely—she couldn't help but admire the view.

They were arrowing directly for a vast blue lake. Around them was low scrub in blackish dirt. Beyond the lake rose a massive volcanic peak—pitch black with iced glaciers trapped in its higher folds like a giant sentinel set to guard against their passage. It blocked out a whole section of the achingly blue sky.

"It's midsummer!"

"Not up there. Cerro Galán is one of the biggest calderas in South America. Besides, we're at 4,500 meters."

"We're *what?*"

She'd been preparing a mental list of problems for Ahmed. Something was eating the Citroën's power. The acceleration had worsened all morning until she felt as if she was gasping as badly as the car. And the power bleed-off response had worsened ten-fold through the day's racing. If they were three miles above sea level—higher than any road, paved or not, in the US—it was no wonder the car was struggling.

Come to think of it, so was she. She'd been so focused on the racing that she hadn't noticed, but now that they were on a straightaway she could feel the oxygen deprivation. Her head throbbed, her butt hurt, and her nose and throat were achingly dry. Drinking water didn't help. Having Luke palm a couple of aspirin for her didn't either.

"Say something," she begged him, needing a distraction.

"Well, according to Liesl, don't drive us into that lake. You might float, because it's way saltier than any ocean, but it also has something like 200,000 times the safe dose of arsenic if we sink instead."

"There *is* a safe dose of arsenic?"

Luke chuckled. She really liked the deep, welcoming sound. It was like his enveloping hugs that she could almost disappear into. "Not in that lake. So no swimming, you hear?"

"Yes, sir, Lieutenant Commander, sir."

"Just trying to keep you safe, Chief Warrant."

And the warmth of that truth sustained her through the rest of the harrowing nine-hundred-and-twenty-seven-kilometer drive. They never did catch the person raising dust ahead of them, but they came close. By the time everyone had rolled into the San Juan bivouac, they were back in third.

22

"*W*hat if he isn't here?"

"He is," Luke tried to reassure her. It was past midnight and her restless flailing had kept them both awake. Seven stages down, they really needed the rest day tomorrow, especially if they didn't get some sleep tonight.

He could hear Zoe was out at her limits. It was a time that every top sailor, and top soldier he supposed, reached. It was a tricky moment. How many strong fighters had he seen hit this wall and tumble back? It was why Hell Week thinned two-thirds of any SEAL class—it's why Hell Week existed. People who couldn't push through those limits might be dedicated fighters, but they'd never be true warriors.

Because of her skills as a pilot, she'd passed into the Night Stalkers, perhaps without ever having tested her limits. Well, driving The Dakar would do that to anybody.

"Maybe he dropped out. Almost a third of the field are already gone. Both of the US motorcyclists have gone out in this last stage."

Luke pondered the grim reports.

One had broken a chain—badly. It had wrapped around the rear sprocket, locking up the wheel at the worst possible moment. How the rider had survived the high-speed flip into a cliff wall had been more miracle than luck. That he'd survived it with only a couple broken ribs and a shattered arm made it God's own miracle.

The other had blown an engine, literally. It was like a bomb had gone off inside it, shattering an entire casing so that the cooling fins had shot like shrapnel into the guy's leg. Dude would be lucky if he kept the leg. Luke had never seen anything like it and he'd seen a lot of bad shit on bikes over the years.

He'd spent an hour checking in with the Malles Motos guys last night. Partly to see how they were doing, but mostly wanting to cheer them up. Neither of the guys who went down had been Malles Motos—they'd both had full support teams—but accidents that bad struck too close to home. Now that he'd seen just what it took to run in the Dakar Rally, he was really impressed that they were doing it solo. If he had to do everything he'd been doing, and on top of it had to service his own ride without any help… Well, he liked the sound of that—what Spec Ops soldier wouldn't—but that didn't make it any less impressive.

But he'd also learned from them that, with only a few exceptions, the first third of The Dakar dropouts were mostly in two categories: amateurs and mechanical failures. Hathyaron's garage said that he was anything but an amateur. And that his ride would be maintained in top form.

"No. Whoever Hathyaron is, he's still running."

She buried her face against his shoulder. "There's got to be some way to find him. He didn't just dematerialize into thin air."

Luke blinked into the darkness, then started laughing.

"What?" Zoe propped herself up on his chest to look down at him despite the darkness.

"You know that you have sharp elbows?"

"Luke!" She was so cute when she tried to growl like a six-foot SEAL warrior.

In answer he picked up his phone and speed-dialed Nikita, then whispered while it was ringing. "Not dematerialize into thin air. But where did he materialize from?"

"Uh," Nikita grunted after the third ring.

"There's a car carrier ship that delivered the cars from France to Argentina prior to the race. When did it leave France?"

"End of November," Nikita mumbled at him.

He could feel Zoe freeze, then she started pounding her forehead against his chest as if she was pounding it against a brick wall. Yeah, it was a real *duh!* moment for him too. But she was doing it hard enough to actually hurt. He wrapped his free arm around her in a headlock before she cracked one of his ribs with her pounding.

She struggled for only a moment before trying to tickle his ribs. Thankfully, he wasn't ticklish there.

"Find out everyone whose car wasn't on that ship. You can cross out Japan and the Americas, too."

"Unless they transshipped through one of those countries to confuse their trail," Zoe mumbled from somewhere around his armpit. He might not be ticklish where her hand was headed, but he was certainly sensitive.

He amended the request to Nikita quickly and managed to hang up just before Zoe latched her hand around him. He grunted hard as she wasn't gentle.

Shuffling her around, he shifted the headlock into a hard kiss. She squirmed against him—closer rather than trying to get away. It was a long wrestling match that left them both with bruises, but much more content.

When she finally slept he wondered how neither of them had seen it. The car carrier ship had left France in November and they'd missed the goddamn arms dealer by only hours in Pakistan on New Year's Eve. He'd had his car *flown* across the Atlantic just as they had—and probably just as clandestinely. Again, his path would be nearly impossible to trace, but at least they'd know that anyone who'd used the ship wasn't their target.

He pulled Zoe more tightly against him and rested his cheek atop her head. It no longer hurt, but he could feel where she'd clobbered him that first time on the beach. None of tonight's bruises would hurt for more than an hour or so— these had been earned in joy, not pain. He wished he could reach down inside her and rip out the pain she carried. Even if he knew it was impossible.

But it didn't stop him from wishing.

23

*N*ikita had the list for him in the morning. Her dark scowl said exactly what she thought about him going back to sleep while she'd done the research and rousted the intel people to get her the ship's manifest. Except he and Zoe hadn't gone right back to sleep for a long, awesome time.

He offered Nikita his best happy smile before returning to his coffee and studying the list. Their layover day bivouac was in Copiapó, Chile, at the southern end of the Atacama Desert. Unlike the heart of the desert—that they'd be passing through tomorrow, which typically received a millimeter of rain per year—Copiapó typically received fifteen to twenty. A whole three-quarters inch of rain per year. Made it a damned weird place to build a city of a hundred and fifty thousand people. Though he supposed the copper and gold mining was enough reason.

He was looking forward to doing the tourism thing with Zoe. Copiapó had jumped onto the world's consciousness with the 2010 Chilean Mining Disaster. It had trapped thirty-three miners seven hundred meters underground for ten weeks—but they all made it out. That was a definite must see.

Did Zoe like flowers and such? There were some nature walks. There were supposedly some great beaches around the high mineral lakes. He wondered if Zoe had that yellow string bikini tucked away in that suitcase of hers. That he *definitely* wanted to see.

Nikita had gone to get some coffee and was already grumbling her way back. One problem with thinking about Zoe, it was an incredibly distracting hobby. He focused on Nikita's list.

Eighty cars and trucks, nearly two hundred campers and assistance vehicles, many of which had a load of motorcycles aboard. That was in addition to sixty media and thirty officials' vehicles. Over three hundred entrants and barely half of the racers had been on that ship. It helped, but it wasn't enough.

He crossed out the dropouts. The overlaps helped, but there were still a hundred possible candidates for the role of Mr. Weapons, the non-Pakistani invisible arms dealer.

Well, they'd have a quiet day to think of something else without having to worry about a stage race. Ahmed and Drake had the Citroën well in hand under Christian's watchful eye. They had whole sections of the car torn open: wheels off and brakes opened for inspection, a full fluids change, Nikita had been set to clean out the carburetor. A local boy was going through with a brush and already removing his second bucket of sand from every nook and crevice of the inside of the car.

Zoe was still sacked out, exactly where he wanted her to be. She had a scheduled couple hours with the media, but that wasn't until after lunch. Then maybe they'd get out of here for a while. Just the two of them.

"Excuse me." A guy who looked like a hippie well past his prime was poking around. "Is this Zoe DeMille's team?"

Luke saw the guy's eyes register the yellow Citroën, so he already knew the answer to that question.

Her fans were being a major pain in the ass. She was still holding top three. Even the slightest mistake by any of the leaders could change that instantly—missing a waypoint, having an on-course breakdown, even getting lost for just a few minutes could change the whole shape of the race. The leaders were just that close.

The media had made sure she premiered in every "Rookie" segment. Actually, she was overshadowing the race leaders; everyone knew they had a hot story. Per their deal, Liesl was the only one who got the personal interviews, but even those, he knew, Zoe carefully censored.

The Soldier of Style Brigade had gone insane. People were flying in to watch the Dakar, easily identified by their lemon-yellow clothing. The racer guys were going wild too, because so many of Zoe's fans were women—both dyed and real blondes. The party atmosphere ramped way up—what happened in Chile remained in Chile—and the male drivers and the rabid female fans were making the most of it together.

And any time Zoe left the bivouac—something she'd stopped doing several stages back in central Argentina, but not soon enough—she was mobbed by fans.

Fans had been getting past security constantly and hunting down Zoe. Christian had even hired some local bodyguards to rebuff anyone who made it this far. And still a few, like this guy, slipped through. Maybe it was because he wore nothing that was lemon-yellow. His hair was as dark as Zoe's part and his eyes as blue. He was a lightly-built man, barely halfway between Zoe's and his own height.

Luke felt a nasty itch between his shoulder blades.

"Who's asking?" Luke rose to his feet and stepped well into the guy's personal space. He shied away with as much spine as you'd expect from a civilian.

"I'm her father, Brian DeMille." He tried holding out his hand, which Luke ignored. "I've always wanted to come to The Dakar Rally, but I never dreamed it would be to see my daughter driving." He was craning around and looking in every direction.

"She said you were dead."

"She...*what?* Why would she say that?"

"You gotta ask?"

The guy squinted at him as if he really did.

"If I were her, I would have said the same thing, rather than admitting to your existence. You're dead to her and it's going to stay that way. Now turn the fuck around and never come back."

"Why would she say that?" Guy was a goddamn broken record.

Nikita was hurrying toward him, holding her palm out vertically in the military hand sign for stop.

"You rape your teenage daughter and you gotta ask why she tells everyone you're dead?"

Nikita skidded to a halt still several steps away with a look of horror on her face.

To hell with her too. It was high time someone confronted the bastard.

"Zoe?" the guy's voice was soft with shock. But he wasn't looking up at him. Instead he was looking off to Luke's left.

He'd been too late to protect her. Luke could feel her there close behind him. He closed his eyes for a moment. The one thing he could do for her was keep her "dead" father away—and he'd failed.

Shit!

"You fucking asshole!" Zoe was screaming.

He opened his eyes, but she wasn't facing her father, she was facing him.

"I trusted you. I trusted you and this is how you repay me? To think I thought that I—" She choked off whatever she was about to say.

The depth of her fury made her clobbering his jaw last week seem mild by comparison.

"Asshole!" She spit it out like an epithet. No tease this time—she was in dead earnest. It hurt worse than Marva's dispassionate slur by a hundredfold.

"Oh, Daddy," Zoe turned to her father. She clung to his arm and began walking him away.

It wasn't right. He'd done that to her and she still clung to him? What was wrong with her?

Nikita stepped up to take Zoe's place in front of him before he could follow. She didn't look furious, instead she looked desperately sad.

"*What?*" He knew better than to try and shove Nikita aside—she was a Team 6 SEAL and looked seriously planted.

"You really stepped in it, sir."

He watched over Nikita's shoulder. Zoe and her father had stopped twenty meters out into the lane between the two sections of the camp. To either side were vehicles being gone over by their teams. There was laughter, camaraderie, and hard work.

Not with them. The two of them were hunched together like they were having a deadly serious conversation.

When her father stumbled back, Zoe gathered him into her arms and held him. The two of them stood there in the shining sun holding onto each other like lost souls in a shipwreck.

"Anything you want to be telling me?" Luke couldn't tear his eyes away to look at Nikita.

"Not my story to tell. As far as I know, there are only two people aside from Zoe who know what really happened, and I'm one of them. At least until you did that. Now there are three."

If her father hadn't known and the guy who did it to her really was dead, then… Clearly he himself didn't know shit. Three would be Nikita, now Zoe's father, and…

"Who's the other?"

Nikita stood silent for so long that he finally looked at her.

"Not your story to tell."

She shook her head sadly. Then she did the strangest thing. Nikita, the warrior woman, rested a hand on his cheek.

"You gotta find a way to fix this, Luke. I've seen you two together. You gotta find a way."

Then as she walked away, he heard her say as if to herself, "I just wish it was possible."

She'd never used his first name before.

*Z*oe didn't return to the camp at all that day.

Luke had waited. After a couple of hours he'd gone looking for her, but the trail was cold. He didn't have Zoe's number because he'd never had occasion to call her. They'd been attached at the hip since the start of the mission, never beyond shouting distance apart.

He tried enrolling Nikita's help, but she flatly refused. "You're my commander, but she's my friend."

Even his offer to help Drake work on the car was turned down.

"Nothing personal, Luke," Drake had assured him. "But Nikita warned me off—though I'll tell you on the sly that I don't know shit. They're close, those two. Anyway, Nikita said it was better if you stewed in your own juices than distracted yourself with work. Guess she wants you to think about things."

Luke tried to think about what he was supposed to think about, but he didn't know what the hell was going on. Except that Zoe had gone off somewhere with her father—who he'd just accused of being a rapist. No, worse. Who'd he'd just told the secret of his daughter being raped when he didn't know.

He couldn't talk it out with Nikita, who knew something but wouldn't say.

He couldn't talk with Drake without betraying Zoe's trust —which wouldn't be acceptable—because apparently he knew even less than Luke did.

No way on Earth was he talking to Christian about anything to do with Zoe.

Luke pulled out his phone again and stared at it. His contact list held the numbers for his team, his commanders, the intelligence agency, and the supply personnel he sometimes needed. Scrolling through the list looking for friends was a fruitless endeavor, but he did it anyway. It had been ten years since he'd needed anyone outside his team. He'd always figured that was all any man needed and he'd been damned lucky to have the one he did. Ten years since Marva had fucked him over by fucking someone else. Her number was still in his phone for some reason. He must be a real mess if he thought for even a single second she might be able to help.

Definitely a mess, he considered it for five seconds before deleting her entry.

The only person he knew well enough to really talk to didn't want to talk to him.

Even if he had her number.

Finally, he figured he'd find her at the nine p.m. briefing if she was still going to be racing. He picked up the next day's Road Book, but there was no sign of the petite blonde who'd punched a hole in his life.

25

"Are you alone?" Zoe whispered when Nikita answered her phone.

"With Drake, but not Luke. Are you okay?"

"Definitely not." Zoe hadn't been this not okay in a long time. She'd just destroyed every fond memory her father had held about his best friend. Mom had been right about one thing at least: Brian DeMille might be a good man, but he was not a strong one.

He was a man with simple needs. He'd loved three things in his life: his wife, his daughter, and his auto business with his best friend. It had been all he'd ever needed. He'd survived Bob's death only because he still had the two of them and the business he loved.

And Luke's accusation had forced her to utterly destroyed all of those happy memories.

Zoe had never been so strong as the moment she managed not to destroy the third. It had taken everything in her to spare him from the last piece of the truth—about his wife, her mother.

The fact that she'd become a target for rape, by his best friend, in his auto shop, had almost killed him. Shattered by that truth, he lay in the medical tent and looked like he'd aged a century. She only *felt* as if she had.

"How's your dad?"

"He's asleep now. The doctors knocked him out. They swear that there's nothing physically wrong with him, but he collapsed like he'd had a heart attack—standing beside me one moment and down in the dust the next."

"Where are you? I'll come and—"

"No, Nikita. I'm okay here with him. But I can't leave him here like this and I can't face Luke. You have to drive with him. Together you can find Hathyaron."

There was a long silence. "I can't."

"Why?"

"I don't have a FIA license. None of us do except for Christian and Luke. You know Christian's back wouldn't survive it. No point in getting a fake one, no one else knows enough to race even if the officials would let us add a team member. Without you, they'll withdraw from the race."

"I," Zoe searched inside and knew the answer. "I just can't."

"You know that Luke feels—"

"Don't tell me!" She didn't want to know. Couldn't know. The blustering bastard had wounded her father past any recovery. In a twisted way, he'd raped her father's past just as surely as "Uncle Bob" had raped hers. She'd thought Luke could protect her; instead he'd permanently wounded the one man she'd ever loved—the only pure thing in her entire life.

"Okay," Nikita's voice was soft. When Zoe didn't answer, "You sure there isn't anything I can do for you?"

"I'm sure."

A long silence later Nikita whispered, "Love you, Zoe."

"Love you." Zoe listened to the soft beep and dead air after Nikita terminated the call. She had one friend in the world. That much she could be thankful for.

26

$\mathcal{L}$uke didn't eat. He didn't go in the camper. Not a chance he'd sleep.

Instead he sat out by the car.

He spent two hours meticulously reviewing and marking the Stage Eight Road Book, knowing it was pointless. Zoe wasn't coming back.

Somewhere way past midnight, Nikita came out to sit with him. She didn't say a word, simply dropped her phone beside his on the table and sat with him in silence.

She knew...something. But a bond tighter than superior officer and tighter than team membership (which was a hell of a bond in ST6) made her keep her silence. She was the closest thing he had to a friend, but she still didn't speak.

This went beyond friendship. Far enough beyond that she hadn't even told Drake—the man she'd married. *Loved* enough to marry.

His need to protect Zoe was an ache that ran through his entire body. Was that reason enough to marry?

Idiot! The one person Zoe needed protection from was

him. Goddess Zoe, running Number Three in her rookie Dakar, needed his protection like she needed a hole in the head.

Nikita said only two people had known who had raped Zoe until he'd opened his yap. He still didn't know. Nikita was one. Which meant the rapist was the other.

But, if her father hadn't known about it... And her attacker was really dead...? Then who was the other person? How many times he'd trodden that loop of reasoning through the long night he no longer knew.

An hour later, he was still nowhere and Nikita still hadn't spoken a word. She'd simply sat like you would with a dead comrade on the long flight back to Dover Air Force Base before they came to bury him in Arlington National Cemetery.

There was a tradition among SEALs. When the coffin lid was closed for the last time but before it was laid in the ground, every SEAL in attendance removed his SEAL trident pin and pounded it into the lid with the side of his fist. When Chris "The Legend" Kyle, the American Sniper, was laid to rest, a hundred SEAL tridents were pounded into his coffin's lid.

He half expected Nikita to pound one into him. At least *that* would make sense. Without Zoe he was a dead man.

Instead, she finally rose to her feet. Reaching down, she tapped the unlock code on her phone and walked away. He could see that it was on the recent calls list. At the very top was Zoe's name.

He watched it for the thirty seconds it stayed lit.

He watched it for the five seconds it dimmed before it locked.

And he watched it lock and go dark.

Luke wanted to talk to Zoe more than anything in the world, but he had no idea what to say.

Just before dawn, Liesl showed up. Apparently a glance was enough for her to assess the whole situation. He couldn't imagine that she was the other person who knew the truth of Zoe's past, so her deep sigh must be for the loss of her insider's scoop. Confirming his guess, she plummeted into the chair. She plinked her fingernail against Nikita's phone beside his. Whether she recognized it or surmised the reason it sat on the table didn't matter.

"Welcome to the human race."

It took him a moment to understand that someone was actually talking to him. He looked over at her in surprise.

"I don't need to be a genius to know that you aren't used to screwing up even if its written all over your goddamn face. I know what you are. Unlike Christian Vehrs, I've covered war zones."

Luke had never been comfortable with Liesl's knowing looks; at least now he knew why.

"You're clearly Spec Ops. SEAL, Delta, maybe Green Beret, but I don't think so. The feel is wrong. You see everything as a threat. Rangers do that too, but they tend to be overeager. I've learned that no one except a Spec Ops warrior sees the world as clearly as a journalist—clearer. Every detail. You probably knew it was me coming just by the sound of my footsteps long before I entered the far end of the lane."

He would have under normal circumstances. The bivouac was dead silent, not even the cooks were awake yet. Instead he'd barely noticed her before she sat down next to him.

"Zoe is a puzzle I haven't quite unraveled yet. Spec Ops in everything but size. Did you know that her standard response to a military fan is that she's a clerk in intelligence? It's brilliant in its way, forestalling all questions. Except clerks can't drive world rally cars in their first-ever race like the very best Dakar Rally racers. She's...ah! She's a pilot, isn't she?"

Luke kept his face neutral.

"But she doesn't see the world the way you do. She walks like a well-trained soldier but also like a civilian. Yet you and she are here together with absolutely no prior history of racing. Yes, I found old rosters that showed neither of you had been in any of the races your vague histories imply you were. What kind of Spec Ops pilot has no field experience? Even the Air Force rescue guys get out of their helicopters once in a while." Then Liesl whistled softly in surprise. "Drone?"

"They prefer RPA—remotely piloted aircraft." Luke couldn't believe that he'd just confirmed every one of Liesl's conjectures.

But she showed none of the triumph he expected. Instead she simply nodded, fitting the pieces together in her neat, journalist's mind.

"You can't—"

"*Nicht dumm!* National security and all that. I'm a German citizen, but I'm not stupid enough to think that would protect my freedom for a second if I were to betray a black ops mission—which is what this has to be. Besides, I don't believe in doing that. I want my sources to tell me their story because they want to, not because they want a moment of fame for revealing state secrets—even if it's anonymous fame."

Luke slumped back in his chair. Could anything else go wrong?

"What will you do if Zoe *kommt nicht zurück?*"

If Zoe didn't come back, there was no chance to

complete the mission. They couldn't stay in the competition. Couldn't be out in the field looking for Hathyaron.

Without Zoe, he—

He couldn't think about that.

"This mission of yours? It's bad?"

The biggest arms dealer in Southwest Asia about to slip through his fingers? The one who'd supplied the opposition in at least the two wars in Iraq and Afghanistan and who knew how many ISIL insurgents and... Yeah, it was bad.

"Does she know that?"

"Better than anyone."

Liesl nodded. "*Gut!* Now you must decide what to do when she comes back."

"But—"

Liesl laughed softly. "How little you know her if you think she could walk away from this. Now you must find a way to make sure that she doesn't walk away from you afterward."

She rose to her feet as if to go.

"Any brilliant ideas?"

Liesl brushed at his hair like he was a sweet little boy. "You'll figure it out."

Then she walked away into the breaking predawn light.

27

*Z*oe stood at the end of the row, watching the team area.

Ahmed was polishing the Citroën—as if it wasn't about to spend nine hundred kilometers traversing the roughest conditions on the planet. Drake and Nikita were breaking down the camp, getting ready to move it to the next bivouac. Christian was hovering.

Luke sat in a lone chair beside the car, as if he had been carved from stone on that very spot. He looked even worse than she felt.

Good!

She checked her watch. Ten minutes until their assigned start time.

Zoe waited until there were only six left, then stepped out into the service lane.

Luke jolted to his feet before she made it three steps. He watched her all the way in. No smile—which was good, because it saved her trying to punch his lights out. No frown. Just watching.

She walked right past him and stepped into the trailer, making sure to lock the door behind her. She allowed herself three minutes to try and wash the sleepless night off her face and get dressed.

At two and a half minutes to the start, she stepped back out of the trailer. She had her knife strapped on the inside of her forearm, in the perfect position to drop into her palm if she needed to stab somebody.

Luke—her prime candidate at the moment—glanced down to it, then back to watch her face.

She barely paused in front of him, "If you say one word not pertaining to the race or the mission, I'll walk away and you'll never see me again."

Zoe didn't even wait for his acknowledgement. She managed to climb into the driver's seat without breaking down, without screaming, without her heart shattering any worse than it already was. But that was all locked away on the inside, and she'd never again share what was inside of her with anyone on the outside. *Never.*

She had the engine started and was already backing up while Luke still had a foot on the ground. He dove in and strapped into his harness while she drove up to the Start Line outside the bivouac's entry.

Waving and smiling to the wild mob of her personal *Brigade* who waited just outside the gates was a strictly mechanical act. Many of them reached out to touch the car as it went by. They were rabidly excited by someone who didn't exist outside of her social media persona. *The Soldier of Style* knew no more about herself than Zoe DeMille did.

However this mission turned out, she was done. She'd serve out this tour and get out of the Army. Maybe she'd go work in her father's auto shop. Having lost herself there, maybe she'd find herself by going back.

The timer handed her their card, then began counting down from ten.

She was done with the Army.

Five.

And she was done with Luke. That was a hard thought— no matter how she hardened herself to take it, the idea was a knife in her already dead heart.

"Zoe?"

"I warned you to shut up!" Her yell at Luke wasn't quite a scream, but it was close.

She couldn't do this.

But as she reached out to kill the engine, Luke pointed silently toward the timer.

He was glaring at her when she turned to face him. "Already ten seconds late. Are you refusing the Start? You know that incurs a fifteen minute penalty."

Zoe did know that. She couldn't imagine why she cared, but she knew that.

She shifted into first and drove away.

When Luke called out the first turn, she let the racing take over. *Just race. Then you don't have to think. Don't have to think about the pain on your father's face when you told him his best friend had raped you repeatedly. And don't think about the half lie you told him when you said you'd kept your silence because you didn't want to hurt him.*

Stage Eight was a blur of snapshots.

Much of the track wasn't dirt, but rock. A whole different technique of driving that she had to learn on the fly.

Cerro Mulas Muertas—the Dead Mules Volcano. Towering up to almost twenty thousand feet, only a little shorter than Denali in Alaska, it dominated the high, arid, *dead* plain.

The names of the local geography leapt at her like personal attacks: Lake of the Dead, Crags of the Dead, Ravine of the Dead Mules, the Dead Mountain... *Muertas. Muertas. Muertas.* It fit her mental state perfectly as she plunged over ash ridges, wove around sharply porous boulders of lava that would as soon shred her tires as look at her, and wondered if she was driving on the Moon...or was simply so disconnected that it felt that way.

She remembered nothing else. Didn't hear that she'd moved up to second. Didn't recall a word she'd said during the mandatory stop in the media interview zone. Didn't care when Christian told her she was the prime feature on today's broadcast.

Didn't even care who carried her to bed in the camper, glad to simply be held for a brief moment in the misery of the last two days.

*L*iesl was looking aloft when Zoe crawled out of bed the next morning. Coffee and *medialuna* did nothing to convince her that consciousness was a worthwhile endeavor.

"How long do I have?"

"Depends if you get your act together today better than yesterday?"

"My act?"

"That is the correct idiom, *ja?*"

"*Ja.*"

"What do you remember about yesterday's drive?" Liesl turned from her inspection of the sky.

Zoe didn't answer, because she didn't have a good one. She remembered little more than the pounding, aching silence in the car as she drove.

Liesl returned to her inspection of the sky. "Is the bottom painted blue to hide it? It is very hard to see as it circles up there so high."

Zoe looked up for a long moment before she spotted the

tiny dot, the only thing moving across the blue sky other than a few early-morning hawks. It was about the size of a dime held three car lengths away. Someone had decided that the mission was important enough for Sofia to fly *Raven* down to South America to help.

The mission.

She hadn't given it a single thought yesterday.

By the time she looked back down at Liesl, she felt as if she was standing there naked with no secrets left in her life. She should have asked what Liesl was looking at, rather than simply accepting her question. Liesl had clearly figured out not only that this was a military operation, but also what Zoe did for a living and that someone would be covering for her.

"No," she replied carefully. "They're a dulled aluminum."

"*Interessant,*" was all Liesl said. "It is time for you to act your act."

"The idiom didn't work there, but I get the point."

"Good. You should also know that another of your compatriots is out of the race."

"Compatriots?"

"United States. He was a car driver with a Brazilian navigator."

Zoe closed her eyes. "What happened?" Still the ground seemed to lurch beneath her feet.

"Frame failure." Not unheard of.

"Grind to halt?"

"In mid-jump. The car came down in pieces. The driver and co-driver are both in the fourteenth hour of surgery."

What the hell was Zoe doing here? She was a pilot, not a racecar driver. She wasn't even that: she'd decided to quit. She'd be a car mechanic. And she'd never get behind the wheel again.

"I am going to warn you now," Liesl was once again staring aloft. "After today's race I *will* be interviewing you about the terribly handsome man who carried you to bed last night and threatened to maim anyone who disturbed you."

Zoe looked around for who that might be, even though she knew.

Luke. Again her protector. And her destroyer.

If only she could find some way to forgive him, but that didn't seem likely.

*Z*oe was far more functional in Stage Nine than she'd been in Stage Eight. She wasn't driving quite as aggressively, which Luke appreciated. He'd never had a death wish, but Zoe had given him a taste of what it must be like to have one.

After he'd put her to bed last night, he'd made a point of going up to Ahmed and Christian and telling them what a magnificent car they'd built. Luke had no question that it had saved his life any number of times during the rough stage.

This morning, Zoe kept leaning forward to the limits of her harness and looking upward—once almost eating a boulder that was in their way as they drove around a scrubby tree.

"What are you looking for?" He risked the question because maybe something was wrong with the car. A crack in the top of the windshield he couldn't see, or maybe the mounting seal coming apart—which wouldn't surprise him after the beating the Citroën had taken yesterday.

"Sofia," Zoe's voice croaked with disuse. It was the first word she'd said to him since her initial threat.

Luke leaned forward to look upward and finally spotted a flash of sunlight reflected off a high-flying craft. He wished it was legal to have a screen in the car with the data feed from the drone, but getting caught with one was grounds for immediate disqualification—which they couldn't afford.

"Hey!" Zoe squawked and slammed on the brakes. She slid to a stop at a Y in the track. There were tire tracks leading up either side, making it unclear which way to go.

Luke checked the Road Book. "Uh, sorry. Left. I guess the trucks must have gone right." The Road Book only told them where to go, with nothing about where other vehicle classifications went.

Cars, quads, and motorcycles almost always followed the same routes, but there were some things ten tons of truck simply couldn't do. So they were occasionally routed off onto another route for part of a stage.

"Maybe best if we both ignore Sofia." Odd, he couldn't even imagine what he'd seen in her before, not with Zoe for comparison.

"I will if you can." It was almost a tease and it made him feel much better.

Then a car overtook them from behind and shot into the left leg of the Y.

"Not for long, buddy!" Zoe had the Citroën spitting dirt in seconds and flew into the lane.

"I TRACKED Legends whose vehicles did not come on the ship from France and who are still in the race." Sofia's liquid tones sounded from the small computer sitting on the camper's cramped dining table.

Nikita sat close beside Zoe, which she found very comforting. Drake sat across from them, craning his neck to see the display. Luke stood with his back against the door to make sure they weren't interrupted.

"I have discounted motorcycles based on Luke's analysis of the tracks departing Hathyaron's Pakistani compound. Even a job box and a pair of motorcycles on a trailer would have been unlikely to make such an impression in the hard soil."

Zoe glanced at Luke to check in with him, but she couldn't read him through his mirrored sunglasses. There'd been a time, a brief time, when she could read every thought on his face, but that was gone. Gone along with her lover. Her choice, so she'd have to live with it.

She turned back to Sofia.

The display was an aerial view of the day's Selective Section. Only eleven lines traced their way back and forth across the screen.

"You lost one here to a broken axle," Sofia placed a yellow circle around a line that ended abruptly in the middle of the course. "And you effectively lost another here," she indicated a line that had zigged wide of the course. Obviously lost, it crossed back and forth several times, losing time and distance. "When they'd finally spotted the track and returned to it, they'd missed two waypoints, which incurred an hour of penalties. They dropped from eleventh to thirty-fourth place."

Zoe knew that could happen to anyone. A single moment of inattention—like her entire day yesterday—could be a race-ending event. Someone had been watching out for her that day and she rather suspected that it was a Team 6 SEAL rather than some unknowable deity. She didn't turn to look at him, but she could feel him there. Watching her. Waiting.

Well, he was welcome to wait until hell froze over.

She turned her attention back to the display. "So we're assuming that Hathyaron is a Legend who is still in the race and still running well."

Nobody answered. It had been her original suggestion.

"I know it's probably fanciful, but it still *feels* right," Zoe answered her own question and no one argued. "So tell us about the remaining nine."

"You can cross out this one," Sofia marked which one she was talking about with a red X.

"Why that one?"

"Unless you and Luke are doing something we don't know about, you aren't suspects."

"Okay, I guess we can make that leap. At least on my behalf. Any dark past you want to admit to, Luke?" She'd turned to face him automatically, until his name caught in her throat. It was the first time she'd addressed him by name since… There was a tightness that clenched her body as if she'd been frozen into a block of immovable ice.

He studied her for a long moment through his mirrored sunglasses before replying, "None that I'm real interested in talking about."

Zoe watched him for the length of a breath. So he wasn't interested in talking. Should they talk? It would be even harder than telling her father about his best friend's dark past. Or was he saying that she didn't need to talk about the past if she didn't want to? Or…

She was going to make herself insane if she followed that back-loop much longer. If they *did* need to talk, it was something she wasn't strong enough to face. Not now. But she hated that it had to be soon.

By brute force alone, she managed to turn back to the display, though it was nothing but a bright blur once she had.

"Three cars and five trucks make up our remaining lines," Sofia continued. As she listed off the names, Zoe tallied them in her head. She knew them all by name and two of the car drivers quite well. She almost told Sofia to cross off their names, but feared that she'd already narrowed the field too much and kept her thoughts to herself.

Sergey Kanski of Poland was currently the race leader in car group—an incredibly able driver—he'd recovered all of the time he'd lost in Stage Two. Perhaps he also had access to Russian military suppliers. He'd have made a splendid Cossack horseman under the Czar—dark and brooding.

Cid and Jabir had recovered splendidly from their float in the river and were currently in sixth. She'd actually have to watch out for them as they were driving like they had something to prove and could well catch up to her before the end. Were they a front for Saudi or Iranian interests? Should she discount them simply because they'd showed a sense of humor at the ford and been glad to chat with her since, despite her success?

Henni was the only other female car driver still in the race. Was her shyness and soft English accent a mask for an evil career? Or was Hathyaron her secretly supportive lover— the team sponsor without being the team driver?

"We need to learn more about the five trucks." She didn't know them well at all.

"Nothing obvious in their bios," Sofia replied. "I'll send all of their names over to The Activity. They found

Hathyaron once, maybe they can find him again from some clue we don't see."

"Thanks. Anything else, anyone?" Zoe had to smile to herself at that one. Sofia was her commander, Drake and Nikita were ST6 enlisted, and Luke was a Navy officer. So how had this become her mission?

When no one said anything, they signed off and stowed the laptop.

She looked around again, forcing herself to look at Luke as well—he was part of the team after all.

Still no one spoke.

"I guess this means we're on to Stage Ten."

Nods and shrugs.

She checked her watch. "Almost time for the course briefing. I'll go," she continued even as Luke turned for the door. And barely managed, "with you."

He stopped with his hand wrapped around the door handle as if steadying himself. A moment later he had the door open and was holding it wide for her and the others to exit the camper as if nothing had happened to make him hesitate.

She hadn't imagined it, but what could make an ST6 lieutenant commander show such weakness?

*L*uke waited by the trailer for Zoe to come out. He'd woken just before dawn, feeling suffocated by the light. The night wrapped about him more comfortably than the day.

Nighttime was the heart of a Spec Ops warrior's soul. It was the environment in which technology truly was winning the war. Night-vision and teams like the Night Stalkers had altered the battlespace for the past thirty years. Their enemies were making giant strides, but even the Russians and Chinese weren't crazy enough to offer their technology to notoriously unpredictable terrorist groups no matter how they were aligned.

Also in the night, Zoe slept and he could lay his pad outside the only door into the camper and sleep—or at least pretend to. By day—when she came to life—it felt as if a piece of himself was torn from his body every time she walked away.

Each morning though, he made sure he was away from the door and sitting by the car long before anyone else woke.

"May I?"

Luke jolted. Again he hadn't heard the person approach. Worse, it was a civilian with no training in stealth. And worst of all, it was Brian DeMille, Zoe's father.

"Of course, sir." What else could he say? *No, go away. Haven't I already hurt you and your daughter enough?* Instead, he sat still and wondered if that simple act might be the bravest thing he'd ever done.

"I still can't get used to her as a blonde."

No, please! He was *not* about to have a discussion about Zoe with her father.

"Only way I've ever seen her, sir." Apparently he was.

"I'm sorry I put on such a show," Brian said as he dropped into the chair as if dropping onto a living room sofa. By the moonlight, Luke could see that he'd passed more than his black hair and blue eyes on to his daughter. Her features were a refined version of her father's: cleaner lines, a narrower face, but just as shapely.

"I'm sorry for my part in it, sir."

"I'm not a sir. I never served like you do. You are in the service, aren't you? With Zoe?"

"Yes, sir." Brian's quick smile acknowledged the "sir" just as Zoe's would have.

"What are you two doing racing The Dakar?"

"I, uh, I can't tell you that, sir."

"Which means you're on assignment? I've never known what Zoe does for the Army."

"I'm afraid that I can't tell you that either, sir." And Luke could see her father slump in the chair. "But I can tell you that she is perhaps the smartest and most skilled woman I've ever met—and when you meet my second-in-command, you'll know just how high a compliment that is." Luke almost assured him that his daughter worked from a place of complete safety—an RPA control coffin—except she'd been right in the fray in Honduras and now was driving in a race that had killed seventy people over the years and injured a hell of a lot more.

"I've always thought she was amazing myself, but then I'm just her father. That makes me totally biased in her favor. So, like, what do I know?" Brian nodded to himself.

They sat in silence long enough for the stars to begin fading with the dawn.

"He was my best friend. How could I not know?" The first light caught the tracks of tears running down Brian's cheeks.

His best friend? Zoe had mentioned that her father was in business with his best friend from childhood. The fucking bastard. Luke fought against the fury that shook him. She'd probably grown up with him as practically a second father. And then he'd betrayed that trust by…

Then other pieces started connecting. Her fear when they'd first started to make love against the side of the Renault on that remote Senegalese beach. The bastard hadn't merely taken her, he must have done it in the family auto shop—staining yet another portion of Zoe's past.

By what unholy strength had she managed to turn her fear around and make love to him there. No wonder she'd wept in his arms afterward. Awash in her past, she'd chosen to purge the memory and create a different future. He didn't know of many SEALs who could face themselves that clearly and make choices that hard. Certainly not him. The less he remembered of his old man and his battering fists, the happier Luke was. Zoe had faced it head on.

"Is he actually dead or did Zoe make that up?"

"He's dead, thank God," Brian's voice caught. "I don't know what I would have done if he wasn't. I know I could never face him again."

Never face him again? Luke was tempted to find the bastard's grave just so he could dig him up and pound on him more than death already had. Hopefully he'd suffered even a tenth of the pain he'd caused Zoe before he finally went down.

"You can take comfort in the fact that she's become an amazing woman, sir."

Brian merely nodded, but the tracks of his tears still caught the light.

More than an amazing woman.

Luke finally knew what was wrong with him, why sleep was more elusive than while on watch far behind enemy lines.

She was *the* amazing woman. If he had a choice of any single woman to spend the rest of his life with, it was Zoe DeMille.

Too bad she wasn't speaking to him anymore.

You gotta find a way to fix this, Nikita had told him. *I just wish it was possible.*

Yeah, him too. But Nikita, who knew Zoe better than any of them, wasn't feeling very hopeful.

This mission had just become the highest stakes of his entire life.

HOVERING JUST inside the camper's door, Zoe watched the two men sitting by the car. Okay, there were worse-case scenarios for how this would play out—she just couldn't imagine what they might be. She'd left her father in a nurse's care thousands of kilometers behind, and now he was here, sitting next to Luke as if it was a perfectly natural thing.

They appeared to be talking as little as men ever seemed to and she prayed that the few words they were exchanging chronicled the weather. *Lost that bet without even gambling, girl. Talking about the next stage? Nope.*

Could she crawl out a back window of the trailer and run away? It would be totally chicken, but she *was* wearing a yellow racing suit.

Taking a deep breath, she stepped out and did her best to be cheery.

"Daddy!" It wasn't hard to be cheery with him.

He lurched to his feet and wrapped her in a hug. He held her hard for a long time. She let herself close her eyes and lay her head on his shoulder just as she always used to. Somehow they'd come through this okay.

"I'm sorry you didn't tell me," he whispered just for her. "I guess I'm glad that I didn't know, for my sake, but I wish I'd known for your sake. I was hurt for a while, but I guess I understand why you didn't say anything."

No, he knew nothing about why she hadn't, and maybe, just maybe, she'd come to terms with the real reason. Or would someday. Preferably sooner rather than later, though she suspected that it would be quite the opposite.

She opened her eyes without raising her head from her father's shoulder.

Luke too had risen to his feet, but he kept his hands jammed into his pockets and his expression blank.

"Morning, Luke."

"Hey, Zoe," she could see him swallow hard. "You doing okay?"

Was she? No longer having to hide everything from her

father was a huge relief, even if there was still one thing he could never know. She raised her head enough to nod, she was okay—in the most basic sense of the word.

She could see the next question as clearly on his face as if he'd shouted it: were *they* still okay? Having no answer to that one, she closed her eyes again and clung to her father for dear life.

3 1

*S*tages Ten, Eleven, and the start of Twelve through the Andes from Chile into Peru were no more than a blur.

Luke kept functioning, but the lack of sleep was really catching up with him. A trademark of a Spec Ops soldier was that they could sleep anywhere, anytime. Helo flight into a life-threatening mission? Perfect excuse for a twenty-minute catnap. Roaring along at thirty thousand feet in a C-130 Hercules, fully dressed for a highly dangerous HALO parachute jump? Better than a sleeping pill.

Being apart from Zoe during those three long nights of the rally had nearly killed him. He'd gotten them lost twice, once for twenty minutes in the trackless dunes of Stage Eleven. The only comfort was that all the teams were so tired that the screw-ups weren't limited to him.

Sergey ran into a boulder and lost time replacing a tire and doing a field repair on the suspension.

Cid and Jabir didn't high-center themselves on a dune ridge, instead they hung themselves out to dry. They'd tried to jump a depression in the sand but hadn't cleared it. Their front end had hit the far side and then the rear had caught on the near side. The car ended up dangling its wheels a meter in the air while its front and rear ends were buried in the sand. It had taken them a long time to dig down enough to free their car.

Henni had busted her top two gears and finished well behind on the Stage Twelve Selective Section. Her crew would be frantically rebuilding her transmission through the night.

Their own Citroën wouldn't still be in the game if Zoe's dad hadn't joined the team. He wasn't merely an ace mechanic, he was an ace racing car mechanic. He and Ahmed functioned together on some level that neither Nikita nor Drake could match.

The Dakar was taking its notorious toll. There hadn't been any deaths this year, but there were sixteen racers and five spectators still in the hospital with injuries worse than Christian Vehrs' back: shattered pelvises, massive concussions, crushed ribs with a collapsed lung—the list was long and gruesome. A kid who'd chased a ball across the road at the wrong moment was going to be playing soccer with an artificial leg the rest of his life. It was by far the worst toll in decades.

The motorcycles were down by a third; though most of his Malles Motos buddies were still in it even if they looked as if they hadn't slept in two weeks. The cars and trucks were down by more than half. A hundred and fifty competitors had been swept off the course by the brutal challenge of The Dakar. Fellow Americans were particularly hard hit and were now few and far between.

They'd started Stage Twelve with a huge sendoff from

Arequipa. Peru's second-largest city sat at seven thousand feet, dramatically close to the foot of the nearly twenty-thousand-foot active volcano El Misti. The historic eruptions of El Misti and the two other nearby monster volcanoes had also made it the most fertile region of Peru. If it ever had more than four inches of rain per year, it would be lush instead of merely green. But even that was a relief to the eyes after crossing the Andes and the high Atacama desert plains.

Here the men in Arequipa traditional dress was brown Spanish bullfight attire with black sombreros. The women's dresses landed mid-calf, but more than balanced out the view with far more vivid colors that the Argentine dancers wore— powerful reds and rainbow stripes.

And the food could kill a man with happiness. The bivouac mess had served massive platters of *lomo saltado*. The grilled sirloin beef was stir-fried with onion, pepper, soy, and yellow Peruvian chilis. The spicy chicken stew, *aji de gallina*, was so good that he just might have to learn how to cook so that he could eat it in the states.

Through it all, Zoe had been pleasant but a mile away. She stayed close to her father and it was a space that Luke didn't dare invade. No matter how tiring the stage, they often worked on the car together with Ahmed. She wholly entrusted him to work up the Road Book—which made it a lonely task.

Stage Twelve had left behind the greenery of Arequipa very quickly. The Selective Section was their most varied stage yet. Up ash hills, down off-*piste* wilderness that threatened to shatter the car and their bodies just from the shaking. A small but particularly vicious set of dunes added variety before they climbed once more into the foothills.

They were racing along a narrow cleft that some ancient

river had carved through the stone—a tortuously twisted path.

"Zoe?"

"Not now!" She snapped out.

"If not now, when?" It just burst out of him as he called the next turn. He was either about to fight her or blow this all to hell, but he didn't know how much more he could take of her silence.

"How about when I'm trying to not kill us?" She dodged a boulder, rode two wheels up and over a rubble pile where part of the sheer wall had collapsed onto the course, then gunned it down a narrow gut with no turns for a few hundred meters.

"Right. Sorry." And she was right. He announced the next turn, even though they could both see it coming.

She had to let there be a time. Now wasn't it, but she had to get over herself and just do it.

At the end of the straightaway, she downshifted hard and was preparing to gun into the corner when Luke called out.

"Smoke!"

Black smoke billowed skyward from just around the corner. She pulled back a gear, then another. She crawled around the curve and still was barely slow enough to not run over the man lying in the middle of the track.

He lay sprawled on his stomach. The marks in the sand showed that he'd crawled from his car. The blood on his face made him unrecognizable.

The gas tank must have breached moments earlier and the car was fully engulfed in flame. Zoe knew from her dad that gas tanks didn't just explode like in the movies, but they could make massive fires.

Killing the engine, she and Luke rushed forward to drag the man farther away from the blazing car. There was no sign of his co-driver.

A brief flutter in the flames, and she spotted the car number. Another US driver, Bernie Cole.

The car that had burned the first day, Andy and Jim Kyle's car burning in Stage Two, the unusual failures of the two motorcycles, the car frame failure, and now Bernie. All registered as entries from the US.

It *wasn't* chance.

"Bernie! Bernie! Can you hear me? Did you see who did this to you?"

Luke was trying to staunch the flow of blood and went shock still for just an instant, then continued his efforts with a sharp curse.

"Bernie? Did you see?" It was a cruel question, his eyes were gone, burned from their sockets. What she'd initially taken for blood all over his face was the black of burns and char.

"Bernie!" She shouted it to avoid being sick. How far had she gone around the bend that she was begging a dying man to help her?

He croaked out a noise.

"Again, Bernie," she leaned her ear close to his mouth. She took his hand, at least it was only bloody and not burnt.

"Man," he croaked softly.

"A man," which was no help at The Dakar where it was ninety-nine percent male. "What did he look like? Help me, Bernie."

"Silver," he gave a struggling gasp. "Man," was the last word he was ever going to say.

She held his hand as one of the race helos came screaming in overhead. It seemed only moments before Bernie was whisked away on a stretcher and the helo was aloft again. Another came in and disgorged men in firefighting gear with tall extinguishers.

They were sent back to their car, "Get moving. Get back in the race. You arrived after the accident, so we can wait until after today's stage to take your statements."

Zoe put it in gear, eased around the fire dying under the blast of the big extinguishers. She slowly worked her way back up to speed, but she felt as numb as she had on that stage after Luke had dumped her past on her father.

"The compound," she finally managed as they rolled into the end of the Selective Section and handed over their timecard. Thank God there was no Road Section today, the Selective Section ended close by the night's bivouac.

Luke nodded. "Hathyaron knows it was US forces that went into his compound."

"So he's killing all of the entries from the United States, but why?"

"In case they— In case we followed him this far."

"So he's just knocking every US entry out of the race— cars, quads, trucks, and motorcycles? But he's never killed before. Maybe that was an accident and he didn't mean to kill Bernie."

Luke's silence was the only reply that was necessary. Then he leaned forward as if looking up at the sky.

"He saw our drone—he'd know to look for it and it's not invisible. He *knows* we're after him."

"And he can't just quit and run because he knows that we'd be on him in a flash."

Zoe eased into the lane and idled her way toward their camp. She parked and turned off the engine but made no move to get out.

Luke waited her out.

She rubbed a thumb at the dried bloodstains on her hands. Bernie Cole's blood. "Why hasn't he come after us?"

"Maybe because you don't look like a Spec Ops soldier?" Luke shrugged. "Or maybe we're next."

32

"At least there are only two stages to go," Luke consoled himself as he tried to find the energy to eat. The price was so high.

It had been just a standard—well, perhaps not so standard—mission. But Hathyaron had just made it personal. Yes, his operation had to be taken out, torn up by the roots and shredded. But Hathyaron himself was going to go down and go down hard.

Too bad Cole's dying words about the "silver man" hadn't helped. There were no silver-painted vehicles still in the race. No one was named silver or wore a silver racing suit. There were some older racers, not many, but none had hair that would be called silver. Salt-and-pepper, gray, white, bald. No help.

"Actually, there's really only one more stage," Christian spoke up. "Stage Fourteen, the final stage, has only a very short Selective Section. It is still a race, but very few changes in the standings happen there. It is more of a parade. No, it is tomorrow's long Stage Thirteen through the Peruvian Andes and down to the beach that will almost assuredly decide the race."

Which meant that tomorrow was their last real shot at finding Hathyaron. Something they were no closer to achieving than three days ago. The Activity had come up blank. Hathyaron had erased his tracks so thoroughly that they might as well be starting with the world's population of seven billion to track him down.

Luke considered burying his face in his plate of rice and shrimp. The tiny town of Nazca couldn't put on a show that could touch a big city like Arequipa, but their food was still damned good. He could tell that, even though he could have eaten cardboard tonight and not noticed.

"Luke?" It was a soft voice, in a tone he hadn't heard in almost a week. A voice that stole his breath.

He turned to look at Zoe, something he'd trained himself not to do anymore because it hurt too much.

"I've got to talk to you," she tipped her head out toward the far side of the bivouac.

He nodded carefully. As he rose to follow her, he glanced at Nikita to see if she had any guidance. She only offered an infinitesimal shrug—perplexity rather than resignation, but still no real help.

Once they were well clear of the group, Zoe came to a stop. Luke estimated they were almost exactly the same distance from their camp as when she'd delivered the news that had shattered her father's life.

"I—" he had to try. "I'm so sorry, Zoe. I swear I'd take it back if I could."

She nodded sadly without looking up.

He couldn't find any more words, so he simply stood and ached that it was no longer his place to console her.

"I have an idea. It could get me thrown out of the military, but I still think it's a good idea."

"No! You can't do that!" He had no idea what her idea was, but that was so wrong. "You belong there as much as Nikita. As much as I do!" Picturing Zoe going civilian was the worst thing he could imagine. "You aren't that fluff ball, Tweety Bird *Soldier of Style* you show everybody. You're so much more than that. You're—" Then she gave him a look that told him to shut the hell up. He could only bite his tongue hard at the restraint she'd just placed on him, but he was going to have his say before this was done.

"But I think it's worth the risk because it might help us find Hathyaron. Also there are still two other US teams out there. We can't risk another innocent," she kept rubbing at her hands even though Cole's blood had long since been washed off.

How did she remain so steady? She was a warrior. Well, so was he, damn it. He took one deep breath and refocused on the mission, then nodded for her to go ahead. She could talk all she wanted, but she *wasn't* risking her career. No way was he letting her just hop out of his life like—

"I'm going to tell Liesl who I really am."

Luke shrugged, "She already knows. She just isn't using it."

"I guess I knew that. I mean that I'm going to have Liesl *report on* who I really am. I'm going to give her the interview she's been begging for by being nice enough to not beg. I won't divulge any secrets or break my officer's oath, but anything short of that is up for grabs."

"Why? Wait…" If Zoe told the media who she was, it wouldn't blow her career—it would fucking nuke it out of existence. Probably get her a dishonorable discharge. Spec Ops served at a whole different level than normal soldiers.

However, if she *did* publicize who she was, Hathyaron would hear about it. He wouldn't be able to help it—Zoe was the talk of race. Luke had descended to pushing Christian to the fore at every opportunity until most people would just assume he was Zoe's co-driver rather than Luke. But Zoe stood front and center.

If Hathyaron heard that Zoe was a Spec Ops soldier, would it spook him? Damn straight. But it would also give him a target—Zoe DeMille.

"You're leaving him only two choices," Luke rolled the idea around, but only found two possible outcomes.

"He drops out of the race at this late date…"

"Telling us exactly who he is," Luke finished her sentence. "Or…"

"He'll come after me," she finished his.

"You're willing to set yourself up as bait? There's an old saying in Maine about how it never seems to work out well for the bait."

"No," she brushed a hand over his crossed arms. Just the lightest of touches, there and gone, but it steadied him more than anything else in a week. "No, I'm setting *us* up to be bait. And I'm banking on you protecting me."

"With my life!" And he absolutely meant it.

"*T*his is Liesl Franks with Reuters, reporting from the heart of the Dakar Rally, the greatest car race of them all, with an exclusive report."

They were all crowded around the laptop. Zoe still wasn't used to watching herself on the screen. She'd never gone back and looked at her own online media vlogs once she was sure they were posed the way she'd wanted. If someone had The Dakar Rally news running and one of her interviews came up, she'd made a point of moving on quickly.

This time she watched intently over Christian's shoulder. Her father stood to one side, with his arm hugging her around the shoulders. Nikita and Drake stood between her and Luke. Liesl was there as well, studying the broadcast as it came out.

"We all know about the most unusual performance in recent Dakar Rally history, the astonishing race being run by Zoe DeMille. In her rookie season—in any rally racing—she is not only the top-ranked Rookie, she's top three in the cars classification."

"Hey, you didn't mention me or my car," Christian piped up.

Everyone shushed him.

"It's my goddamn car," Christian grumbled, but everyone ignored him. Zoe had insisted that he not be mentioned, not in this interview. She wanted to protect Christian as much as possible from what was coming next. No one knew what that was except Luke and Liesl.

"Today I confirmed another startling fact about Ms. DeMille's past, or should I say, her present. And I'm hoping to confirm it with Ms. DeMille herself in this exclusive interview."

Several people in their group glanced her way. Zoe ignored them.

The camera pulled back to reveal a very serious Zoe standing beside her. Her hair, rather than falling in its normal ripples down to her shoulders, was pulled back in such a severe ponytail that she almost didn't have hair at all. No thick-rimmed sunglasses, she'd borrowed Luke's mirrored Ray Ban aviators, which were too big for her face. You could see the camera reflected in them as if she was part cyborg. She'd opted to retain the yellow racing suit, zipped up to choke-her high. She looked dangerous, which was a good trick when she was only five-four, but Liesl had a good man working the camera.

"Thank you for your time, Ms. DeMille. Are you enjoying the race?"

"Oh yes. There are such fantastic competitors, they've just been great. And the challenges that the race committee set out have been beyond demanding. I just love this kind of driving."

"And you're very good at it."

"Thanks!" Merry, happy, everyone's friend Zoe DeMille was about to go away.

"Ms. DeMille, I recently found out that you have a very interesting day job."

"What have you heard?" Zoe had shut it down hard. Listening now, she sounded too severe. For a lack of any better idea, she had tried her best to sound like Luke. Her voice wasn't much lower, but the words were sharper, clipped until they were no more than honed, rapid-fire projectiles.

"Is it true that when you aren't driving at The Dakar, you work for the United States Army?"

Zoe had paused a long moment before snapping out an uncharacteristic monosyllable, "Yes!" At least uncharacteristic for her persona.

It was such a contrast to her earlier interviews—the bright and ever-cheery-no-matter-how-she-actually-felt *The Soldier of Style*—that it should really catch everyone's attention. That had been one of Liesl's suggestions on how to make the interview more memorable.

"And not just your average position either, but rather an officer in military intelligence?" She *was* a chief warrant officer, and she hoped that Command—who were sure to see this—would forgive her Luke's suggested white lie. She wasn't technically in an intelligence branch of the service, but her drone certainly was a tool for tactical intelligence even more than it was a lethal weapon.

"I'm unable to confirm or deny that information," her voice now carefully deadpan.

"I understand that you work for an unnamed agency who is deeply involved in supporting Special Operations Forces."

Nikita and Drake gasped in surprise at the on-air revelation.

Her father and Christian spun to look at her.

She stared at the screen as she'd stared at the camera during an intentionally over-protracted silence—could feel that her lips and her expression were just as tight now as they were on her on-screen persona.

"We're done here!" she'd finally snapped out, then stalked off-camera as if immensely irritated. And she had been irritated. She might as well have admitted to being a foreign spy who was operating in a friendly country without permission. Then, and now watching herself, Zoe could feel viscerally just how much she was risking. Thrown out of the military, her working relationship with Luke and Nikita and all of the others would be cut off. She'd known it would be a risk, but if she caught Hathyaron with the trap, maybe it would be worth it.

By airing the interview just before the start of the stage, it wouldn't give the wheels of injustice enough time to chew her up, but now she felt a cold chill radiating from the Pentagon already. The possibility of losing her career felt painfully real.

"Yes," Liesl continued on screen. "Never a dull moment here at the magnificent Dakar Rally. This has been Liesl Franks reporting for Reuters from Nazca, Peru. Next up, our coverage of the start of Stage Thirteen, the penultimate stage of this brutal two-week challenge."

Everyone starting asking questions at once.

She glanced over at Luke.

He offered her a single nod—it just might have been respect.

If Hathyaron was out there listening, she'd certainly lit the fuse. Now to see where the explosion hit.

34

*L*uke was having a very hard time not smiling. It was as if someone had jammed a cattle prod up the entire event's backside. Or maybe an armed explosive that had no visible timer.

The crew in the next pit over, who'd been as friendly as any seasoned racer ever was with a high-performing rookie, had lowered a curtain of silence as certainly as if it was made of steel.

The Brigade had all saluted her in unison as she'd rolled by them. Most of them were sloppy civilian attempts, but he saw several that appeared authentic. The other media cameras were positioned to eat it up. Liesl was among them, but she was filming the crowd's responses whereas most of the others were filming Zoe. Luke made sure to keep his head tilted down so that no one got a decent angle on his face past the brim of his helmet.

When even the route timer treated them differently, Luke couldn't stop the laugh.

"Fine for you," Zoe snarled as she accelerated off the

start. "You're not the one with the bullseye painted on your racing suit."

"We actually *are* Spec Ops, Zoe, not just some intel group. If Hathyaron comes at us, he's in for a very rude surprise. Besides, I got us a little extra help." He glanced aloft, but it wasn't time yet.

"And what's to stop him from using a sniper rifle or a missile on us?"

"He hasn't survived this long by being stupid. He knows that if he does that, we'll have him as point of origin. Sofia has *Raven* down to thirty thousand feet. Hathyaron probably already knows it's there, but he absolutely can't miss it now. Not with his training."

Zoe grumbled, but seemed to relax into the drive. Which was a good thing, the course designers had created a particularly challenging penultimate stage.

The narrow track behaved as if it had stomach cramps. One moment twisted up, the next it unraveled completely only to snarl up in a new direction. It plunged into a dry arroyo and slalomed along a channel barely wider than the car. Worse, it crossed and re-crossed other classification's tracks. One moment they were racing among cars and motorcycles, then the next they'd merged with the truck course. Then, in the blindest, dustiest areas—where it would be natural to follow a massive racing truck through an intersection—their courses would suddenly diverge again, enticing the drivers to choose the wrong route.

The navigation was a nightmare. Motorcycles—who had to read their own Road Book on a small scrolling display at the center of their handlebars—frequently strayed off-course and had to double back to pick up the track. Soon the motos, quads, and cars were hopelessly intermixed.

Then, when the track had been closed in on both sides by thick masses of brush like an English hedgerow, the Road Book had the symbol HP with a slash through it—off-*piste* forbidden. They had to stay on the track now or suffer severe time penalties.

"No HP," he called out.

"Guessing this won't be good," Zoe slammed through the gears. The course was so challenging that she was shifting at twice the rate she'd done on any other stage. There wasn't a moment where being in a particular gear was at all useful in the next moment.

They were in a twisting green tunnel several meters taller than the Citroën and never more than twice as wide.

"S-curve ahead," he called out.

A tight right-hander was immediately followed by a sharper left-hander.

Then the car nosed down hard and a brown cloud billowed out forward of the car.

"*Fesh fesh!*" They cried out in unison. Luke slammed the internal vent closed, but already there was a whirl of brown in the cockpit despite the filters.

Fesh fesh was a dirt so fine that it acted like water, splashing out in every direction. It also acted like dust, hanging in the air and creating blinding brownouts. Finally, it acted like actual dirt. Tires sinking down through its watery quality could easily high-center a car on its dirt-like quality.

There was only one answer: power, and lots of it. Of course that only stirred it all the more. *Fesh fesh* clogged air filters, blocked vision, and coated everything like glue. Windshield wipers could help a little, as long as no water was used. Any water instantly turned the fine dirt into an impenetrable mudpack.

To make matters even worse, it was almost impossible to see other vehicles that hadn't made it through the mess and were stuck in the trap. Not colliding with a downed motorcycle or a stuck car was a major road hazard.

In half-second gaps in the brown swirl, they both tried to assess what lay ahead of them.

Then the Citroën's nose would plow into the next dip, Zoe would pound on the accelerator, and another brownout cloud was thrown aloft.

Races had been won and lost in *fesh fesh*. It was only a miracle that no one had ever died in the stuff.

They were still in it deep when the Citroën jerked hard.

"What did we hit?" Zoe cried out.

Nothing that Luke had seen. Instinct had him glancing back to see if they'd run over someone, though they'd already be invisible in the dust cloud. What he saw in the rear window was the massive grill of one of the racing trucks. In fact it was *all* he could see out the rear window, with the truck's logo dead center like a stainless steel branding iron ready to stomp on them.

"Who do we know who drives a MAN SE?"

Zoe swerved around a motorcycle that Luke didn't see until it went by mere inches from his side window. The woman apparently had built-in radar.

"MAN SE? About a third of the field, why?"

"Guy's an asshole. He smacked us."

"You're kidding, right? The trucks are the only ones high enough to see clearly in this crap." She cut sharply right to avoid a mired car and bounced off the green wall of thick growth on Luke's side.

Another slam shook them.

"Well, at least I won't be getting stuck in this. If I do, he'll just shove me back into motion."

"Or run over the top of us."

"You're right," Zoe tried accelerating to the very limits of even semi-safe visibility. Then he clobbered them again.

"I guess we're not going fast enough for him."

"Well I'm getting sick of this. I can't risk a look in the back mirror. Tell me the moment before he's going to hit us again."

Luke twisted in the seat enough to see him. Nothing but brown cloud.

Then the window-filling black radiator emerged from the latest wall of *fesh fesh*.

"Ten meters."

"Five and coming hard."

"Hang on!"

Luke turned, braced himself against the seat, and grabbed the handles.

Along the *fesh fesh* route, officials were stationed in any of the wide spots to try and keep everyone safe.

Zoe steered way wide of the track and was on the verge of ramming one of the official trucks. She twisted them sideways at the last second, almost brushing steel down her entire length as she plunged back into the *fesh fesh*, throwing up the biggest cloud yet.

The MAN SE truck—whose driver must have only been focused on following them—wasn't nearly as maneuverable and it plowed into the official's parked Hilux Toyota pickup before slamming to a halt. Then the brownout closed in behind them. No way to see who it was.

"Do you think—" Zoe left the question open as she managed a jump out of a patch of *fesh fesh*.

"That Hathyaron drives a MAN SE truck? Yeah, I do." Then Luke had to chuckle even though it twisted in his throat.

"What?"

"Picture a MAN logo. What color is it?"

"Silver," Zoe gasped. "Oh, poor Bernie." He'd seen his death coming as the silver MAN logo on Hathyaron's front grill.

Their next landing plunged them back into another patch that exploded outward in billowing clouds.

35

<hr />

     *I*t was another hundred kilometers before a MAN SE truck came near them again. They were out of the track country and hopefully clear of any more *fesh fesh* holes. If he never ate *fesh fesh* dust again in his life, it would be too soon.

Behind them, the Peruvian Andes drew a massive wall that extended along the entire eastern horizon. Someday he was going to have to come back to this country when he could move slowly enough to admire it.

They were deep in dune country. These weren't the monster dunes like the last time they'd hit them in Chili, but they weren't in nice linear rows either. Their directions could best be described as confused—like a confused sea that had no directional wave pattern after a hurricane. It was as if they'd been built by contrary and battling winds, duking it out on a colossal scale with fifty- and hundred-meter-high dunes. With no clear direction, it was anyone's guess how best to cross through this topography.

Apparently Zoe's guess was to run perpendicular to the

dunes: racing up one face, jumping the crest, then flying down the other side. The MAN SE appeared as if by magic, racing along the valley between the dunes at right angles to their own track.

"Goddamn it," Zoe swore vehemently. "It's Goldfarb out of the Netherlands. I wouldn't have guessed him in a hundred years."

Luke agreed, except he'd met enough men who presented one face, then tried to stab you in the back while wearing another, that he didn't trust anyone. The SEAL operator who'd been fucking Marva in Luke's bed had been one of Luke's most eager and friendly companions in the bars.

"Take the bastard out."

"He's ten tons, we're less than three. Any suggestions?"

"If you can't figure it out, just get me close enough and I'll shoot the bastard."

"With what?"

Luke simply growled at her, even if she was right. All racers were subject to surprise inspections for illegal navigation equipment. They would freak if they found lethal weaponry aboard. Still, his palm itched for something more dangerous than his working knife.

They continued converging at right angles. They were definitely going to get within shouting distance.

"I can't think of anything to do except outdrive him and run away again."

Luke didn't know either, but then he saw the truck more clearly and relaxed.

"What?" Zoe must have noticed the change in him as easily as he noticed every single change in her. Again, encouraging.

"It's not him. His front end isn't all bunged up from ramming us."

Goldfarb waved as he raced past not far in front of them.

Luke only barely resisted giving him the finger in response. He was convinced that someone was indeed after Zoe now, and that was unforgivable even if it was part of the plan. Luke wanted a piece of whoever it was and he wanted it now. At the moment he hated Goldfarb simply because he wasn't Hathyaron.

36

*T*he dunes continued to be mayhem. Zoe was passed by motorcycles going the other way, who would then circle and head back and race by her, assuming she knew what she was doing and they were wrong. It was a marginal bet at best.

She did feel sorry for them. The dunes between Nazca and the finish line at Lima were far too close to sea level. This was no high-altitude course. The sun was blazing hot, cooking the sands to sun surface temperatures. Every time they turned so that the sun shone in the windshield, it felt as if their air conditioner had broken. The guys on the bikes must feel like burnt toast.

Zoe really wished she hadn't thought of that analogy. The image of Bernie's face came back to her.

"Where is that bastard?" she finally snarled out. She wanted a piece of him. A big one.

"We'll get him," Luke said with all the stupid calm of his I'm-just-a-patiently-waiting-SEAL-super-warrior thing.

Fat chance, how could they find Hathyaron when she

didn't even have a clue where they themselves were? The Road Book had uncharacteristically provided a compass heading and nothing else on a thirty-kilometer run...too bad they couldn't drive in a straight line across this terrain. Going a kilometer southwest to skirt an uncrossable dune, then two klicks due north to find a pass over the next, when her true heading was supposed to be northwest...

She was just thankful that Luke was navigator. He gave each direction change with such easy confidence that she couldn't decide if he was making it all up or if SEALs had built-in little magnets in their heads—just like fish that used the earth's magnetic field to navigate. Maybe Navy SEALs had to be half-human and half-dolphin to be let in.

Though there'd been nothing fishy about his lovemaking. He'd been magnificent and she'd missed it every night. When he'd shattered her father's world, she'd been so furious. And as she sat by Dad's bedside holding his hand alone through that long, long night, the thing she'd wished the most was that Luke was beside her, holding *her* hand.

Her life was an utter mess.

She wasn't a field operative.

She wasn't a rally driver.

And she was no longer Luke's lover.

Who the hell was Zoe DeMille?

The Soldier of Style. That much at least she knew for certain. Except what had Luke said? *You aren't that fluff ball, Tweety Bird Soldier of Style. You're so much more than that.*

Zoe took a moment to glance at Luke while he was staring off into the distance doing his aligning with the Earth's magnetic field thing. He clearly didn't think much of *The Soldier of Style.* She'd spent so many hours over the years perfecting that persona that she didn't know who else Zoe DeMille might be.

Luke saw her as the opposite of how she saw herself: a woman capable of being a field operative, a rally driver whom he'd cheered on at every turn (not once in the two weeks had he pulled the I'm-the-guy-so-I-should-drive card), and...

She didn't know what else was in that *so much more* that he'd called her. Probably because she was no longer on speaking terms with him outside the bounds of the race. Shutting out the best lover—the best man—to ever enter her life because he'd done what, told the truth?

Not exactly your best move, girl.

Well, she'd never been one to let sleeping dogs lie. "Luke, I—"

That's when she almost died.

She'd been clawing along a dune's slip face, looking for the right spot to turn upslope, when a vast shadow blocked out the sun. If not for that shadow, she *would* have died.

Instinct had her yanking the wheel to turn downslope and stamping on the accelerator. With an ear-deafening roar, the Citroën leaped ahead. Maybe it was a sand avalanche. Or a—

Just as she pulled clear of the shadow, she glanced upward —and stared into the undercarriage of a massive racing truck. The long drive shafts to the front and rear axles seem to spin in slow motion. Each tread of the huge tires was going to be imprinted upon her mind's eye forever.

Then it thudded down into the sand close behind her like an elephant with dreams of being a pouncing lion. It had just jumped over the dune and nearly landed on top of her.

It was an accident. Just bad luck that had nearly killed her—or rather it was good luck that she'd survived.

Now running downslope, she could see the truck slam into the dune's flank once more after bouncing up from its landing, then come zooming toward her.

A MAN SE.

With a badly mangled front bumper. Maybe he'd hit a rock or maybe…

Zoe veered north.

"Hey, where are you going?"

The truck turned hard on her tail.

"Does the view behind us look familiar?" Zoe could hear the thinness of her voice. She wasn't the sort cut out for near-death experiences.

Luke twisted to look back between the seats. Out of the corner of her eye, she saw his smile and it looked truly evil.

"Who's number 507?"

She glanced back herself. All she could see was the dented metal of the bumper, the bent front grill with its shining silver MAN emblem, and a small white rectangle bearing the truck's Dakar Rally entry number—507.

Zoe sighed. "What is it with you and women?"

"What do you mean? Oh." At least Luke wasn't slow.

"Maybe she's trying to kill you for turning her down. Maybe I'm not the target at all."

"Or maybe she wants you out of the way so that she can have her way with me." Luke was actually teasing her and she couldn't help smiling at him.

Tammy Hall, with her long *naturally* blonde hair (that Zoe hated her a little for) and her killer body (which Zoe hated her *a lot* for), was definitely on the warpath. Not so much with being the sweet lady from Texas.

Zoe made an attempt to cut north, but Tammy sliced up onto the dune's face to block her. Zoe didn't necessarily want to get away, but she didn't want to get sandwiched somewhere either.

"Any bright ideas?"

"Yep!" was Luke's cheery reply. "Just keep us alive for the next five minutes or so."

"That's not helpful." And not terribly likely. Tammy was a masterful driver, currently running Number Two in the truck classification. If Zoe could get up on the dune's slip face, she'd have some advantage because she was more agile. But Tammy knew that and kept closing the door with her truck's massive power. Zoe should be able to outrun the truck, but Tammy must have some sort of illegal system hidden in her engine. She was accelerating like she was using nitrous oxide—a totally illegal option. To go along with whatever illegal tracking equipment had let her find them.

"Try," was Luke's only suggestion.

"You know, if you were any kind of a decent SEAL, you'd pull out an MP7 or a howitzer or something right now."

"Didn't think the inspectors would appreciate finding a submachine gun aboard. And howitzers are Army shit. I'm hoping for something a little more subtle."

With nature's vicious sense of perfect timing, Zoe plowed into soft sand. Not *fesh fesh*, but soft enough that Tammy had just gained a major advantage with her massive fifty-inch wheels.

Tammy managed to clip the Citroën's rear corner and they spun wildly—almost tumbling had they caught an unseen hummock.

The recovery was whip-snap vicious. Why was there never a race official around when you needed one? That's when she realized they must be well off their original vector. Some routing that Luke understood and she didn't had taken them away from most of the field.

Was it a strategic racing move or did he know that Tammy couldn't resist hunting her down given the opportunity? Had the woman also installed illegal tracking equipment in her truck?

"Are you *trying* to get me killed?"

"Nope," was the extent of Luke's infuriatingly cheery reply.

Zoe shot over the top of a dune. It was a bad choice, leading to a harsh landing, but it bought her a few moments before Tammy's truck lurched over the crest as well. Annoyingly, she didn't roll, flip, or even get stuck for a moment. Instead the resilient suspension had popped the big truck out of the deep sand in a single bound and put Tammy back on Zoe's tail.

"Please tell me you didn't screw her."

"Never even considered it."

"Good!" At least that tiny thing had gone right with her sex life.

She cut south, hoping to get back in view of the media helicopters. Except there weren't any in the air. For twelve days they'd buzzed along the course like a pack of gigantic mosquitos and now when she needed one, they were nowhere to be found.

"Where are all the damn helos?"

"Grounded." Luke seemed sublimely calm. Too calm. What did he know that he wasn't telling her? With the amount the man *didn't* speak, that could be a very long list.

"Grounded? Why?"

"There are several hobby drones flying along the course at the moment."

Zoe knew that the small hobby drones could down a helo —turbine engines spinning at three thousand rpm didn't like it when they ingested the heavy lithium batteries inside hobby drones. So if someone had launched some small drones, all of the usual helos would have been told to clear out for safety until the perpetrator had been found.

As she slewed down a graveled slope at the lowest point between two dunes, with Tammy still hot on her tail, Zoe wondered how Luke could possibly know that. They weren't allowed a radio or any other messaging device except for the emergency satellite phone.

Unless of course he'd arranged for them to be launched beforehand.

But launched by whom? And why?

The answer to the second question was obvious once she thought about it. Sofia, far aloft, would have tracked the truck ever since it had beat on them in the *fesh fesh*. And when they ended up far off the course together, she'd have known the final confrontation was coming and signaled the release of the hobby drones.

Then the answer to the first question flew by close over her head. Even at the speed she was racing, the downdraft of the Black Hawk made the Citroën shudder.

And it wasn't any standard Black Hawk. It had the stealth configuration that only the 5E flew. She recognized the piloting from the hundreds of missions she'd watched over them—Rafe and Julian. Funny, wild, and fantastic pilots.

Suddenly Tammy had other things to worry about.

"If he shoots her, I'm going to get arrested for it," Zoe didn't like that at all. "And if they decide that it was a military operation, I'm going to end up in a National Directorate of Intelligence dungeon and I'll never be seen again. I don't want to end up in a Peruvian jail, but I *really* don't want to end up in a dungeon."

"He's not that foolish."

Then what?

"Get some distance on her."

Easier said than done. Zoe decided to slow down, slow until Tammy was so close that all her rearview mirror showed was bent radiator grill.

Then she shoved in the clutch and dropped down a gear. Tammy's blow, while the Citroën was in neutral, shoved the car ahead whiplash hard.

Zoe responded by popping the clutch and hammering down on the gas. It wasn't much, but it was a gap.

And into that gap, Julian dropped a pair of gas cylinders. Knock-out gas.

It was brilliant. They were far off course from the other racers, there were no other helos in the air because of the drones that they'd launched from the Black Hawk, and they'd just sleepy bombed Tammy and her crew.

Except it didn't work at all.

Tammy blew through the cloud and kept right on coming. She must have guessed what was happening at the last moment and closed the outside air intake just as she would if driving through *fesh fesh*.

Luke grunted unhappily.

The valley between the dunes was narrowing rapidly.

In a desperate move, Julian eased down until his skids were beside the top of Tammy's truck. Zoe watched in the rearview as he tried to flip her onto her side, but she was too canny for that. Instead, she counter-steered sharply into the helo's skids at the last moment, catching him by surprise.

For five seconds, ten tons of elite military helicopter and ten tons of Dakar racing truck shoved against each other. But Julian's traction was only air and Tammy had four massive tires on the ground. With a sudden twist of the wheel, she almost flipped Julian onto his side. How he managed to recover without plunging a rotor blade into the side of a dune and crashing was one of the most impressive pieces of flying she'd ever seen.

As he moved up and back to recover and think of something new, Zoe focused ahead.

The dune to her left was the obvious escape route. The face was climbable to a low pass. She might even be able to outpace Tammy, at least to the crest.

To her right…

*Z*oe recognized the dune's shape and prayed she could pull off the maneuver a second time. This dune was a monster, a Mother of All Dunes that rose for hundreds of meters above them.

No time to ask Luke. No time to pray. No time to even think.

Zoe kept her foot down to the floor and cranked the wheel to the right. Five hundred horsepower responded with all the heart she'd come to expect from the Citroën.

Tammy was hot on her trail. Any respectable, legally configured truck would have petered out around the halfway mark. Tammy just kept climbing, so close to Zoe's tail that she could feel the blonde breathing down her neck.

The race to the top was going to be close. A sand slip threatened her advantage. Then some hard-pack gave it back.

Back at the Huckfest, by flying with all those overeager boys and men, she'd seen dozens of attack methods for an up-dune climb.

Some thought it was all about raw power.

Well, neither she nor Tammy had a real power advantage.

More advanced jumpers thought about the angle of their attack on the dune's slope, sometimes angling slightly to the left or right to use the edge of their tires like the edge of a water-skier's skis. They carved their way to more traction as they climbed.

The very best, who consistently achieved the best jumps after the long run-up ramp, made constant little adjustments. They trusted to their instinct and the instant-to-instant feel of the sand communicated through the steering wheel.

By each moment a patch of sand was giving way, she was already turning the other direction.

The tiniest flattening of slope was met with eased acceleration, which let her spin less and gain another shred of speed with improved traction.

Steeper? Hit it with raw power.

"Holy shit!" Luke muttered softly and she could see him brace himself against the handles. He didn't call her off. He didn't tell her she couldn't do it.

Luke understood what was about to happen. And he trusted her to do it.

This had better work. There were a lot of things she still wanted to say to the man beside her. Because whoever the hell Zoe DeMille was, she knew one thing about herself. She was totally in love with Luke Altman.

It wasn't just because he trusted her.

He knew her better than anyone—far better than she knew herself.

And still he believed in her. She didn't know how that was

possible, but she wanted more of that like she wanted air to breathe.

Tammy was too far back. The massive truck was hitting its limits.

Zoe needed her to be too close to hesitate when they reached the dune crest.

She didn't ease off on the gas, instead she let a small sideslip bleed off a tiny bit of the Citroën's speed.

The gap closed.

The crest came nearer.

Five car lengths away.

"Luke, grab the handbrake. Pull when I tell you."

He reached out one of those big wonderful hands and wrapped it around the tall handle.

Two car lengths.

Tammy was positioned perfectly.

Zoe hit the crest but didn't let the car fly. Instead, she threw it into a sideways drift.

"Now!" She screamed it out as she fought the wheel while dropping a gear.

For just an instant, she was staring out her door's window straight into the truck's massive bumper. Roll cage or not, the truck was going to shred her.

She looked up into Tammy's eyes.

Tammy had the big steering wheel clenched in her hands and was leaning forward to look down at her. Zoe offered her own best feral smile in response, then popped the clutch and jammed down on the gas.

Without needing to be told, Luke released the handbrake.

The Citroën hesitated for a long moment, spewing a twin rooster tail of sand out the back. Then it caught and jolted forward.

The MAN SE clipped the rear of the Citroën, knocking both rear wheels across the crest.

Zoe managed to keep one front tire hooked over the edge of the crest exactly as she had the first time. The instant she was clear, she stopped and both she and Luke turned to watch.

The MAN SE didn't pause at the crest. Even over the Citroën's engine, Zoe could hear the roar of the truck's engine. It never decelerated.

Just like that dune in Stage Two, the back was a carved bowl that was impossibly steep. The sand, in some form of hyper-stability, was close to vertical.

The truck leapt out into that void.

It was a humongous jump. This was the Mother of All Dunes. The truck continued its long arcing flight with its nose to the sky. The front wheels twisted one way. Impossible to fix now. The truck seemed to hang forever as it fell.

The record jump at Huckfest had been after she left for the Army. Mike "Hollywood" Higgins had jumped 169 feet with a hang time of well over a second. He'd done it in a highly-modified pickup truck engineered to be as light as possible.

Tammy blew that away in a lipstick-red ten-ton racing truck.

For six full seconds, Truck #507 fell fifty stories out of the sky.

It didn't crash on impact, it disintegrated.

The impact also destabilized the slip face. The dune avalanched over the wreckage. A thousand, a *million* tons of sand spilling over the shredded scrap metal.

"*Z*oe!" Luke screamed.

She saw what had alarmed him and didn't waste time responding. Zoe herself skipped right over alarmed and went straight to terrified.

She could feel the rear end of their car sagging downward.

Despite gunning the Citroën, she couldn't crawl back to the other side of the dune. Everything she and the car had weren't enough to escape the crumbling of the Mother Dune's crest from under her wheels.

But she was on top of the dune's collapse, not under it.

Giving in to the slip, she aimed downslope and fought for high ground. She really wished she'd surfed as a kid because some practice would really help right about now. Every moment of the massive sand slide, the surface shifted. To hesitate was to be buried forever—or at least until the winds rolled the dunes aside, which could be centuries.

Dodging from spot to spot on the back of the ongoing slip, she was sometimes on top and sometimes wheel-deep.

The slip couldn't have lasted more than another twenty seconds, but all she knew was that it was the longest drive of her life.

She came to in darkness, gripping the wheel with both hands. The silence broken only by her own desperate breath and the creaking of the car's metal.

The engine was dead.

And so were they. Buried under a million tons of sand. She'd almost rather have died like Tammy, in one great pyrrhic leap—the victory of the beautiful jump somehow worth the horrific cost. To die of suffocation beneath the sands of Peru didn't have quite the same panache to it.

"Now that," Luke spoke softly from beside her, "was *most* excellent."

Zoe turned to look at him by the faint glow of the dashboard lights.

"Are you nuts?"

"No, I'm absolutely serious. If we get out of this alive, I'm so adding a sand course to SEAL driver training. And what you just did? I hope that Julian or Sofia got video of it just to show what's really possible."

"You *are* nuts. I've killed both of us." She hadn't saved anything.

"Ain't dead yet."

He had a point, but she wouldn't be placing any bets. "Let's see. There's no way to open the doors. The moment we smash one of the windows, it would end us. The sand would pour in and bury us before we could climb out. This is sand, not even *fesh fesh.*"

"Too bad this isn't Dune, the desert planet," Luke sounded…cheerful. When had he started doing that?

"You're being unusually happy, Luke. What's up with that? We might as well have been eaten by a sandworm."

"I'm always happy at the successful end of a mission."

"You've got a weird definition of success."

He cocked an ear to one side, "Maybe. Maybe not."

She listened too. Somewhere outside the car was a low muffled thud like a heavy heartbeat. No, like a Black Hawk helicopter.

Less than thirty seconds later, a clear *clank* sounded along the car's frame from the rear. And moments later they were hauled from the sand, dangling butt first from a Black Hawk helicopter's lifting cable. In the whole massive sand avalanche, she'd managed to keep them near the surface.

The sunlight was a shock as thorough as being born anew. Like...huh! Like someone finally opening the garage doors wide enough to purge all the shadows. She liked the sound of that, the feel of that, a lot.

Luke just grinned at her as they dangled from their harnesses while the Black Hawk lowered them to the flat area at the bottom of the dune.

"You were right."

"I was?" Luke pretended to sound shocked.

"Most excellent."

And their shared laugh—only a little bit laced with hysteria—might well be the best sound she'd ever heard.

"GOT THE WHOLE THING ON VIDEO," Rafe bubbled as the four of them met on the sand.

Luke high-fived him.

"Seriously, girl," Julian agreed. "That's some wicked-cool

moves you got there." He mimicked driving a car half like a racer and half like a bronc rider.

"You landed ass up, so we were able to snap on a cargo hook."

"Told you that you had a cute ass," Luke whispered in Zoe's ear and enjoyed seeing the bright blush.

"Whoa!" Rafe remarked. "When did that happen?"

"What happen?" Zoe asked but blushed harder.

Julian waved his index finger between them, "Seriously? Okay, totally getting the cutest couple of the year award."

"Better shut up, you two," Luke grinned at them. "Or next time Zoe may guide you straight into the side of a mountain from her RPA."

"Oh, I'd never do that," she said sweetly. "I'd send them right over an enemy's gun emplacement instead. Then no one could say it was my fault."

Rafe and Julian groaned.

The crew chiefs who'd been working in the back of the Black Hawk stepped out onto the sand with small remote control boxes. In moments, they were landing hobby drones on the sand and packing them into padded cases.

"Time's short," Julian checked his watch, then clicked on his radio. "Sofia? Did we get them?"

"Roger that. Drake and Nikita have the other four members of Truck #507's team in captivity. We told the officials they were needed for questioning over an illegal customs issue. They've handed them over to the CIA, who'll have them airborne back to the States within the next twenty minutes. And the team's leader has a Pakistani passport, as well as several others. We think he's American, but we don't know. All of the others have Pakistani stamps in their various passports, including the truck's three crew members."

"Thankfully not our problem. Thanks and out," he clicked off the radio.

"That's your cue," Rafe tossed him the satellite phone from the unearthed Citroën. "We're out of here."

Luke wrapped his arms around Zoe and turned his back to the sand kicked up by the helicopter's down-blast. In moments, it had slipped away along the valley and even the echoes were dying. Silence.

To hold Zoe for even that second was such a joy. But it was also a liberty he should never have assumed so he let her go before she could complain.

He turned his back on her so that she couldn't see how badly he wanted her and how badly he wished he could undo what he'd done.

Luke punched the speed dial on the phone. When the safety officer answered, Luke spoke.

"I'd like to report an accident."

And he hoped like he'd never hoped for anything in his life that Zoe would forgive him for the accident he'd made with her father.

*H*e almost didn't recognize her; wouldn't have except that he'd memorized everything about Zoe DeMille during those long days they were apart. She couldn't hide her walk as she strolled past the massed members of *The Soldier of Style Brigade* without any of them noticing, but everything else was so changed it was hard to believe.

She'd erased the buoyant Tweety Bird—completely.

It also didn't hurt that the party at the Lima, Peru, finish line had been in full swing for hours and sobriety had gone south long before the final riders made it to the Dakar Rally's finish line. Christian was thrilled to take the accolades for the highest finish his car had ever achieved. They'd held on for fifth despite their long sidetrack and delay waiting for the race officials to arrive once they'd overcome their fear of the tiny hobbyist drones and dared fly their helos again.

It was doubtful that anyone would pay for the operation to unearth Truck #507 or the remains of its three-person crew—it would cost a fortune.

After the race, Zoe had simply disappeared.

Now she was back, but she was no longer *The Soldier of Style.*

Her blonde hair with the black part was now all the same jet black as her father's. It made her deeply blue eyes shine forth. She'd shed her yellow sunglasses as well, a pair of mirrored shades just like his were pushed up into her hair holding back the straight glorious fall. In fact, there wasn't a single thing about her that was yellow. Blue jeans, red tennies with pink shoelaces, a matching red Dakar t-shirt, and a lightweight black leather jacket that made her look terribly sleek and urban in the dusk of the cool Peruvian evening.

She walked up to him without comment and, more importantly, without any of the media noticing. She looked so different, like...she was finally herself.

Liesl, who'd been standing right next to him, was most of the way through introducing herself before she startled in recognition and reached for her camera. Then she hesitated for half a moment before lowering it again and offered a radiant smile.

"I want the last-ever interview with *The Soldier of Style.*" Liesl spoke as if they The Soldier of Style and Zoe were two different people.

And she was right in some respects, but so wrong in most of them. Maybe Luke was the only one who saw that.

"Too late, she's already gone," Zoe declared her line in the sand. "But she just might have taped a few final thoughts on video for you to post as part of your wrap-up story." Zoe handed her a thumb drive. "When you're done, the crosslink will be her site's last-ever post."

Liesl bounced it on her palm a few times before pocketing it and turning to Drake and Nikita, "Let's go get drunk somewhere. You've never really been to Lima until you've gotten hammered—that is the right word, *ja?*—on Pisco Sours."

Drake had been talking to Ahmed and apparently missed Zoe's near-miraculous transformation. Christian was off with the other Legends. Nikita didn't even blink, pausing just long enough to give Zoe a hug as if nothing had changed. He supposed it was just more inexplicable women shit that he'd never learned.

"Where's your father?"

"I sent him home. The race is over and he was really terribly homesick. I don't know if he's ever left southern California before."

"Just remember, he came for you and he stayed for you." Nikita hugged her again and moved off with the others.

Now they were alone in the middle of a crowd that was surging up and down the main plaza.

Zoe simply stood and waited him out.

"I'm...so sorry," Luke finally dredged up the only apology he could think of for what he'd done to her father.

She reached out and tentatively touched a hand on his crossed arms. When she left it there, hardly trusting himself, he unfolded one of his arms so that he could rest his hand over hers. She didn't pull away.

"I believe you, Luke. And I'm sure that if I'd told you the truth about my father and his best friend, you'd never have betrayed that trust."

Too late to argue that one way or the other. He'd already done the damage so he kept his mouth shut.

"Maybe if you spoke more, asked me a question once in a while instead of swallowing it down so hard that it was choking you, I'd have told you the truth and we'd have avoided the whole mess. Though maybe not. It was locked away awfully deep."

He started to nod, then decided to speak instead, "Yeah, maybe."

"Wow! Three whole syllables, Luke. That was masterful."

Rather than speaking, he offered her a triumphant smile. And why not? He was feeling pretty damn triumphant. They'd survived The Dakar for a fifth place finish. And they'd taken out Hathyaron—who turned out to be a father/team manager and his daughter, Tammy the driver.

"Oh, that's why it's Hathyaron, the plural, not Hathyar," he finally got it.

"Weapons, not weapon," Zoe blinked in surprise. "We never thought to look for a family team—Dad-and-daughter Gunrunners Incorporated."

They shared a smile.

And there was Zoe, the real Zoe—shining in the look she'd been born with—right here with him.

"One last thing I have to tell you. You can never talk about this except with me or Nikita. You can never let *anyone* else know."

"The one question I've never asked," Luke knew it couldn't be anything else.

"...My mother," Zoe just said it flat, though he could see her eyes closing down and her struggle to not do that.

Her *mother*? *She* was the one other person who knew about the horrors of Zoe's past? Luke didn't know what to do with that. He'd never have guessed that in a hundred years. He reached for her, but Zoe raised a hand to stop him. She left it on the center of his chest, anchoring him in place—at a safe distance. No, so she could watch his face.

"I went to her first. I could see the shock, the horror, then she sort of shook herself, like a duck shaking off water."

"She didn't *believe you?*" Luke wasn't going to *not speak* to her, he was going to strangle her until she felt even half the pain her daughter had.

"I think that she *couldn't.* She knew what it would do to my father. If you think he's a gentle dreamer now, you should have met him twenty years ago. It absolutely would have destroyed him, as it almost destroyed him this time. If Mom is smart, she'll never admit a thing to him when he tells her about it. Because without her, I know my father would never survive."

Luke could only sigh. She was probably right. He'd ended up liking Brian DeMille, but her father was not a strong man used to facing life's harsh realities.

"Mom and I were never close, I was always a daddy's girl. Let's just say we've been even less close since then."

Without thinking, Luke finally pulled her against his chest this time and held on. Soon he could feel the hot tears through his t-shirt. She wasn't sobbing or shaking, she was crying as gently as her father had because she was absolutely Brian DeMille's daughter.

"*I'm sure you misinterpreted what happened. Bob would never do such a thing,*" Zoe managed in a dead voice that sounded nothing like her. "That's what she said to me. Told me to not exaggerate things all the time. I'd been a fanciful girl up until that point—perhaps *too* much like my father. But I didn't misinterpret a thing. I was only eleven when it started and I barely understood what was happening to me. He was… Uncle Bob. Somehow convincing me that it was my fault he couldn't keep his hands off me. It went on until I was fourteen—the pain and the fear had become my new normal.

Then one day I sort of woke up in mid-attack and went after him with a shop knife. After that I always wore a blade and I made sure he knew it. Don't mess with me in a knife fight, Luke. I've taken a lot of classes. From Spec Ops instructors too."

"You took control of your own life." Luke also made a mental note to heed her advice on the knife.

"I guess," she sniffled against his chest. "I abused myself, went full-on slut for…far too long. *The Soldier of Style* was my way out of that, though I didn't really understand that until very recently. I just knew that if I kept reinventing myself, I never had to look at my real self."

Luke knew she was strong. He'd learned that one the hard way. But did she know, really know that about herself as she was now?

He stepped her back enough to look at her. He combed his fingers through her lovely pure black hair, then brushed at the tears still trickling from those brilliant blue eyes.

"You are so goddamn beautiful, Zoe. You, not the mask you raised," he stroked her cheek. "And I'm not talking about your lovely face. Though please tell me I get to keep looking at you for the rest of our lives."

She nodded once, like a puppet jerked on a string. Then, as his words sank in, she threw her arms around his waist and pulled herself tightly against him once more. This time the hot tears didn't worry him, he'd seen the bright flash of joy in her eyes.

The words that should have been a shock—*What idiot believes in long-term commitments?*—felt perfectly natural now that he'd said them.

The most classic Maine joke—*Cain't get thea from hea!*—

oddly didn't apply at all. You could get there from here, as long as there included Zoe DeMille.

"Had an idea," he mumbled against her hair.

He could feel her hold her breath.

"Next year. The Dakar."

And her happy sobs turned into delighted giggles. Damn but he loved this woman.

"Though," Luke dragged it out enough to make her pause. "Unless you want to be mobbed by *The Soldier of Style Brigade* again, you might want to consider changing your name. At least your last one."

"I do that and you *will* be stuck with me for life."

"Works for me."

"Zoe Altman," she whispered as she snuggled more tightly into his arms. "I like the sound of that. We'll make one hell of a car team."

"Malles Motos."

She kept her arms tight about him, but leaned back enough to look up at him with those sparkling blues of hers. "But I don't ride motorcycles."

"They're the best. I'll teach you."

"Okay," she smiled at him so sweetly, he could feel himself melting. "Or maybe, if you're a good boy, I'll teach you how to really drive a rally car. Then, instead of competing against each other, we can race together. I bet I can talk Christian into being a team manager and financing us."

Luke had to admit that he liked that image, "Your dad as our mechanic."

Her little gasp of delight told him it was the perfect thing to say.

Zoe pulled him down into a kiss and he could feel her

smile. He knew he'd just lost that coin toss—rally car it was—but he was still buying her a motorcycle as soon as they hit US soil.

"I guess we're gonna do it. I know by now that there's nothing you can't do once you set your heart on it."

"I like that, Luke," she whispered against his lips. "I've got my heart set on you—a lifetime's worth. And you're actually pretty good with words. Don't stop, okay?"

In answer he simply held her. He'd been right the very first time he'd met her: there was no other woman like Zoe DeMille. Which was good, because one of her was about all he could handle.

If you enjoyed the adventure and romance,
don't miss the Firehawks Smokejumper series:
Wildfire at Dawn
(excerpt follows).
And we love getting reviews, too!

WILDFIRE AT DAWN
(EXCERPT)

IF YOU ENJOYED THIS, YOU'LL LOVE THE FIREHAWKS SMOKEJUMPER SERIES!

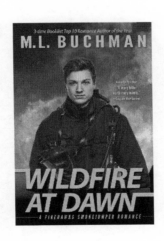

WILDFIRE AT DAWN

EXCERPT

ount Hood Aviation's lead smokejumper Johnny Akbar Jepps rolled out of his lower bunk careful not to bang his head on the upper. Well, he tried to roll out, but every muscle fought him, making it more a crawl than a roll. He checked the clock on his phone. Late morning.

He'd slept twenty of the last twenty-four hours and his body felt as if he'd spent the entire time in one position. The coarse plank flooring had been worn smooth by thousands of feet hitting exactly this same spot year in and year out for decades. He managed to stand upright...then he felt it, his shoulders and legs screamed.

Oh, right.

The New Tillamook Burn. Just about the nastiest damn blaze he'd fought in a decade of jumping wildfires. Two hundred thousand acres—over three hundred square miles—of rugged Pacific Coast Range forest, poof! The worst forest fire in a decade for the Pacific Northwest, but they'd killed it off without a single fatality or losing a single town. There'd been a few bigger ones, out in the flatter eastern part of Oregon state. But that much area—mostly on terrain too steep to climb even when it wasn't on fire—had been a horror.

Akbar opened the blackout curtain and winced against the summer brightness of blue sky and towering trees that lined the firefighter's camp. Tim was gone from the upper bunk, without kicking Akbar on his way out. He must have been as hazed out as Akbar felt.

He did a couple of side stretches and could feel every single minute of the eight straight days on the wildfire to contain the bastard, then the excruciating nine days more to convince it that it was dead enough to hand off to a Type II incident mop-up crew. Not since his beginning days on a hotshot crew had he spent seventeen days on a single fire.

And in all that time nothing more than catnaps in the acrid safety of the "black"—the burned-over section of a fire, black with char and stark with no hint of green foliage. The mop-up crews would be out there for weeks before it was dead past restarting, but at least it was truly done in. That fire wasn't merely contained; they'd killed it bad.

Yesterday morning, after demobilizing, his team of smokies had pitched into their bunks. No wonder he was so damned sore. His stretches worked out the worst of the kinks but he still must be looking like an old man stumbling about.

He looked down at the sheets. Damn it. They'd been fresh before he went to the fire, now he'd have to wash them again. He'd been too exhausted to shower before sleeping and they were all smeared with the dirt and soot that he could still feel caking his skin. Two-Tall Tim, his number two man and as tall as two of Akbar, kinda, wasn't in his bunk. His towel was missing from the hook.

Shower. Shower would be good. He grabbed his own towel and headed down the dark, narrow hall to the far end of the bunk house. Every one of the dozen doors of his smoke teams were still closed, smokies still sacked out. A glance down another corridor and he could see that at least a couple of the Mount Hood Aviation helicopter crews were up, but most still had closed doors with no hint of light from open curtains sliding under them. All of MHA had gone above and beyond on this one.

"Hey, Tim." Sure enough, the tall Eurasian was in one of the shower stalls, propped up against the back wall letting the hot water stream over him.

"Akbar the Great lives," Two-Tall sounded half asleep.

"Mostly. Doghouse?" Akbar stripped down and hit the next stall. The old plywood dividers were flimsy with age and gray with too many showers. The Mount Hood Aviation firefighters' Hoodie One base camp had been a kids' summer camp for decades. Long since defunct, MHA had taken it over and converted the playfields into landing areas for their helicopters, and regraded the main road into a decent airstrip for the spotter and jump planes.

"Doghouse? Hell, yeah. I'm like ten thousand calories short." Two-Tall found some energy in his voice at the idea of a trip into town.

The Doghouse Inn was in the nearest town. Hood River lay about a half hour down the mountain and had exactly what they needed: smokejumper-sized portions and a very high ratio of awesomely fit young women come to windsurf the Columbia Gorge. The Gorge, which formed the Washington and Oregon border, provided a fantastically target-rich environment for a smokejumper too long in the woods.

"You're too tall to be short of anything," Akbar knew he was being a little slow to reply, but he'd only been awake for minutes.

"You're like a hundred thousand calories short of being even a halfway decent size," Tim was obviously recovering faster than he was.

"Just because my parents loved me instead of tying me to a rack every night ain't my problem, buddy."

He scrubbed and soaped and scrubbed some more until he felt mostly clean.

"I'm telling you, Two-Tall. Whoever invented the hot shower, that's the dude we should give the Nobel prize to."

"You say that every time."

"You arguing?"

He heard Tim give a satisfied groan as some muscle finally let go under the steamy hot water. "Not for a second."

Akbar stepped out and walked over to the line of sinks, smearing a hand back and forth to wipe the condensation from the sheet of stainless steel screwed to the wall. His hazy reflection still sported several smears of char.

"You so purdy, Akbar."

"Purdier than you, Two-Tall." He headed back into the shower to get the last of it.

"So not. You're jealous."

Akbar wasn't the least bit jealous. Yes, despite his lean height, Tim was handsome enough to sweep up any ladies he wanted.

But on his own, Akbar did pretty damn well himself. What he didn't have in height, he made up for with a proper smokejumper's muscled build. Mixed with his tan-dark Indian complexion, he did fine.

The real fun, of course, was when the two of them went

cruising together. The women never knew what to make of the two of them side by side. The contrast kept them off balance enough to open even more doors.

He smiled as he toweled down. It also didn't hurt that their opening answer to "what do you do" was "I jump out of planes to fight forest fires."

Worked every damn time. God he loved this job.

THE SMALL TOWN of Hood River, a winding half-an-hour down the mountain from the MHA base camp, was hopping. Mid-June, colleges letting out. Students and the younger set of professors high-tailing it to the Gorge. They packed the bars and breweries and sidewalk cafes. Suddenly every other car on the street had a windsurfing board tied on the roof.

The snooty rich folks were up at the historic Timberline Lodge on Mount Hood itself, not far in the other direction from MHA. Down here it was a younger, thrill seeker set and you could feel the energy.

There were other restaurants in town that might have better pickings, but the Doghouse Inn was MHA tradition and it was a good luck charm—no smokie in his right mind messed with that. This was the bar where all of the MHA crew hung out. It didn't look like much from the outside, just a worn old brick building beaten by the Gorge's violent weather. Aged before its time, which had been long ago.

But inside was awesome. A long wooden bar stretched down one side with a half-jillion microbrew taps and a small but well-stocked kitchen at the far end. The dark wood paneling, even on the ceiling, was barely visible beneath thousands of pictures of doghouses sent from patrons all over the world. Miniature dachshunds in ornately decorated shoeboxes, massive Newfoundlands in backyard mansions that could easily house hundreds of their smaller kin, and everything in between. A gigantic Snoopy atop his doghouse in full Red Baron fighting gear dominated the far wall. Rumor said Shulz himself had been here two owners before and drawn it.

Tables were grouped close together, some for standing and drinking, others for sitting and eating.

"Amy, sweetheart!" Two-Tall called out as they entered the bar. The perky redhead came out from behind the bar to receive a hug from Tim. Akbar got one in turn, so he wasn't complaining. Cute as could be and about his height; her hugs were better than taking most women to bed. Of course, Gerald the cook and the bar's co-owner was big enough and strong enough to squish either Tim or Akbar if they got even a tiny step out of line with his wife. Gerald was one amazingly lucky man.

Akbar grabbed a Walking Man stout and turned to assess the crowd. A couple of the air jocks were in. Carly and Steve were at a little table for two in the corner, obviously not interested in anyone's company but each others. Damn, that had happened fast. New guy on the base swept up one of the most beautiful women on the planet. One of these days he'd have to ask Steve how he'd done that. Or maybe not. It looked like they were settling in for the long haul; the big "M" was so not his own first choice.

Carly was also one of the best FBANs in the business. Akbar was a good Fire Behavior Analyst, had to be or he wouldn't have made it to first stick—lead smokie of the whole MHA crew. But Carly was something else again. He'd always found the Flame Witch, as she was often called, daunting and a bit scary besides; she knew the fire better than it did itself. Steve had latched on to one seriously driven lady. More power to him.

The selection of female tourists was especially good today, but no other smokies in yet. They'd be in soon enough…most of them had groaned awake and said they were coming as he and Two-Tall kicked their hallway doors, but not until they'd been on their way out—he and Tim had first pick. Actually some of the smokies were coming, others had told them quite succinctly where they could go—but hey, jumping into fiery hell is what they did for a living anyway, so no big change there.

A couple of the help pilots had nailed down a big table right in the middle of the bustling seating area: Jeannie, Mickey, and Vern. Good "field of fire" in the immediate area.

He and Tim headed over, but Akbar managed to snag the chair closest to the really hot lady with down-her-back curling dark-auburn hair at the next table over—set just right to see her profile easily. Hard shot, sitting there with her parents, but damn she was amazing. And if that was her mom, it said the woman would be good looking for a long time to come.

Two-Tall grimaced at him and Akbar offered him a comfortable "beat out your ass" grin. But this one didn't feel like that. Maybe it was the whole parental thing. He sat back and kept his mouth shut.

He made sure that Two-Tall could see his interest. That made Tim honor bound to try and cut Akbar out of the running.

LAURA JENSON HAD SPOTTED them coming into the restaurant. Her dad was only moments behind.

"Those two are walking like they just climbed off their first-ever horseback ride."

She had to laugh, they did. So stiff and awkward they barely managed to move upright. They didn't look like first-time windsurfers, aching from the unexpected workout. They'd also walked in like they thought they were two gifts to god, which was even funnier. She turned away to avoid laughing in their faces. Guys who thought like that rarely appreciated getting a reality check.

A couple minutes later, at a nod from her dad, she did a careful sideways glance. Sure enough, they'd joined in with a group of friends who were seated at the next table behind her. The short one, shorter than she was by four or five inches, sat to one side. He was doing the old stare without staring routine, as if she were so naïve as to not recognize it. His ridiculously tall companion sat around the next turn of the table to her other side.

Then the tall one raised his voice enough to be heard easily over her dad's story about the latest goings-on at the local drone manufacturer. His company was the first one to be certified by the FAA for limited testing on wildfire and search-and-rescue overflights. She wanted to hear about it, but the tall guy had a deep voice that carried as if he were barrel-chested rather than pencil thin.

"Hell of fire, wasn't it? Where do you think we'll be jumping next?"

Smokies. Well, maybe they had some right to arrogance, but it didn't gain any ground with her.

"Please make it a small one," a woman who Laura couldn't see right behind her chimed in. "I wouldn't mind getting to sleep at least a couple times this summer if I'm gonna be flying you guys around."

Laura tried to listen to her dad, but the patter behind her was picking up speed.

Another guy, "Yeah, know what you mean, Jeannie. I caught myself flying along trying to figure out how to fit crows and Stellar jays with little belly tanks to douse the flames. Maybe get a turkey vulture with a Type I heavy load classification."

"At least you weren't knocked down," Jeannie again. Laura liked her voice; she sounded fun. "Damn tree took out my rotor. They got it aloft, but maintenance hasn't signed it off for fire yet. They better have it done before the next call." A woman who knew no fear—or at least knew about getting back up on the horse.

A woman who flew helos; that was kind of cool actually. Laura had thought about smokejumping, but not very hard. She enjoyed being down in the forest too much. She'd been born and bred to be a guide. And her job at Timberline Lodge let her do a lot of that.

Dad was working on the search-and-rescue testing. Said they could find a human body heat signature, even in deep trees.

"Hey," Laura finally managed to drag her attention wholly back to her parents. "If you guys need somewhere to test them, I'd love to play. As the Lodge's activities director, I'm down rivers, out on lakes, and leading mountain hikes on most days. All with tourists. And you know how much trouble they get into."

Mom laughed, she knew exactly what her daughter meant. Laura had come by the trade right down the matrilineal line. Grandma had been a fishing and hunting tour guide out of Nome, Alaska back when a woman had to go to Alaska to do more than be a teacher or nurse. Mom had done the same until she met a man from the lower forty-eight who promised they could ride horses almost year-round in Oregon. Laura had practically grown up on horseback, leading group rides deep into the Oregon Wilderness first with her mom and, by the time she was in her mid-teens, on her own.

They chatted about the newest drone technology for a while.

The guy with the big, deep voice finally faded away, one less guy to worry about hitting on her. But out of her peripheral vision, she could still see the other guy, the short one with the tan-dark skin, tight curly black hair, and shoulders like Atlas.

He'd teased the tall guy as they sat down and then gone silent. Not quite watching her; the same way she was not quite watching him.

Her dad missed what was going on, but her mom's smile was definitely giving her shit about it.

Keeping reading Wildfire at Dawn.
Available at fine retailers everywhere.

ABOUT THE AUTHOR

M.L. Buchman started the first of over 50 novels and even more short stories while flying from South Korea to ride across the Australian Outback. All part of a solo around-the-world bicycle trip (a mid-life crisis on wheels) that ultimately launched his writing career.

Booklist has selected his military and firefighter series(es) as 3-time "Top 10 Romance of the Year." NPR and Barnes & Noble have named other titles "Top 5 Romance of the Year." In 2016 he was a finalist for RWA's RITA award.

He has flown and jumped out of airplanes, can single-hand a fifty-foot sailboat, and has designed and built two houses. In between writing, he also quilts. M.L. is constantly amazed at what can be done with a degree in geophysics. He also writes: contemporary romance, thrillers, and SF. More info at: www.mlbuchman.com

Join the conversation:
www.mlbuchman.com

SIGN UP FOR M. L. BUCHMAN'S NEWSLETTER TODAY

and receive:
Release News
Free Short Stories
a Free Book

Do it today. Do it now.
http://free-book.mlbuchman.com

Made in the USA
San Bernardino, CA
28 May 2020